THE OLD FLAME

A MAXIM ULTRA NOVEL

J. DOUGLAS SIMPSON

EDEN'S HOLLOW PRESS

Eden's Hollow Press

www.jdouglassimpson.com

Cover Image courtesy of NASA

For Gwen, Laura, and as always, Mia

AUTHOR'S NOTE

This book is late. It's really annoying too, because I've had this story mostly plotted out in my head for years now. I always wanted to do a story that exploits the fact that on Earth, Max essentially has a secret identity and I decided that this would be the novel that covers that idea. So, this one isn't all interstellar slam-bang action, though there's plenty of that too. This one gets into some more feelings, maybe, than the last. But, yes, this book is late. After I published *Great Big World: The Misplaced Children* in late 2020 after *Maxim Ultra* in 2019, I thought I was on a roll. Unfortunately, the need to pay bills and life in general interceded and this one took much longer to complete than I had anticipated. So, if you've been waiting patiently for this one, I thank you for sticking around. I hope you'll enjoy this Max adventure as much as or more than the last one.

I have to extend a gigantic thank you to my editor on this one, Erin Hodge, who gave me some great advice and helped me trim this thing down a bunch. I also have to thank my loving family, without whom I couldn't function at all. And, as always, thank you to you, the reader, for taking a chance on an indie author and his favorite creation.

My next novel is already underway, but I'm hoping you'll see more of Max sooner rather than later. I may be doing the third adventure before I finally tackle *Great Big World 3*, but I haven't completely decided yet. As always, the news will hit my website when I've made a concrete plan.

As I said last time, I love writing these characters and I hope you'll enjoy reading them just as much. Thank you so much for returning to Max's world with me.

If you'd like to keep up with me online and want to ask questions or just chat about the book, you can find me at the following places:

www.jdouglassimpson.com
facebook.com/jdouglassimpson
doug@jdouglassimpson.com

Thanks again for reading. I hope you enjoy the adventure!

- J. Douglas Simpson
  July 2024

THE OLD FLAME

CHAPTER 1

A macabre hellscape greeted Matthias Glintock as his shuttle started landing procedures. Chaos reigned on the ground. Fires burned everywhere. *The Gallant*—the tallest residential building on Aval—had been reduced to cinders.

"Terrorism" was the buzzword circulating in the wake of the catastrophe. Matthias couldn't fathom the evil required to incinerate over five thousand civilians. *The Gallant* held no political or strategic importance. Even a psychopath like Kalen Vandeir employed *some* kind of warped reasoning for his killings. *Vandeir*. The name left a sour taste in his mouth. It reminded him of the pile of *nakra* he'd been forced to eat for the last year since the Memta case.

His communicator trilled in his ear. He looked at his handheld. *Veck*. "Yes, Brontin?"

"Excuse me, Agent Glintock?"

Matthias clenched his teeth, thankful it wasn't a video transmission. "Yes, Captain Brontin?"

"That's more like it."

He could hear Brontin's smug smile. In the aftermath of the Memta case, Matthias had been demoted and placed under the direct supervision of Brynden Brontin—Matthias' worst nightmare. Brontin ensured the reality surpassed his imagined horrors.

Brontin lorded his power over Matthias by sending him on frivolous, dead-end cases. It was this penchant for wasting his time that had Matthias worried. Why had Brontin sent him here, to an important crime scene? He could only imagine what Brontin *hadn't* told him.

"No disrespect, Captain, but is there a reason for this call?"

"*I'd watch that insubordinate tone, Glintock. That's what got you where you are now.*"

Matthias suppressed every expletive that came to mind. "All I meant…*sir*, was that I've only just arrived. Is there any new information?"

"*No, I was looking for your initial report.*"

Again, Matthias gritted his teeth. The call was a power play, designed to remind him who was in charge. "It's a vecking mess down here."

"*That matches Dilton's report.*"

"Wait, Dilton's here?"

"*Yes. Get up to speed, and report back to me.*"

The connection went dead. After a year under Brontin, Matthias wondered how much more he'd have to take.

He set his shuttle down in a staging area amid a sea of emergency vehicles. Medical personnel covered the area like an invading army; several fire brigades fought the remaining flames. A haze of smoke hung in the air accompanied by the stomach-turning stench of burning flesh.

Matthias wiped his watering eyes with the back of his hand as he approached a uniformed GAC officer. "Glintock, GAC."

The fresh-faced officer pointed to the cluster of people and vehicles that made the makeshift command center. "You'll want Dilton."

Matthias headed over. Officers swarmed the portable tables laden with communications and monitoring equipment. He opened his communicator and reviewed Dilton's personnel file—his unwanted partner had a spotless record. Dilton was either strictly by the book—which he could deal with—or a bootlicker that would report his every move to Brontin.

As he neared the command center, he was hailed: "Agent Glintock!"

He turned. A human woman dressed in a sharp black suit with a long black coat approached him. She held out her hand. "Agent Varra Dilton." Her slightly slanted green eyes flashed in the firelight.

He took her hand, which looked even paler against his dark skin. "Agent Matthias Glintock."

"I've heard a lot about you, Agent Glintock." Her handshake was firm and warm.

"All good, I hope."

She tilted her head with a half-smile, running a hand through her shock of white-blonde hair. Her expression didn't fill him with confidence.

"What have you found so far?" he asked.

She gestured around. "All this isn't enough?"

"I don't suppose this was all an unfortunate accident?"

"No way. Not this level of destruction. The tech teams are trying to tap into the old video feed."

"What should we do while we're waiting on them?"

She smiled. "This way."

He followed her across the street to a small café which was still open to emergency responders. Matthias looked from the café to the rubble of *The Gallant*. The café *should* have been pulverized, yet there was almost no damage.

Dilton watched him intently. From her coat, she produced a gold flask. She took a swig and held it out to Matthias.

He hesitated. "If I drink that, does it go in a report to Brontin?"

Her smile widened. "Ah, so we're going to have this talk?"

"I like to know who I'm dealing with."

"Likewise." She took another sip. "I know you probably don't want it this way, so if you're unwilling to work within these parameters, there's always—"

"Returning to my shuttle?"

She paused. "Resignation."

"Is that what our partnership is? A suggestion to resign?"

"I don't know what the veck Brontin's trying to do. This isn't exactly my dream assignment either."

He hadn't considered that. His fellow agents probably saw him as fairly toxic in the wake of the Memta case. Matthias had not received the praise he'd expected after averting a galactic calamity. Instead, the heads of the Galactic Authority Commission blamed him for losing the Memta statue. Though he'd argued against it, Matthias had come around to Maxim Ultra's thinking that the statue was better off with the Revash people. Of course, he'd never tell Max that.

Ultimately the bosses admitted that he'd stopped the threat and Kalen Vandeir. Still, he'd cost them a powerful weapon. Brontin was his punishment.

Had Dilton run afoul of Brontin too? "So, why offer me the drink?"

"I figured you'd need it with what we're walking into." She tucked the flask back in her coat.

They stepped inside the café. A few first responders milled about, but Matthias's attention locked on the haunted man behind the counter. "The proprietor?"

Dilton nodded. "He saw everything. Well, except for who did it."

"It's never that easy."

"No, it never is."

Matthias and his partner approached the owner. He was short and paunchy with flecks of gray in his dark mustache.

"Mr. Delod," Dilton said. "Can you please tell my partner here what you saw?"

"Y-yes, I think I can do that. I had six patrons inside at the time. One moment, everything was fine. The next, everything was lit up like day time. I rushed to the windows and I saw *The Gallant* burning. But, the fire swirled up into the sky, like the building was in a bottle."

"Did you see anyone—?"

"Running away? Yes, everyone! Some took refuge in my café, others continued up the street."

"No, did you see anyone suspicious?" Matthias finished his actual question.

"In a crowd of people? Impossible."

Matthias thanked the proprietor for his time and he and Dilton stepped back outside. "Does that sound like an accident?" she asked.

"No, not at all."

Dilton's communicator trilled. She touched her ear. "We're on our way." She looked at Matthias. "We've got video."

"How'd they manage that?" he asked as they walked back to the command center.

"None of the surveillance footage was stored locally. It's all backed up on a server off site."

"Lucky for us, I guess."

"You don't sound so sure."

Matthias nodded. "I think that whoever pulled off a crime this massive would have known that."

"Well, I guess we're about to find out." They arrived to find several people huddled around a bank of monitors. "What have we got, Beattie?"

The techs and personnel parted to reveal Beattie. Matthias recoiled. She was Dilton's exact duplicate, but Beattie was literally plugged into the computer terminal.

A bot. Matthias had a checkered history with robots and synthetic beings.

Dilton picked up on his obvious discomfort. "Yeah, sorry about that. I read that you're not the biggest fan of bots."

He glared at her. This was *definitely* Brontin's reason for pairing them together. He knew Matthias' history. Dilton wouldn't need to report on him when she had a duplicate capable of recording everything. "How do I know which is the real you?"

"Are you kidding? Beattie would never answer to such an unfortunate name as Dilton," she said with a smile.

He didn't share her humor.

"Are you two quite finished?" Beattie asked. "May I proceed?" Her voice sounded like Dilton's, but colder; more monotone. There didn't seem to be any digitizing. She was clearly top of the line.

"By all means," Matthias said, trying valiantly to keep his feelings in check.

"We were able to recover most of the video surveillance in and around *The Gallant*," Beattie said.

Dilton leaned in closer. "Great work, Beat. Have you scanned the footage?"

Beattie rolled her eyes. Matthias clenched his jaw. *An emote. This gets better and better.*

"Of course I scanned the footage, Varra. There is not much worth seeing, but I have cued up the most pertinent portion." With a tap of the keys, a video stream played. The image was muddy and dark.

"What are we looking at here?" Matthias asked, leaning closer.

"This was the main exit just prior to the explosions," Beattie said.

A shadowy figure stepped into frame. It looked masculine, but Matthias couldn't be absolutely sure. "Who is that?"

"We think it is the perpetrator. Give it a moment," Beattie replied, annoyed.

The figure stepped into more light and looked directly at the camera with a smirk. Matthias' heart stopped. Without meaning to, he gasped audibly.

"What is it?" Dilton asked. "You see something?"

Matthias didn't know what to say. "I think I recognize him."

"You should, Agent. This man was central to your case last year." Beattie paused, as if waiting for an answer. When Matthias kept his mouth shut, she said, "It is Maxim Ultra."

CHAPTER 2

The *Sequel*'s loading ramp settled on the ground. For the first time in several years, Maxim Ultra took a breath of Earth's air. He was home.

The landing had been tricky, dodging passenger jets and international radar, but Max was back on Earth. Since Earth wasn't a member of the GAC, spaceships weren't a regular sight. So, the *Sequel* had to be parked out in the middle of nowhere. A united world government would change that, but Max didn't see that happening anytime in his lifetime. Snooping eyes wouldn't have much time to spy the ship or the crew, though. Once Max and Roeger were on their way, the others planned their own vacation to blow off some steam. It was for the best. Due to their completely alien appearances, Litning and Gerry wouldn't be very welcome on Earth.

Shanta Morrico, the *Sequel*'s new first mate, piloted the Rover out of the ship. Roeger carried some bags after her, grumbling that he felt like a pack mule.

Litning towered over the bot. "I like this place, Roeger. Very serene," the Revash said. Despite his loose clothing, Litning's gray, furry exterior would more than likely get him mistaken for Bigfoot than anything else.

"That's because we landed out in bumblefuck," Max said. "No spaceports here, but the cities might drive you nuts anyway."

"As long as there are places like this, Earth would make a fine home," Litning said.

Max looked at the scenery. The forest surrounding them was beautiful and peaceful; only the cicadas broke the silence. The trees swayed in the gentle breeze. Max had truly missed his home planet.

"You would have to live in hiding here, Litning," Roeger said. "Even though primitive robots exist on Earth, I have to hide myself."

"That's because you're more advanced, bud," Max said.

Roeger blinked twice, slowly. "Really? I thought it was due to my wit and sterling personality."

Litning roared with laughter as Roeger moved to the parked Rover with the bags.

"Always the comedian," Shanta said as she approached. "Wouldn't Litning be happy in the northwest? Less people there."

Max grinned. "Someone's been doing her research."

"I'm always prepared, Max. Hell, I probably know more about Earth than you."

"I wouldn't doubt it. Where's Robbie?"

Shanta looked back at the *Sequel*. "He, ah, wasn't interested in leaving the ship."

Max followed her gaze. "I'd better go talk to him." He made his way to the *Sequel*'s common area and stopped at the telltale shuffling of Gerry approaching.

"*Chutho*, Max," the Glutob said. Gerry's body was amorphous. With concentration, he could be any shape he wanted; at rest, he was a big, lovable blob. When they'd met in prison on Aval, Gerry had been a cook. Now, he was the resident chef on the *Sequel*, as well as a highly skilled mechanic and tinkerer.

"How's it going, Gerry?"

"I thought you would be on your way to your mother's by now."

"Yeah, almost. I have to talk to Robbie first. You heading out to take a look at Earth?"

"Yes. I enjoy seeing the different worlds we visit. I would be remiss if I did not experience your home world." He paused. "I hope we can visit mine soon."

Max winced, recalling an earlier promise. "We will, Gerry. Soon, I promise."

As Gerry slinked off, Max headed for the cockpit. Soft jazz echoed down the stairwell. Max predicted Robert was well into his third or fourth drink. He entered the cockpit to find his friend in the pilot's seat—a drink in one hand and an old photograph in the other. The woman in the picture was Jenine, Robert's ex-wife. German-born, she met Robert while he was on active duty in the U.S. Air Force.

"You know, if you're going to be flying my ship, I'd appreciate you not being blasted," Max said, leaning against the co-pilot's seat.

Robert waved him off. "Shanta's flying us to wherever we're going—and Christi can handle simple flying," he said, referring to the *Sequel*'s A.I.

"Shanta said you weren't interested in seeing our home world."

"There's nothing out there for me. I can see enough from here." Robert had lost the weight he'd packed on while captain of the *Galactic Dream*, but he'd replaced food with alcohol.

"That was some fancy flying to get us down undetected. Thought it might make you nostalgic. Why not let the others go do their thing and we stay here? We can even see Jenine if you want; maybe to tell her how you still feel about her?"

Robert glared at him, taking a drink. "You *know* I can't do that. Remember last time?"

"I do. She's married."

Robert tucked the photo in his shirt pocket. "So, what difference would it make, Max? I lost her. She's gone."

"Well, Robbie, that may be true, but you'll never know until you try. I'm just worried about you, buddy."

Robert paused. There was a glimmer in his eyes. "I appreciate it, Max, I really do. Thank you."

Max put his hand on his shoulder. "Always, pal. Always."

He left the cockpit and met the rest of the crew outside. Litning helped Roeger load the bags, while Gerry took video of the scenery.

"We'll take care of Robbie, Cap. Don't worry," Shanta said, her long, black braids tied back from her face. She was shorter than Max and solidly built. Her violet eyes set off nicely against her light chocolate skin. "The Rover is all charged up. You should be good for the week. The holo projectors are functioning properly, so it'll look like you're driving on regular rubber tires. Just…don't let anyone take a close look."

"Right. Will do." He didn't know how he could have survived the last six months without Shanta.

The two of them had been brought together by Pepper, one of Max's father's old crewmates. He now ran the *Con-3* in Marina on Modan. Max had been in dire straits when they'd met. Alesha, his on-again-off-again partner and former first mate, had taken off with her own crew. The Memta job had taken its toll on Alesha. She'd lost so much. Max hadn't seen her in the six months since. He missed her desperately.

Shanta was exactly what Max needed in the wake of Alesha's departure. She didn't fill Alesha's shoes in *every* department—Max wasn't her type—but she kept his ship in order.

"Where are you guys headed?" Max asked.

Shanta smiled. "We're going to a little pleasure planet I know, Majis, so I can find a couple of honeys and let off some of this stress!"

"It hasn't been that bad, has it?"

"We've had some close ones, Cap. That last job was no joke."

She wasn't lying. They'd been hired by an old associate, Murrall, to find a friend, Blix. They found Blix, murdered by a fervent sex cult that wasn't too keen on outsiders. Escape had been dicey, to say the least.

"Well, hope you all have a grand time," Max said. "We all set, Roeger?" Roeger didn't answer as he struggled to cram an overstuffed bag into the overstuffed trunk.

Litning stepped up to Max. "I should accompany you."

"Why?"

"Protection."

"That's probably a bad idea, Fuzzy."

Litning snorted in response to the loathed nickname.

"First off, you stand out too much for Earth. Second, I'm home—what kind of trouble am I going to get into that would require Revash help?"

"If you have not been paying attention, Maxim, you attract an overabundance of trouble."

"Not here I won't. I appreciate the offer, but trust me. This planet is the safest place for me in the galaxy. Roeger and I are going to visit with my mom. You go with the crew and have a blast."

Litning folded his arms, exhaling forcefully. "I do not like this."

"What's not to like? You're going to have a great time."

"I am trying to put my…great times behind me."

Max's expression softened. "I know you are, buddy." In the last year, Litning had tried valiantly to exorcise the demons that had plagued him since his exile from his home planet, Revjekt. While it was true he wouldn't need Litning on Earth, Max didn't reveal that he wanted the Revash to keep an eye on Robert and for Shanta to keep an eye on them both.

Max hated leaving the ship. It wasn't that he didn't trust his crew—he trusted them with his life—but, the *Sequel* was his identity.

"We'll take excellent care of her, Cap," Shanta said, empathy in her eyes. "You hired a highly competent babysitter."

"I know. Thanks, Shanta. Have fun."

"You too, Cap. We'll see you in a week."

He turned and walked toward the Rover. Roeger already sat in the passenger seat, tapping his fingers impatiently.

"Hey, Cap," Shanta called as Max reached his vehicle. "Be careful."

"Why does everyone think something bad is going to happen? We'll be fine!"

* * *

Forty Minutes Later…

"Maxim, the police," Roeger said.

"Jesus fuck." The flashing red and blue lights flooded Max's rearview.

"We need to pull to the side."

"Yes, thank you, Mr. Obvious!" Max snapped. He didn't fear the police, but police complicated things for someone in his line of work. He pulled off the road and slowed to a stop.

The officer emerged from the patrol car and Max reached into the panel serving as his glove compartment. His hand closed over the documents he needed and he sent up silent thanks to Shanta.

"Okay Roeger, you know what to do."

"What would that be?" The robot's flat tone was always the same.

"It's time for Stupid Robot Tricks."

"Must we?"

Max rolled his eyes. "You know it's the only explanation for the locals. Come on, it's fun!"

"For you, maybe."

"Stop being a baby."

The officer stopped at Max's door. Behind his sunglasses, he gave Roeger the once over. "License and registration, please." Max said nothing as he turned over the requested documents. "What's with the robot, Mr. Thompson?"

Max took a moment to respond to his given name, having used his professional one for so long. "Ah, I'm a hobbyist. Robotics. Say hello to the nice policeman, Roeger."

Roeger didn't say anything for a moment. Then he folded his arms and looked at the cop. "Hello."

The cop chuckled. "That's pretty neat. He do anything else?"

"I also knock over banks and jewelry stores," Roeger said.

Max was horrified as he turned to Roeger. The robot's face was expressionless, but Max felt him smirking.

The cop laughed. "That's funny! Well, I haven't heard of any robot heists of late, so I guess I won't have to haul you in. Unfortunately, Mr. Thompson, you *were* speeding."

Max smiled as innocently as possible. "I'm sorry about that, Officer. I'm heading over to my mother's for a family dinner. I'm running a little late and I'm a little excited to see everyone."

The officer looked at him a little more, nodding his head slowly. "How's your driving record, Mr. Thompson?"

"Uh, no tickets in the last few years." Max knew that was true—he'd been in prison on Aval for most of that time.

"All right, just sit tight for a minute." The officer walked back to his vehicle, leaving Max to wait impatiently.

"I feel cheap and degraded," Roeger said.

Max gave him an incredulous look. "You didn't exactly help matters."

Roeger paused a moment. "I told you I was not interested in playing 'Stupid Robot Tricks.'"

Max bit his bent finger so he wouldn't explode. He wasn't worried about getting a ticket—his job negated the citation's ramifications—but dealing with law enforcement made Max nervous. Well, any law enforcement except Glintock. He was the only lawman Max trusted.

The officer returned. "All right, Mr. Thompson, I've got another call, so I'm going to let you off with a warning on the speed."

"Thank you, Officer. I appreciate that." He considered that if a black man like Robbie had been driving, he wouldn't have received the polite treatment.

"You should take that robot on tour. It's something else."

"I'll think about that, thanks."

"All right, drive safe now." The cop walked back to his car and Maxim let out a long slow, relieved breath.

"Did you really think a citation would be a problem?" Roeger asked.

"Of course not. It's just a hassle we don't need." The cop peeled off, lights flashing, and Max pulled back onto the road. "Not much farther to go."

"I know, Maxim. I have a computer for a brain."

Max ground his teeth.

Max pulled up to his mother's house about ten minutes later and parked on the curb. He recognized the van in the driveway as Sam's, but an older truck sat beside it. Max was about to inspect the truck when a child's scream came from the backyard.

Reaching into his jacket, he produced a three-inch box that was two inches wide. He pressed a button on the box. It extended and contorted to reveal its true nature as a pistol. It was sleek and black and there were no seams or hinges to suggest that the weapon was collapsible. Alesha had given it to him as a parting gift.

"Come on, Roeger," Max said, moving swiftly to his right. He stopped at the house's front corner and peered around it toward the backyard.

"Maxim, what are we doing?" Roeger asked, standing beside him.

"You didn't hear that scream?"

"Of course I did, but is this the proper reaction? We are on Earth."

"Bad things can't happen on Earth? Come on." They moved down the empty side of the house. Voices floated from the backyard. Nothing sounded amiss, but he couldn't shake his bad feeling. He stopped when he heard a child's laugh.

Max leaned against the side of the house. He released a deep shuddering breath and lamented how paranoid his job had made him.

"A child's laughter. How terrifying," Roeger said.

Max gave him a look. He pressed the button that transformed his gun back into the non-descript box and tucked the weapon back in his jacket. He ran his hand through his short brown hair, and forced a smile. As he passed the corner of the house, he caught sight of a man with a white beard. He immediately spun around and pushed Roeger back.

"What is wrong, Maxim?"

"There's somebody here I don't recognize. Some old guy."

"What is the problem?"

Max balked. "He can't see you. How do I explain that?"

"The same way you explained it to the police officer."

Max closed his eyes. At times, dealing with Roeger was like dealing with a toddler. "That's a completely different situation and you know it. I know you, Roeger. You're too social to be left out. You'll blow your cover for sure."

The robot's metal flaps that served as his eyebrows went down. He wasn't happy. "What about all the neighbors? Have they seen too much? Do we need to murder them?"

"Just go upstairs and sit in my room. I'll send the kids up to play with you later."

Roeger didn't move for a moment. He then stomped off to the front of the house, grumbling all the way.

Once Roeger had turned the corner, Max stepped into the backyard. "Hey!"

A cheer went up from the guests. His mother, Kate, stood on the deck with the mysterious man and Sam's wife, Cindy. Standing in the backyard were Sam's kids, Stevie and Abigail, and the man himself. Sam had been Max's best friend in high school and his pilot before Robert. He was the only person Max had ever told about his father's secret profession. When Max left for space, Sam had gone with him. Sam had returned to Earth with two prosthetic legs, leaving Max with a mountain of guilt.

His friend embraced him warmly. There was an almost imperceptible hitch in Sam's step; the off-world prosthetics were more advanced than anything Earth engineers could offer. "How are ya, Max?"

"I'm good, Sam. You?"

Sam gestured around, his messy brown hair shifting in the breeze. "I'm livin' the dream, Max. Livin' the dream."

"Hi Uncle Max," Stevie said with a smile.

"Hey, bud! Gosh, how old are you now?"

"Nine."

"And Abby?" he asked, turning to Abigail.

"Six!" the little girl responded.

"Then I guess you don't really remember me, do you?"

Abigail shook her head and danced away.

"You've been gone five years, Max," Sam said. "How was it?"

Max glanced over at the deck. "Looks like I can't tell that story. Who's Whitey?"

Sam grinned. "I'll let your mom field that one."

The comment hit Max in the gut, but Cindy descended from the deck and wrapped him in a hug. "So good to see you!"

"You too, Cin."

Cindy's expression was sympathetic. "Your mom told us about Alesha. We're so sorry."

"Thanks, Cindy." He wasn't interested in discussing his broken heart. "The kids are so big!"

"Would you like to take them back with you? For a week?" Cindy knew all about Max and Sam's past adventures.

Before he could answer, his mother embraced him. "I've missed you so much," she whispered.

"I missed you too, Mom."

They held each other for a few moments, then his mother pulled away. "I have someone I want you to meet."

The man with the white beard was tall and thin, looking to be about his mother's age. Like his beard, his hair was white and cropped short. He held out his hand and out of habit, Max took it.

"Max, this is Billy. Billy, this is my son, Max."

"Nice to meet you...*wulp!*" Billy had pulled him into a bear hug.

"Good to meet you, son!" Billy grinned. "Your mom's told me so much about you!"

"Max, Billy was an old friend of your father's."

Max's stomach twisted. "Oh, really? Did you know he's dead?"

A shocked silence followed.

Kate was the first to recover. "Maxim, apologize!"

"You're right Max, he is," Billy said. "Your dad and I were in the service together and when he moved the family, we lost touch."

"At least until his wife was widowed, right?"

His mother grabbed his arm so tightly, it hurt. "Come with me."

She marched him into the house. Max was angry, but unsure why. Had he expected her to mourn his father forever? The deck door slammed behind them.

"Really didn't need this right now, Mom."

"I'm sorry, Max, but when should have I told you? While you were in prison? Or while you were away from home?"

Her questions cut him. He couldn't admit why he hadn't come home. True to her word, Alesha had stayed long enough to help Max kick his addiction to rimi. He'd gone through absolute hell, but he beat the demon that he'd embraced in prison and had, to date, avoided the hallucinations that were common among addicts. He wasn't prepared to make that revelation to his mother—this was supposed to be a happy day. All he felt at that moment was shame—shame for his actions off-world and for his outburst outside.

Max needed more information. "Does he know? Does he know what I do—what Dad did?"

"No! No, he thinks you're working out of the country."

The shock started wearing off. "Good. So, how'd you hook up with this guy?"

"He heard about your father and called with his condolences. Then, we just kept in touch."

"How long have you been seeing him?"

"After the last time you were here. So…a while."

Max's expression softened. One more thing to feel guilty about—his time away.

"I wish you'd give Billy a chance."

Max said nothing in response. His father had been dead for fourteen years, but for Max, the wound was still fresh.

Kate put her hand on his shoulder. "Max, I'll always love your father, but he's been gone for a long time. I think he would have wanted me to be happy."

"Are you?"

She smiled sadly. "Getting there."

He nodded. "This was just a shock, that's all. I'm sorry."

She embraced him. "I know, honey. I know."

"I miss him." Tears stung his eyes.

"So do I, Max. God, so do I." She patted him on the back. "Okay, make yourself presentable."

"Why, what's up?"

"Your surprise is here."

"This wasn't enough of a surprise?"

"No, this one will be far more pleasant for you."

He heard the door open behind him and he spun around.

"Hi, Max." It was Gina Rivio, his high school girlfriend.

CHAPTER 3

Before Alesha Cabal, there had been Gina Rivio. Max couldn't believe his eyes. There she stood, in his mother's kitchen, more beautiful than he'd remembered. Her light brown hair hung just below her shoulders, but her always dazzling smile started to fade; he realized he was gawking.

"Gina, hey! Wh-what are you doing here?"

His mother explained. "Gina and I run into each other all the time. I told her you were going to be in town this week and invited her over."

Gina was embarrassed. "I hope that's okay."

"Yes, of course! It's great to see you!" They shared an awkward hug.

"Sorry to spring this on you," she whispered. "But, your mom insisted."

"She does love her surprises," he muttered. "Well, come on, say hi to everyone." As he led her outside, he looked back to his mother, who positively beamed.

"Holy crap! Gina Rivio!" Sam said as he ascended the deck stairs. "What are you doing here?"

"Mom invited her," Max answered. "You remember Sam, right?"

"Of course. You two were inseparable in high school. How are you, Sam? Are these adorable munchkins yours?" Gina asked.

"Indeed they are. And this is the only woman who will have me, Cindy. Cindy, this is Gina, a friend from high school."

"A pleasure, Gina," Cindy said, shaking Gina's hand.

"Uncle Max?"

"Yes, Stevie?"

"Where's Roeger?"

Max and Sam's eyes went wide. "Uh…."

Upstairs in Max's old bedroom, Roeger sat on the bed, staring into nothing. He sighed. This was not how he envisioned his vacation going. He could have gone to Modan to work on his comedy.

Kate's black cat, Lacy, hopped into Roeger's lap. He blinked at the cat, who nuzzled him, purring.

Roeger gently put his hand on the cat's back to pet her. "Hello, kitty cat."

Again, he sighed.

"What's a Roeger?" Gina asked, clearly clueless.

Stevie began walking around like a robot. "A super cool robot man!" He added sound effects to his stilted movements.

Gina gave Max a questioning look. He shook his head. "Kids, right?" It didn't help that Abigail imitated her brother.

"Hey, kids, let's see if Mrs. Thompson has cookies!" Cindy said, gently pushing the children toward the sliding glass door. The whole way over, the kids continued moving like robots.

"What was that all about?" Gina asked with a chuckle.

"Ah, I've been trying to get them into *Star Wars*," Sam said. He winked at Max as he and Gina moved to the patio table. They hadn't worked out a concealment plan. Max had no idea they'd need one.

Max pulled out Gina's chair as the trio sat down. "Always the gentleman," she said.

"What, this guy?" Sam joked.

"He used to do that for me all the time when we dated," Gina said. There was a brief pause. "Then I didn't see him all that much."

These weren't the old times Max wanted to relive. "That's…a long story. I'm more interested in finding out what you're doing now."

She smiled. It was sincere, but he could see in her eyes that she was still sore about how he had broken things off. There was nothing he could have done. The off-world work with his father had picked up and he had been too busy for a girlfriend, no matter how much he wished it had been different. He regretted how it had ended.

"Yeah, Gina, what are you doing these days?" Sam asked.

"I, ah, work for the government."

"Oh yeah? Doing what?" Max asked.

"Oh, you know, just an office gig. Boring, paper-pushing."

Max *didn't* know. It seemed like she was holding back, but he wasn't going to ruin the evening by interrogating her.

"What about you, Sam? How's family life?"

"Fantastic. Really, we couldn't be happier. I made a killing in the market and I'm a stay at home dad now. Cindy still works, to cover our monthlies and stop herself from going crazy."

"Stock windfall, huh? Lucky you," Gina said.

Max kept his mouth shut. He had shared in the treasure that made up Sam's windfall. Unfortunately, he hadn't been able to hold onto it as well as Sam. Regardless, he was happy for his friend.

"And Max? What are you doing with yourself these days?" she asked with an expression that told him she was far more interested in his current situation than Sam's.

"Y'know, still working the family business." *How vague can you get?*

"What is it you do again?"

"Logistics—you know, getting things from point A to point B." His answer was practiced for situations like this. No specifics. Deflect all questions. It was exhausting.

"I was sorry to hear about your dad," Gina said. "I know that must have been hard."

Melancholy swept over him. "Thanks. It was. I miss him a lot. Even today." He paused. "How are your folks?" he asked, shifting the focus back to her.

"They're good. Real good. Relocated to Florida and loving it."

"That's great." Max looked back into the kitchen and saw Billy with his arm around his mother while they talked to Cindy.

"Anyone special in your life, Gina?" Sam asked.

Internally, Max rolled his eyes. Why was Sam encouraging this? His job kept him in *outer space* the majority of his time. How the hell could he have a productive romantic relationship on Earth?

"No, no one in particular. A few dates here and there. What about you, Max?" Her tone was even. Was she just curious or eager to know?

"Not at the moment, no. My last girlfriend left to…pursue her career." It was true enough.

"I'm sorry to hear that. Dating's hard at our age. You're very lucky, Sam," she said.

"Don't I know it? Cindy is awesome."

She raised her eyebrows. "Are you two planning on going to the reunion?"

Max looked at Sam, who had suddenly found something very interesting to look at in the backyard. "I'll probably be out of town. When is it?"

"This week. I'm surprised you don't know about it. I mentioned it to your mom," Gina said.

Max grimaced. *The reunion? Really?* "I'm guessing you're going?"

"Oh, totally," Gina said. "Any chance I can get to reconnect with old friends."

"And Sam," Max said, his eye practically twitching. "Are *you* going to the reunion?"

"Huh? Oh, um, well…yeah. I mean, Cindy wants to go, so I guess."

Max narrowed his gaze at his friend.

"Well, if you'll excuse me, I'll go see if I can help your mom in the kitchen," Gina said. She walked back into the house.

"You need to get on that, dude," Sam said.

"What? That wouldn't do anybody any good. I'd never be here."

"Then stick around a little more. She's a keeper."

Max could see Gina talking and laughing with his mother. The last time he'd been on Earth, that had been Alesha.

"So, where *is* Alesha? Was what you said true?" Sam asked.

"Yeah. She has her own crew now. I'm really proud of her, actually. I just…miss her. The last several years haven't been great, bud."

"I know. Your mom filled me in on the details." Sam paused and took a drink. "Is Alesha coming back?"

He shook his head. "I have no idea."

"But, you're holding out hope."

Max shrugged. "I guess. I've been with her basically since we met. I'm supposed to chuck that because my high school girlfriend wants to reconnect?"

"Right, but Gina's here, and Alesha's not."

Max waved Sam off. "She's here to see my mom, not me."

"Come *on*, man. Gina doesn't want to hang out with your mom. She made the effort to come here and see you. You ask me? You need to take her out, see if there's any spark, and then escort her to that reunion, because there will be plenty of guys there trying to re-introduce themselves to Ms. Gina Rivio."

"Yeah, the reunion. Thanks for the heads up on that one."

Sam laughed. "Yeah, I knew you'd be thrilled about that. It'll be fun to see everybody. Stop pretending it won't."

"I'll have to come up with a very detailed cover story." He dreaded it.

"Like you haven't done that before. Max, we used to come back to Earth every month back in the day. No reason you can't do that again."

Max looked at his friend for a moment. "How are you doing for money?"

"You heard what I told Gina. I'm fine. We're fine." Sam looked at Max, who wore a concerned expression. "Honestly, we're fine. That Cellex Nine job set me up for life. Cindy really only works so we don't have to dip into the nest egg. Also, I do freelance stuff from home. We're good."

"I'm sorry I've been out of touch for the last few years."

"Max, you were locked up in a *prison* on *Aval*. You're forgiven."

"I know, but I always promised that I'd look out for you, especially after…."

Sam patted his prosthetics, which were safely concealed by his jeans. "After these? Buddy, you have got to let yourself off the hook for that. I knew the risks. I don't blame you."

"Maybe. But, I blame myself."

"You shouldn't. These legs are great. My life is great." Sam leveled his gaze at Max. "You're like my brother, Max. I love you. You deserve happiness too. I think you need to ask Gina out."

"Sam's right, Max. You do deserve to be happy," his mother said. He hadn't heard her come back out.

Sam patted Max on the shoulder. "I'll let you two talk. Think about what I said."

"I will, Sammy. Thanks."

Sam got up from the table, gave Kate a quick hug, and headed into the house.

"Max, we need to talk," his mother said.

Just what he *didn't* want to do. "Is he living here? That'll make it a little difficult for Roeger."

She frowned. "No, Billy doesn't live here. He stays over quite a bit, but he and I agreed, before you insulted him, that while you're here, he will only be visiting."

He nodded. "Look, I'm sorry I lost my shit. I was just shocked, that's all."

"I shouldn't have sprung it on you without warning, but…Billy makes me happy, Max. And to be perfectly frank about it, you have no say in the matter." Kate gripped Max's hand. "All I ask, is that you try. Get to know Billy. You'll probably be surprised to find how much you have in common."

He kept his comments to himself. "I'll be nice, Mom. You deserve to be happy too."

"Thank you, sweetie."

The glass door slid open and Billy stood in the open doorway with a plate of burgers and hot dogs. "All done? The kids are getting antsy."

Max looked at his mother. "We are. Let me give you a hand there, Billy."

The older man was surprised by Max's offer. "Uh, sure. I think I'd like that."

The rest of the evening went off without incident—Roeger only called Max's communicator seven times. As everyone gathered in the driveway to say their goodbyes, Max embraced Gina warmly.

"It was really great to see you, Max."

His stomach flip-flopped. "I'd love to see you again while I'm in town."

She smiled brilliantly. "I thought you'd never ask."

"How about dinner tomorrow night?"

"How about this? You agree to escort me to the reunion, and I'll go to dinner with you."

He winced. She drove a hard bargain. "Go out to dinner with me tomorrow night and I'll let you convince me to go to the reunion."

Her gaze narrowed, but she maintained a playful smile. "Deal. Your mom's got my number. Give me a call."

"I'll do that."

"And I'll see you tomorrow night."

She got in her car and drove away, leaving Max with a ball of excitement in his chest. At that moment, he didn't believe that anything in the galaxy could get him down.

CHAPTER 4

Cornered and outnumbered, Matthias sat in the passenger hold of his shuttle with his new partner, Dilton, and her synthetic doppelganger, Beattie. His belief in Maxim's innocence in the Aval bombing had been met with skepticism. Unfortunately, streaming in on holo video was the biggest proponent of Maxim's guilt, Brynden Brontin.

"*I'm confused, Agent Glintock,*" Brontin said, his fat, pasty face filling up the holo image. "*Why are you still on Aval when our bomber is on the loose?*"

"*Alleged* bomber. We're still investigating."

"*I found the evidence to be more than persuasive,*" Brontin said.

Matthias leveled a glare at Beattie, who had sent Brontin their findings without running it by him.

"*Are you investigating the crime, or looking for a way to get your friend off the hook?*"

"That's out of line, Brontin!" Matthias caught himself. He didn't lose his composure often and regretted it when he did.

Dilton shifted in her seat, a look of unease on her face. Beattie gazed at him with cool detachment.

"*And I believe I made it clear, Agent Glintock, that you were to address me as 'Captain.'*"

That made Matthias' temperature rise. "Look, *Captain*, you're not listening to me. Ultra is incapable of committing this crime! It's not in his nature."

"*And I suppose you're the Maxim Ultra expert?*" Brontin asked. "*One case and you've got it all figured out?*"

Matthias wasn't about to reveal to Brontin that he'd been in regular contact with Maxim since the Memta case. It was a benefit to have an independent contractor available. Brontin had one thing right, though. Maxim was Matthias' friend. Was that blinding him to the obvious evidence? *No, there's got to be another explanation*. Unfortunately, Maxim had been disconcertingly unreachable.

"Agent Glintock," Beattie said. "Subsequent video showed a laden Ultra entering *The Gallant* before the explosion. We should be searching for him."

That bit of evidence was inconvenient. "I'm telling you, he couldn't do this. He wouldn't."

"*He was imprisoned there for almost three years. It's understandable he'd have a grudge*," Brontin said.

"Grudge enough to kill thousands of innocents? I don't buy it." Matthias was incensed. What would it take for these people to believe him? Maybe if he erased their memories that the highly incriminating video evidence existed.

"*Maybe he's working for someone else. He* is *a mercenary, after all.*"

Before Matthias could counter Brontin's latest theory, Beattie came in with another. "Perhaps the Memta entity infected him.

The being could be using Ultra as a vessel for her own wrongdoing."

Matthias shook his head. "Was there any photographic evidence of his crew on Aval? Was his *ship* even here? Videos can be faked."

"We have determined with ninety-five percent probability that the person in the video is Maxim Ultra," Beattie said in her emotionless tone.

Matthias closed his mouth. He wasn't going to win this one. He looked to Dilton. "You've been quiet. What do you think?"

Dilton looked at him with sympathy. "I think the evidence has given us a solid lead and we should pursue it."

Though he barely knew her, her proclamation crushed him. He'd hoped that the other investigator in the room would be on his side, not on the side of a robot and a vengeful supervisor.

"Not that I was looking for any kind of majority of opinion, but that seals it," Brontin said. *"I'm putting out a galactic alert for Maxim Ultra and his ship…what's it called again?"*

When Matthias was slow with the answer, Beattie filled the void. "The *Sequel*, Captain."

"Thank you, Beattie. And an adjoining alert for any of his associates. Maxim Ultra is now Galactic Enemy Number One."

Matthias protested. "That will alert every bounty hunter in the galaxy."

"We need all the help we can get to bring this scum to justice."

"And how did working with Talon Merthane on the Memta case shake out for you?" Matthias asked.

Brontin glared at him. *"My mistake was working with Merthane directly. This general alert will call in* all *the hunters— every individual for themselves."*

"Captain," Dilton spoke up. "That's liable to make our job *very* difficult."

"*We need eyes, Agent Dilton, eyes on Maxim Ultra wherever he is hiding. That's not necessarily where the GAC's gaze falls. We must cast the largest net possible. Any problem with that, Agent Glintock?*"

Matthias gave Brontin his phoniest smile. "No problem at all, *Captain*." It was all happening too fast. GAC investigations usually did, especially when one of the bosses smelled blood. He glared at Beattie and Dilton. They had been zero help. It was all right, though. Matthias had other allies at his disposal.

CHAPTER 5

Egar Kowas had known that leading a revolution against the corrupt ruling party of Iswat would create a host of enemies. However, he never imagined one would pursue him through his home.

After overthrowing the Commandant, the planet's citizens had insisted that Egar, their new leader, take possession of Iswat Palace. As he raced down another of the palace's countless corridors, he gave silent thanks to the people for forcing him to live in such a spacious residence; eluding his pursuer would be much easier. He didn't get a good look at the intruder. All he saw was a masked figure looming over his bed when he started awake. The fate of his companion for the evening was unknown to him.

Though he'd gained some weight since his lean days in the resistance, it wasn't enough to slow him down. What troubled him was the lack of security around the palace. Egar eschewed the use of mechanical guardians, preferring the presence of real live defenders. However, they were nowhere to be found as he scrambled from one empty hallway to the next.

"Help! Help! Alert the guard!" he cried out through his panting breaths.

"*No one is coming to help you, Kowas,*" a digitized voice echoed around him. It sounded feminine.

"Why? Why are you doing this?"

"*Mostly the money, but I do love to take out despicable vecks like yourself.*"

He wished he didn't know to what the intruder referred. While the former ruling party hadn't been popular with the people, Egar wasn't doing well. It had only been two years since he'd been installed as Iswat's leader, but many were already calling for elections to replace him. Though he'd never admit it to anyone, the power was intoxicating. Yes, he had enemies, but enemies venomous enough to send an assassin after him? The GAC certainly hadn't looked kindly on his revolution. That corrupt husk despised things that upset the status quo, even on planets, like Iswat, that were not members. He'd heard rumors of another organization rising to challenge the GAC, but there was no way he could appeal to those people to help him now—if they existed at all.

Egar ran through the cavernous receiving room, where he held events, receptions, and yes, orgies. Perhaps one of the many women he'd courted had a jealous husband? The marble floor was cold on his bare feet. He turned left. The front doors of the palace were tantalizingly within reach. Two moons lit the room through the skylight. He dashed toward the palace exit.

A lithe figure flipped down from the upper level and landed in his path. The intruder caught Egar by the waist and tossed him. He crashed into the low table in the middle of the room, smashing plates and glasses.

His hand closed on a handle. He threw the gold-plated knife at the intruder, but she dodged it easily. He scrambled to his feet, but she fired a laser bolt at the floor from the pistol strapped to her leg. It stopped him in his tracks.

"*You're not going anywhere, Kowas,*" the intruder said.

The black mask had large tinted orbs where her eyes would be. Her body was covered in a form-fitting jumpsuit. Even in the moonlight, Egar could see that the outfit was made of deca-weave—heavily armored fabric; strong enough to absorb a laser blast. Two scabbards were secured to her back and several devices attached to her belt. As she sauntered over to him, she laughed, the mask's vocal digitization making her laughter all the more sinister.

"Please! Don't! I'll give you anything!" he begged.

"*More than my client is already paying?*" she asked.

"Oh…almost certainly. All I ask is that you tell me who hired you." Excitement built in his chest. He could still turn the situation to his advantage.

"*Why would I tell you that?*"

"A condemned man does not deserve to know who wants him dead? I assume that's why you're here. You look a bit over-dressed to simply be delivering a message."

"*Oh, a whole lot of people want you dead, Kowas.*"

"So, what is the harm in telling me?"

Her blank orbs stared at him for a moment. "*The truth? I don't know who it is. This one wanted to keep it anonymous.*"

"The people will avenge me." He knew he was lying to himself.

"*Not from what I hear. I may not know who's paying me for this job, but I do know that you're not very popular these days.*"

"Apparently, you do not know who I was before I became Iswat's ruler, girl."

She shook her head. "*Such disdain for women. No wonder you abandoned your friend upstairs.*"

"And I suppose you killed her too?" he spat.

"*Why would I kill her? She's not part of the contract.*"

Much to Egar's shame, he envisioned himself running back upstairs and using his companion as a human shield. His pride stirred. Once, he was known as the Blade of Iswat. He would not fall without a struggle. Looking down at the table, he spotted two sharp knives. In a swift motion, he swept the knives into his hands. As he took a fighting stance, the assassin drew one of her swords. The blade crackled with energy.

He charged at the assassin with an Iswati war cry. She stood her ground and sidestepped his flurry of attacks before swinging her sword upwards, slicing one of his knives in half. In his panic, he threw his good knife at her and she knocked it aside with her blade. He attempted to attack her with his hands, but she kept her sword at her side and wrapped her leg behind his, tripping him. As soon as he hit the floor, Egar scrambled backwards on his hands, attempting to put as much distance between the two of them as possible. He didn't get far.

She fired a high-tension cord from the gauntlet on her left wrist. The cord wrapped around Egar's neck, choking off his air. The pain of the cord cutting into his flesh was unbearable.

"*If you worship any god, I would make peace now,*" she said.

"You...vecking *horvorka!* You'll pay for this!" His words were strained.

"*A gentleman to the end, I see. And I'm already* getting *paid for this.*" Before she could taunt him any further, the orbs in her mask lit up with blue light. The symbols he saw looked like letters and numbers. The orbs clearly served as some sort of heads up display. *"Ultra?"* she whispered. *"Finally."*

Whatever she'd seen had captured her attention. Egar inched away, hoping that her distraction would relax the cord. Immediately, the assassin snapped to attention and yanked the cord tight.

For Egar, his universe ended in darkness.

CHAPTER 6

Shanta sighed, contented. The pleasure planet Majis was as advertised. She burrowed her toes in the warm sand of one of the planet's innumerable beaches. The lapping of the waves paired perfectly with the soft nibbling of her companion, Haina, on her ear. Her other companion, Deera, placed soft kisses on her neck. Both women were Panchan—humanoid, with pointed ears and long, prehensile tails. Shanta shivered in delight as she recalled what those tails had gotten up to the previous night.

As was customary on Majis' beaches, Shanta's companions were naked, their tantalizing and ample breasts exposed. Shanta, however, remained in her shorts and tank top. Despite her hedonism, she was far too paranoid to parade around in the nude. Experience had taught her that it was always smart to know where your clothes were; you never knew what was coming.

Yes, Shanta was pretty content. She had a stable job with a good crew and was able to take time away like this when she needed it. Majis had endless activities in which she could partake, but she preferred to find two girls, veck them until they couldn't move, and relax on the beach. She wasn't interested in exotic tours or death-defying stunts, she got enough of that with the job.

It hadn't always been that way, though. There had been a lot of lean times growing up on Vale. Shanta had no idea who her father was. Her mother had raised her alone and served in local law enforcement, which didn't pay much. Things had improved when her mother secured a position with the GAC. However, a few years later, her mother had been killed in the line of duty.

The GAC never found the perpetrator, so Shanta chose not to follow her into the world of law and order. Instead, she embraced the less reputable half of the galaxy. Part of that had to do with an old girlfriend of hers who showed her the ropes. They parted amicably and still saw each other now and then.

Before hooking up with the *Sequel* and Max, Shanta had bounced from crew to crew doing all sorts of jobs to survive. She wasn't proud of all of it. With Max, though, it was different. He did some shady jobs, but mostly, he wanted to help people. It was the closest she'd ever felt to being on her mother's path. Max wasn't law enforcement by any means, but he was a good guy. She felt her mother might have finally been proud of her life's direction.

Her communicator trilled in her ear. She groaned. "Why are you interrupting my vacation?"

"*Technically, it is* our *vacation*," Litning said, gruffly.

"All the more reason for you *not* to interrupt it."

"*We need you over here, post haste.*"

"What's the problem? Is Robert fall down drunk again?"

"*That, I could deal with. Please come. Now.*"

She switched off her communicator in disgust, but knew that tone in Litning's voice. He wouldn't have used it unless he really needed her.

Shanta huffed, patting her Panchan beauties on their bottoms. "All right, ladies, time to head out."

Deera nuzzled her neck. "Time for more lovemaking?"

Haina worked on the other side. "We can just do that here."

If there was one thing Shanta prided herself on, it was keeping work time and playtime separate. Litning's tone implied it was time to go to work. So, with a supreme effort, she patted the girls again and got up. "Head back to the hotel and get cleaned up. I have to meet my crew over at *The Undertow*. I…wouldn't be upset if I saw you two there, later."

Haina smiled at her. "We may just do that. Come, Deera, let us bathe together." Deera walked off hand-in-hand toward the hotel with Haina, leaving Shanta to feel nothing but regret.

"This better be worth it, Fuzzy," she grumbled as she trudged toward the bar.

Majis was a popular vacation spot. The whole planet, as well as other pleasure worlds, was owned by Baron Zeth. It was a heavily featured stop on many of his galactic cruises. It seemed the only thing you *couldn't* do on a Zeth Pleasure World was get away from people.

Shanta moved through a gaggle of sightseers to *The Undertow*. The bar's slogan was, "Once it sucks you in, there's no escape." *Probably not great for Robert*, she thought.

She entered the bar and was assaulted by noise. It was a party bar, which she despised. She was more of a "quiet drink with friends" type. The place was a tourist trap and packed—the antithesis of her quiet beach with her lovely ladies.

She spotted the boys in the corner. As was usually the case when the crew hit the town, Litning sat with his back to the wall, so he could see every exit. Gerry sat on Litning's right, eyeing the crowd with suspicion. She was surprised that Robert appeared alert. He'd been so down since they'd dropped Max off on Earth, she had fully expected to find him face down on the table. The fact that he wasn't disconcerted her.

Shanta pulled a chair to the table. "Hello, boys."

Gerry smiled. "Chutho, Shanta." The alcohol he'd consumed so far swirled in his mid-section like a brewing storm.

"Anybody want to tell me what this is about?"

"There is a couple sitting over there," Litning said, his eyes flicking to his right. "They keep staring at us."

Shanta glanced over and saw that a well-dressed, human couple—a dark-skinned female and a tanned male—was indeed gawking at the *Sequel* gang. She laughed.

"What do you find humorous?" Litning growled.

"Of course they're staring at you! A human, a Glutob, *and* a Revash? I'd be staring too, if I didn't have to live with you!" She saw the humor in the situation, but inside, she seethed. *For* this *I gave up my Panchan angels?*

"Normally, I'd chalk it up to Litning's paranoia," Robert said. "But, they're *watching* us."

The accusation coming from Robert, a *sober* Robert, held far more weight. She glanced at the couple again—still staring.

"Okay, let's say they're watching us. Why? What for?"

"*That* is the question," Litning said.

Both the man and the woman were dressed in dark suits. In the middle of Apex on Modan, that might not be strange, but on a resort planet? It was a little odd. "Do they look familiar to any of you?" All three shook their heads. "Me neither." She glanced around the bar. "Anything else out of the ordinary?"

"Not that we can tell, no," Robert said. "But, that doesn't mean they don't have allies."

"Are we in trouble with anybody? Did we not pay the docking fees for the ship or something?"

"No," Robert said.

"*Shanta*," Christi's voice came in over her communicator. "*I have been monitoring your discussion. There are similar individuals outside the ship.*"

"Christi, lockdown. Everything," Shanta said.

"Friends," Gerry said. "Why is Maxim on the video screen?"

The other three followed the Glutob's eyes to one of the many screens throughout the bar. Instead of relentless advertisements, there was a smoldering heap of metal and glass on Aval in one box and in the other, their captain, Maxim Ultra. The words, "Galactic Enemy Number One," were printed under his picture.

The four crewmates turned back to each other with stupefied expressions. *How* was this possible? As far as Shanta knew, the last time Max had been on Aval was when Glintock had gotten him out of prison. He had sworn he'd never go back. And besides that, they had literally just dropped Max off on Earth! How could he have gotten to Aval to perpetrate such a horrific crime?

Shanta watched the screen; according to the news blast, the destruction on Aval had occurred while they'd been traveling to Earth. Despite what the GAC thought, there was no way Max could have been involved. They had to get word to Glintock and sort the whole thing out. But first, they had to protect their captain.

"Let's, ah, let's head back to the *Sequel*," she said casually, rising from the table. The others nodded and did the same, but Robert froze.

"Don't move!" came a harsh, female voice.

Shanta raised her hands instinctively and turned her head toward the couple slowly. Both man and woman had pistols drawn on the crew. "This is a misunderstanding."

"Tell it to the victims' families on Aval," the man said.

"We had nothing to do with that," Robert said. "And neither did Max."

Two more patrons moved in from the right, brandishing their weapons. Tourists started screaming and running. Clearly, the armed people were GAC—weapons weren't allowed to be carried on Majis. All the crew's weapons were locked up on the ship.

"Keep your hands where we can see them," the woman said.

"I'll note that you haven't identified yourselves yet," Shanta said.

"Put the pieces together," the man said. "We're planet security and you're under arrest, horvorka."

Shanta gave him a look of shock. "That was uncalled for, *sir*. There's a nicer way to do this." Her eyes flicked to Gerry, then to Robert, and finally to Litning.

"I only count four," Gerry said.

"Same," Robert said.

"Good," Shanta said before nodding at Litning.

In the blink of an eye, Gerry squished down and Litning flipped the table over him at the first two agents, knocking them to the floor. Robert and Shanta turned and swung at the second pair of agents, who had trained their weapons on Litning. They both connected, knocking the agents down.

"Let's get the *veck* out of here!" Shanta yelled, leading the way out of *The Undertow* through the throng of fleeing patrons. As she hit the door, she found herself blinded by sunlight and surrounded by a dozen armed security agents.

"Give it up, Morrico!" one of the agents yelled.

There was no escape. Shanta raised her hands slowly in surrender. "*Veck*."

CHAPTER 7

"Son of a bitch," Max muttered as he unknotted his tie for the third time.

"Shall I assist you, Maxim?" Roeger asked as he sat on Max's bed.

"No, it's just been a while, that's all." It had been about a year. With Alesha.

"You know that is false," Roeger said. "If I did not know any better, I would say that you are nervous about your rendezvous with Gina."

Max grimaced. "Don't call it a rendezvous. That makes it sound dirty. It's a date. That's all." He undid the tie again. "Dammit!"

"I think Roeger's right," his mother said, appearing in the doorway.

"*Pfft*. Why would I be nervous? It's dinner with Gina. I've known her practically my whole life." He was sweating like a pig.

"*But*, you haven't seen her in years and you two were very close."

"Mom, don't push."

She smiled self-consciously. "I know, I know. But, is it so wrong for me to want to see you happy?"

"I *was* happy."

"I know you were, honey, but if I understood you right, Alesha's not around anymore."

"She'll be back. She always is." Though he said the words, he wasn't sure he believed them.

"Max, you know I love Alesha, but your relationship has always been…turbulent, to say the least."

"What are you trying to say?"

"I just don't want you putting happiness on hold because you're waiting for something that's not going to happen."

When Alesha had taken off six months previously, Max had never doubted she'd return. This was the longest he'd gone without hearing from her, outside of going to prison. Worry was settling in—for her safety and their relationship. He remembered what it had been like when he was imprisoned on Aval. The scarred edges of that emotional hole were starting to itch. He wondered if he'd ever see Alesha again.

Perhaps his mother was right—before Alesha, Gina had been the object of his affection. Could that flame be rekindled? It seemed like she was game. Was it fair to start something with Gina when he felt the Alesha situation wasn't resolved? Though Alesha often laughed at his "Earth beliefs" when it came to relationships, they were ingrained. She definitely wouldn't care if he took up with Gina, but he'd feel weird about it.

His mother smiled at him as he finally knotted the tie. "So handsome."

"You're biased. But, thank you." He pulled on his sports jacket and adjusted his shirt cuffs.

She put her hands on his shoulders. "Just relax and have fun. Whatever happens, happens."

He smiled at her. "I'll be fine, Mom. It's just a date."

Twenty minutes later, his leg bounced like a pogo stick as he pulled up to Gina's house in the Rover. *Nope, not nervous at all*, he thought. He hopped out of the vehicle and opened the door for her.

"Thought I'd save you the walk," she said, embracing him.

"Oh, no worries." He hugged her back warmly. She felt right in his arms.

"Interesting car," she said. "I've never seen one like it."

"It's custom," he lied.

"*Really?* Where did you get it? I'd love to own one."

"Ah, picked it up in Europe, actually. Not readily available." At that moment, he wished he had kept an Earth automobile in his mother's garage. Keeping track of the lies was the worst part about returning home.

"You look nice," she said with a smile.

He shrugged. "Just jeans and a sports jacket. No biggie. You look beautiful, though." That was *not* a lie. She wore a cream-colored sundress with purple flowers on it. Her hair was down around her shoulders.

"Thank you. You need to learn to take compliments, mister."

After a mostly silent fifteen-minute drive, Max pulled into the parking lot outside *Rascals Steakhouse*. You could get a great steak there, but there were no peanut shells under your feet. Within minutes they were seated and ordering their drinks.

"I'll have a glass of Zinfandel," Gina told their server.

"And for you, sir?"

"Just water for me, please."

"Okay, I'll get those out to you right away."

"Just water?" Gina asked, a hint of disappointment in her voice.

"I don't drink," Max replied. He didn't like the way it made him feel and he couldn't stand the taste.

She shrugged. "No problem. More for me, I guess."

A moment of silence passed between them. It felt like an eternity. *I fucking hate dating.*

"I have to apologize for blindsiding you yesterday," Gina said. "Your mom was so cute, wanting it to be a surprise."

"No apology necessary. It was a pleasant surprise. I was thrilled to see you."

She smiled.

The server returned with their drinks and they ordered their entrees.

Gina looked around the restaurant. "Slow night tonight. This may be a quick date."

"Only if you want it to be."

She arched her eyebrow as she sipped her wine. "That remains to be seen."

"Oh, I see," he said with a chuckle.

"So, why don't you want to go to the reunion?"

He winced. *This* will *be a short night.* "I don't know. I…just really don't want to hang out with a bunch of people I haven't seen in fifteen years. I couldn't care less if I never saw them again."

"Is that how you feel about me?" she asked.

"No, of course not."

"Because, if I hadn't run into your mom at the store, we wouldn't be sitting here right now. I mean, you wouldn't have reached out to me, would you?"

He felt cornered. "I…I didn't even know you were still in the area."

"That's the point, Max. Aside from Sam, you haven't kept up with *anyone*. You're not on social media. Hell, when your number came up on my phone, it's 'restricted.' You're like a ghost and I'm…curious why."

"What can I tell you, Gina? I'm bad at keeping in touch. I travel a lot for my job and—"

"But me, Max? You cut *me* out?"

I know where this is going. "What do you want to know?"

"I want to know why. I want to know why you broke things off with me—with a really piss-poor explanation, I'll add—and have barely spoken to me since."

His heart broke. "It wasn't you, Gina, believe me."

"Oh, I *know* it wasn't me. You were an idiot for letting me go, make no mistake. So, why?"

He hesitated, unprepared for the ferocity of her assault. "It's hard to explain. I was really involved with my dad's work and helping him."

"Oh, you mean when you go into space?"

He laughed. "What are you talking about? Space? Where'd you come up with that?"

She folded her arms. "I know about the spaceship, Max. I've seen it."

His eyes grew three sizes as he stared back at her, speechless.

CHAPTER 8

"Gina…I…I don't know what to say."

"Well, you can stop lying to me."

He looked down at his food, which had shown up immediately after Gina's revelation. Suddenly, he wasn't so hungry. "How did you find out?"

"At least you're not denying it. I was suspicious of how your dad made his money. You guys were always taking work trips and while your parents weren't extravagant with their money, you could tell they had it."

"Maybe I had a rich uncle," he offered.

"That's true, but it didn't explain the constant work trips."

"You thought my dad was running drugs."

"Or something like that, yeah. I wasn't interested in seeing my boyfriend get caught up in some DEA sting, even though you broke my heart."

He grimaced at that memory. He hadn't wanted to break up with Gina, but believed he had no other choice.

"So, one night, I followed you and your dad to the farm where you kept the ship."

He smiled fondly. "The *Hunter*."

"I...I couldn't believe it. An actual spaceship. I can't even tell you how long I stayed in that field after you left." Her eyes were filled with wonder, but clouded over. "Then I realized how angry I was."

"With me?"

"Yes. I was angry, because you chose to break up with me instead of sharing this incredible part of your life."

He nodded. "I'm sorry about that, I truly am, but you've gotta understand, Gina, the work my father did—the work I do—it's secret."

"You told Sam, clearly."

He squinted. "Sam's my best friend...in the *galaxy*. I couldn't hide it from him. I had to tell *someone*."

"And you couldn't trust me with that information?"

"Gina, look what happened. We broke u—"

"*You* broke up with *me*, *because* of this."

He held his hands up to her. "Fair. But, what if something else had happened and we broke up anyway? I couldn't have you telling everyone my family's business." He wanted to word that differently as soon as he'd said it, but he had to make her understand.

From the look on her face, his words clearly had their unintended effect. "I would have never done that to you."

He sighed. "That came out wrong. All I meant is, how many high school relationships last?"

"I couldn't come with you?"

"Would you have? Would you have left your family and friends, never knowing if you were ever coming back?"

That seemed to dampen her fire. "No...no, I guess not. There's no way you could have known that, though."

"We were friends first, Gina. We'd only just started dating. It was all so new. There was no guarantee that it would last."

"There are no guarantees in life, Max."

He hadn't wanted to bring out the big guns. "Did you notice Sam walks with a hitch in his step?"

She was wary. "Yes."

Max swallowed hard. The story was still difficult to relate. "He lost his legs while out there with me. I made a decision, he lost his legs. It's my fault. And he's not the only crewmember I've lost out there. He's one of the luckier ones. My friend, Gage, was killed during a job. Now, his bounty hunter father, who used to run with my dad, hunts me down and makes my life miserable whenever he can. That's my life."

Gina's eyes were wide, but it looked like she was fascinated. "Jesus...."

"My father had warned me of the dangers out in space; how death lurked around every corner. I didn't want to risk anything happening to you, so I chose what I thought was the least painful option."

"I...I had no idea...." She looked away for a moment, pensive.

"I'm sorry I didn't tell you, but I thought it was for the best. You have to understand, it's not a secret just because we wanted it that way. The Earth's governments *want* it that way. The Galactic Authority Commission—"

"*Galactic Authority Commission?* Who are they?"

"They, ah, kind of run the galaxy. They're like the CIA, FBI, and UN all rolled into one. But, they don't approach a planet for inclusion until it's unified under a single government."

"Fat chance of that here."

"Exactly. Most of the world governments know that the GAC exists and they're not too keen on the general populace finding out."

She paused. "Wouldn't that unite the world?"

"Well, I've been gone a while, but you tell me. Would it?"

"No. Probably not." Her hands started to fidget. "Max, I'm sorry."

He waved her off. "You had every right to be angry with me."

"No...what I mean is...I'm jumping all over you about being honest, but I haven't been totally truthful with you."

"Oh?"

"Um, yes. The truth is, I'm not just a paper pusher at a government agency."

"No?"

"No. I actually work for the FBI."

Max's jaw went slack.

"JAMES MAXIM THOMPSON," came a booming, but familiar voice from across the room.

Max looked up and immediately covered his face with his hand. "Jesus fuck."

Greg Wilson, a classmate of theirs from high school, approached the table. They were *not* friends. That didn't deter Greg from stopping at their table, wearing a gigantic shit-eating grin.

"What have we got here? Max Thompson and Gina Rivio out to dinner the week of the big reunion? Does this mean that you two will be hittin' the reunion together?"

"Hi, Greg," Gina said with a less than genuine smile. "I'm definitely going, but Max is only in town for a short time. He may miss it."

"That true, Thompson? You're here for the lead up, but you're not going to seal the deal?"

Max couldn't hide the disgust on his face. "Still on the fence, Greg."

"I guess that means Gina will be attending alone? Bonus for the Greg-meister."

Gina grimaced. "So, what have you been doing with yourself, Greg?"

"Oh, I'm killing it, G. I'm one of the top sales guys at my company, hittin' the gym every day, and I'm not unpleasant to the ladies, if you know what I mean." He literally waggled his eyebrows. Max couldn't believe he was seriously talking to a living cartoon.

"That sounds great, Greg. Congrats," Gina said.

"How about you two? Haven't seen you in ages, Thompson."

"I travel a lot for work."

"Oh really? What do you do?"

"Ah, I'm in logistics."

"But are you killin' it, bro?"

Max looked at Gina, who smiled at him, laughter in her eyes. "Yeah. Yeah, Greg, I guess I'm…killin' it."

Greg's demeanor shifted as he turned his attention to Gina. "And what about you, G? Are you…killin' it?" His tone was softer, almost flirty.

"I work for the FBI, Greg."

The unwanted visitor immediately stood back. "Whoa, nice! That-that is very cool!" Clearly, whatever Greg was "killin' it" in, he didn't want to associate with the FBI. Max chuckled.

"You here by yourself, Greg?" Max asked. He'd already spotted the busty blonde in the tight, hot pink dress.

"Uh…no. I'm here with my co-worker, Sharon." Sharon obviously wasn't dressed for a business dinner.

"Well, we'll let you get back to her," Max said pointedly.

Greg seemed to regain his composure. "Good to see you, Thompson." He winked at Gina. "And I'll see you Saturday."

Gina gave him the fakest smile Max had ever seen. "Only if I see you first, Greg."

Greg departed. Max looked at Gina. "*That's* why I don't want to go to the reunion."

"Oh, Greg's harmless."

"He's a gigantic douchebag."

"Well, he is that too," Gina admitted with a laugh.

"So, are you investigating me?" he asked, bringing their conversation back to Gina's second bombshell of the night.

"You're…a side project of mine."

He arched his eyebrow. "What does *that* mean?"

"The FBI doesn't consider extraterrestrials as a high priority. So, I do it on the side. It really sucked that my key informant has been away from Earth for years. Where *have* you been? Your mom said she hadn't seen you either."

Max looked around, making sure no one was eavesdropping. "Prison."

Her eyes went wide. "You were in *prison?*"

"Yeah. Almost three years on a hellhole called Aval."

She was fascinated. "You were in prison on an alien world?"

"You don't have to be so thrilled about it."

She covered her mouth. "I'm so sorry. It's just…another planet! You were on another planet!"

"Gina, I *live* on another planet."

"Oh my god, that's so exciting!"

Her enthusiasm was cute, but he had to remember what a big deal traveling off-world was for people not named Maxim Ultra. "So, this was never really a date. Was it? You just wanted me to confirm your theories?" He was surprised by the pang of regret.

She was shocked. "No, Max, no! I really wanted to see you. I…missed you."

When he thought about it, he'd missed her, too. Their failed romance had irrevocably damaged the strong friendship that had previously existed. Sometimes, when he and Alesha were on the outs, he'd wonder whatever happened to Gina Rivio. "I missed you too, Gina."

"I know you can't go on the record about this stuff, but it confirms what I suspected."

"Which is?"

"That the government *definitely* knows something they're not telling the public."

"The public doesn't want to know about this, Gina. They *think* they want to know, but they don't. The general public thinks that the first official meeting with aliens will be with E.T. I have rarely met kind aliens. They're mostly all assholes."

"Then why keep doing what you're doing?" She paused for a moment. "Wait, what is it you even do anyway?"

He chuckled. "I…find things for people—artifacts, items, *people*—it all depends on the client."

"So, you're like a private detective?"

"Ah, a little bit, yeah. There's definitely an investigative component to my work. It can definitely be dangerous, but I…really like what I do. I don't see myself coming back to Earth."

"I'd love to go out there."

"Again, you think you do, but…."

"Don't tell me what I want, Maxim Thompson," she said.

"I didn't know you were so into space."

"Well, I wasn't until I found out my ex-boyfriend had his own spaceship."

"Ah, I see. You want to use me for my ship."

She grinned. "Can I see it?"

"You can when my crew returns to pick me up. They just dropped me and Roeger off before heading off on their own vacation."

Her brow knitted up. "What's a Roeger?"

"My robot pal."

She covered her mouth and laughed. "Oh my god, you were serious about that? Can I meet him?"

"Of course. He's literally just hanging out at my mom's house. He's the reason why I got into the family business in the first place."

"Really? How did that happen?"

He shrugged. "He was lonely and woke me up in the middle of the night when I was twelve. After that, my fate was sealed."

She chuckled. "What is he doing right now?"

"Probably playing *Scrabble* with my mother."

Her chuckle became a full-on laugh. "Yeah, right!"

Across town, Roeger sat at the kitchen table with Kate, a *Scrabble* board between them. She looked at her letters, lamenting her lack of options. Then she realized she did indeed have a word.

"Here we go. V-E-C-K and that gives me a triple word score." She smiled, proud of her quick thinking.

Roeger looked at the board, back at Kate, and at the board again. "Katherine, *veck* is not a valid word."

"What? Of course it is. Max says it all the time."

"Veck is an off-world swear word. It is not based in American English, much less Earth. The word is invalid."

She looked at him with a deadpan stare. "Roeger, I love you, but you're a pain in the ass as a gaming partner."

"Maxim calls me a stickler." He sounded very proud.

Kate grumbled as she cleared her letters off the board, back at square one.

"I'm sure my mom would love to see you, too," he said.

She got a flirty little smile on her face. "Maybe later. I wanted tonight to be just us."

That piqued his interest. He'd been so focused on Alesha, he'd forgotten what it was like to connect with anyone else. He'd felt a thrill when he first saw her at his mother's house, but the look in her eyes now was intense. Apparently, she *was* interested in rekindling an old flame. He felt a hot blush creeping up his neck.

"So, where do you live now?" she asked.

"On a planet called Modan in a city called Marina."

"How far is that from here?"

"About a hundred light years."

"And that is…?"

"Far."

She chuckled. "Got it. What…what's it like out there?"

He paused. It was scary, even terrifying at times, but it was never boring. "Incredible."

She sighed. "All the nebulae and stars. It must be difficult to take your eyes off of it."

"Sometimes, yeah. There is definitely a lot of beauty in space. So, besides me, what have you investigated for the Bureau?"

"Mainly domestic terrorism. White nationalists and all that."

"Those fucking idiots still haven't learned yet?"

"I don't think they ever will."

"Let them go a few rounds with a slobbering Inwain. They'll be embracing all the colors of the rainbow."

"*See?* That's why people on Earth need to know about what's going on up there! If they know we're not alone in the universe, then…."

"Then they'll just hate someone else. Knowledge of the denizens of the universe doesn't cure hate, Gina. I know this firsthand." He winced. "Sorry to 'mansplain' it to you like that."

"No, no, it's okay. This is something you *actually* know about and, *literally*, no one else does. So, I'm not sure if 'mansplaining' covers it. This time." They both laughed. "I know we can't do anything until your crew comes back, but I really want to go up there with you some time. What I want to do *right now* is a little closer to home. My home."

He got a nervous flutter in his stomach. "But, I wanted *dessert*," he said in his whiniest voice.

She arched her eyebrow. "Oh, there will definitely be dessert."

About thirty minutes later, Max and Gina pushed through her front door, lips locked together. As the door closed after them, she pulled at his tie, clearly not realizing what a struggle it had been to get it right. Her fluffy gray cat wailed as they crashed onto the couch, chasing him out of his napping place.

It all came flooding back to Max. His desire for her, the sneaking around to avoid parents, stolen kisses by the lockers, all of it. He moved his lips back to hers and she accepted him eagerly.

She gently pushed him back. With a sultry glint in her eye, she pulled her dress up over her head and left it crumpled on the carpet. Then she moved to kiss him again, wrapping her legs around him.

It wasn't their first time by any means, but Gina was definitely more aggressive than he'd remembered. He liked it. He'd missed having her in his arms.

Time melted away until the two of them were left sweaty and spent on the couch, breathing heavily.

"Okay," Max said. "I'll go…to the reunion."

Gina weakly raised her arm in victory. "Yay."

CHAPTER 9

The facility alarms blared throughout the halls. Red lights flashed as Torrin and his squad raced to intercept the intruders. Even after countless drills, he did not feel sufficiently prepared to deal with an armed assault. However, the plasma rifle in his hands was very real and he was fully expected to use it to defend life and property—the company's property.

His squad entered the freight lift. Already, he heard screams floating down the lift shaft. He hoped they belonged to the intruders. Behind the tinted shields of his comrades' helmets, Torrin could see wide, frightened eyes. He wasn't alone in fearing that they were unprepared.

The lift rose. Torrin and his comrades shifted uncomfortably. The ride felt like an interminable death march. His eyes caught the company logo on his uniform. A bitter taste filled his mouth. Torrin seriously doubted that Baron Zeth would lay his life on the line for anything, except to squeeze more money out of something. He'd never met the man personally, but had seen plenty in the gossip vids and news reports. Zeth wasn't the kind that valued the lives of his employees.

The lift came to a stop. The squad held its collective breath. As the gate opened, they were greeted with a scene out of their worst nightmares. Their comrades lay dead on the ground, their bodies broken, bloodied, and burned. The floor was a dark shade of crimson where the blood coated the dull, black tiling. Little fires filled the lobby with smoke.

The masked invaders wore black. Their uniforms were bulky with equipment, and all carried laser rifles. Though many of Torrin's co-workers attempted to fight, the intruders picked them off with frightening accuracy.

Despite the horrific scene, Torrin's eyes were drawn to the woman at the center of the invading horde. She had longish red hair, a skin-tight black uniform, and eyes that glowed with a turquoise light. The energy bolts she fired from her hands were the same color and sparked new fires where they fell. Whenever one of Torrin's allies took a shot at her, one of her cohorts stepped in front of the projectile, taking the damage. They behaved like members of a fervent cult, protecting their leader.

If I could just get a bolt through that wall of bodies, Torrin thought, *this could be all over*. He wasn't sure what he was thinking. A hero he was not.

"Push forward!" the woman cried as she fired off another energy bolt.

Torrin looked for a superior, hoping at least *one* person knew what they were doing. He spotted one of his comrades doling out orders.

"Torrin! Get your squad over here!" Mittels called out.

Torrin waved the rest of his troops behind Mittels' barricade and took cover. "Where's the Lieutenant?"

"Dead," Mittels responded. "All the ranking officers are gone. They knew who to hit."

Torrin's gut twisted. "We have to take out the woman."

"Hah! Easier said than done. You take a shot at her, she makes sure you regret it."

"Well, we can't beat them in a firefight. They're too good."

"Planetary Defense are on their way, but gods know when that'll be."

Torrin swallowed hard. "We may be dead by then."

"And these *petches* will walk off with the Brupheen energy cores."

Brupheen cores—the most powerful manmade energy sources in the galaxy—were manufactured exclusively by Zeth Enterprises. One core could power a small city. If a force this large was storming this Zeth facility, they weren't looking for just one. The intruders' unknown intentions sent a shiver through Torrin.

Mittels' grim look said he'd come to the same conclusion. "We have to stop them here."

At Mittels' command, all the remaining security guards fired their weapons at the invading force. Torrin kept his sights on the woman, which was why the last thing he remembered was a torrent of blue flame filling his vision.

Torrin had no idea how much time had passed. He was prone on the floor in excruciating pain. He managed to lift his head just enough to see his charred body. Bile rose in his throat. He tried to look around. His squad was dead. Mittels' lifeless eyes would haunt him for the rest of his short life.

He watched as the intruders used hover-lifts to move the Brupheen Cores out of the facility. Where was Planetary Defense? Torrin's stomach dropped at the thought of all the unarmed individuals in the facility. Had the invaders killed them too?

"Oh gods, you're still alive!" a female voice sounded from his left.

Despite the blinding pain, he turned his head to see the woman standing over him. Her eyes no longer glowed blue. Torrin tried to speak, but no sound came from his half-moving lips.

She knelt beside him. "Shhh, shhh, shhh…. Save your strength. You're going to need it." She pulled a thin metal cylinder from her belt and stuck one end of it into his neck. A cooling sensation spread from the injection point through the rest of his body. "Now, I want you to tell everyone what you saw here."

"Wh…who…?" he struggled to ask.

"You don't need to know that. The people who do, will." She winked at him, the turquoise gleam returning briefly to her eyes. Then, she and her comrades were gone. Torrin remembered her words and when the Planetary Defense forces finally arrived, he repeated them for all to hear.

CHAPTER 10

"Vecking Brontin," Matthias said for about the hundredth time in the last hour.

"What's the problem?" Dilton asked.

"He's vecking up this investigation just to veck with me."

"How do you figure?"

"By plastering Maxim's face all over the info vids, he's made it impossible to do this quietly. Now we have to deal with an annoyed *Sequel* crew and *hope* we get some answers!"

Dilton leaned back in the cushioned seat of their private hover car. Beattie piloted the vehicle through the streets of the pleasure planet, Majis. "The only person trying to derail this investigation is *you*."

He flinched as if she'd slapped him. "*Excuse me?*"

"'Maxim?' To us, he's 'Ultra.' You're working so hard to prove his innocence, you're not seeing what's right in front of you. Clear video evidence of him committing the crime...."

"*Of him leaving the scene.* If I'm not allowed to have a biased view of the events, neither can you."

She nodded. "The point is, he *is* suspect number one and his crew just tore up a resort drinking establishment to escape security agents."

Matthias couldn't argue with that. But he needed their side of the story. He was on his way to a meeting—an interrogation—of people whom he considered to be, if not friends, than colleagues. He had to remain professional and distant, but somehow let the *Sequel* crew know he was on their side.

"We are approaching the GAC field office," Beattie reported.

Matthias set his expression to appear impartial. He still had no idea to whom Dilton reported. Beattie, he was positive reported to Brontin. He didn't know why, but he felt that if he could get Dilton alone, he'd be able to convince her to see things his way. The damn bot was always in the way, though.

Their vehicle pulled into the covered parking station and they took a lift to the main security office. The field office was very modern, but he wondered if the office's paradise location had resulted in lax procedures. From what Matthias understood, the GAC was little more than an advisor to Zeth's private security. The GAC would step in on major crimes, but otherwise, they kept their noses out of Zeth's business.

"Agents Dilton and Glintock, welcome." A short man with olive skin and very short black hair offered his hand. He wore a standard, dark blue GAC uniform with white boots and white piping. His nameplate read, "Vantross," and he wore a commander's insignia pin. He looked like a real ladder-climber.

Matthias took his hand. "Commander Vantross." The man's handshake was firm, but brief. "Thank you for welcoming us."

"Always nice to have fellow GAC family members visit."

Yes, he's a real *ladder-climber.*

Dilton smiled uncomfortably as she also took Vantross' hand. "Quite a facility you've got here, Commander."

The commander's smile broadened. "It's definitely not a hassle to come to work every day. We're very proud of it."

"Do you *get* much crime on a pleasure planet?" Matthias asked.

"You'd be surprised. A lot of folks feel like they can come to places like this and do anything they want, and by anything, I mean *anything*."

"It must be difficult when that's exactly what Zeth sells in his advertisements," Dilton said.

"Let's just say…we have a good working relationship with Zeth Enterprises."

Matthias' brow furrowed. It sounded as though the ladder-climber wasn't afraid about getting his white boots dirty on the way up.

"Can I give you the grand tour?" Vantross asked.

Matthias and Dilton shared a glance. "Actually, we're quite pressed for time," Matthias said. "Where are the, ah, detainees?" He avoided calling the *Sequel* crew prisoners.

Vantross' smile faded a bit. "Right this way." He led them down a hallway to another lift. They entered the compartment and the commander pressed the button for a lower floor.

"How long have you been stationed here, Commander Vantross?" Beattie asked.

"Five years." His response was clipped, cold. Matthias was never going to be a best friend to bots, but Beattie was a fellow member of the GAC and to be treated with respect.

The lift stopped and the door opened onto a dark hallway. Along the walls were illuminated cells. "This wraps around the entire level and the next several below us."

"Is this a field office or a prison?" Dilton asked, horrified.

"A field office, but as I said, people think they can get away with anything here. Take Maxim Ultra's associates, for instance. They tore up a drinking establishment. Why? Because we wanted to ask them some questions about their murderer friend?"

Matthias didn't like Vantross' line of thinking. "Does Zeth's private security force make use of these cells as well?"

Vantross frowned. "It's like I said, we have a good working relationship with Zeth Enterprises."

This whole place needs an audit. Gods only knew who Zeth had locked up in this fortress. They passed one of the illuminated cells and Matthias did a double take. Behind a force field, locked in massive manacles encasing his hands and feet, was Litning. Matthias stopped cold. "What's he doing in there?"

Vantross came to a halt and turned around. "Well, he's a prisoner."

Matthias looked at Dilton with incredulity, but all she could do was stare up at the hulking Litning. "I thought Ultra's allies were being held for questioning? Why is he chained up in there?"

Vantross leaned closer, as if he were imparting proprietary knowledge to Matthias. "I'm not sure if you're familiar, Agent Glintock, but that is a Revash."

"Not only am I familiar with Revashes, Commander Vantross, I am intimately familiar with this *specific* Revash. I ask again, why is he chained up?"

"He could kill everyone in this field office," Vantross replied in a low voice.

"*Has* he killed anyone? Has he even assaulted anyone?"

"I threw a table," Litning said, his deep baritone reverberating in his cell.

Matthias' lips pursed. He wasn't angry with Litning, but with his own GAC colleagues. "Let him out."

Vantross scowled. "Not to pull rank, *Agent* Glintock, but you don't really have the authority to demand that."

Indignant anger lanced through Matthias. "Oh, I don't? Understand *this*, Commander, we are investigating the deaths of over five thousand souls. I need this Revash's cooperation to continue this investigation. Chaining him up will not make him very compliant. Release him."

"Agent Glintock," Litning's voice echoed. "I am fine here. This little man holds no power over me."

Matthias looked up at the Revash, defeated. Before he'd been placed under Brontin's thumb, Matthias wiped Litning's slate clean with the GAC. Litning had done horrible things to retrieve the Memta statue, but he'd also helped to save the galaxy from goddess' wrath. After some intense soul-searching, Matthias saw it as a wash. He didn't want to fail him here.

"Trust me, Agent," Litning said.

"Where are the others?" Matthias asked.

"Shanta Morrico is being questioned by our investigators. The others are in a holding room."

"Then you'd better show us the way, *Commander*."

Vantross gave Matthias a dirty look and prompted them to follow him. Muffled yells emanated from behind a door around the corner.

"You *horvorka veckers!*" Shanta screamed as the door snapped open. Her gaze traveled from her interrogators to Matthias. "*WELL*, look who decided to *finally* show the *veck* up! Come in here, Glintock! You two, get the veck out and stop wasting my time!"

The two much-abused investigators looked at each other and then at Matthias, who motioned for them to leave. He turned to Dilton. "Give me a minute with her."

"Unacceptable," Beattie said.

"I wasn't asking *you*," he replied with a cold glare. He looked back to Dilton. "I know these people. I *may* be able to get information out of them, if the locals haven't completely vecked it up."

Dilton stared at him. "Fine," she snapped. "Two minutes. Then we do this my way." Dilton and Beattie left the room and Matthias took a beat before closing the door behind him.

"Hoo boy, Glintock, boss lady's got your nuts in her hand," Shanta said with a laugh.

"Hardly," he replied, taking a seat opposite her. "Do you mind telling me what the hell is going on here?"

"Don't *you* know?" she asked in surprise. "We were enjoying our vacation and these goons arrested us!"

He looked at her sternly. "Where is Maxim?"

"He's...not here," Shanta said haltingly.

"I can see that. Where is he?"

"He and Roeger are...*away*," she said. Her tone indicated she was trying to tell him something more.

"Do you understand the peril he's in right now?"

"Glintock, do you really believe Max returned to Aval, the single place he hates most in the entire galaxy, to commit a heinous crime, *and* got caught on camera while doing it? Come on!"

"That evidence is pretty damning."

"It's all circumstantial, unless you have a holo of Maxim Ultra actually setting the explosives. It's also a little too easy."

He lowered his voice to a harsh whisper. "You think I don't know that? I am *trying* to help you here!"

"Then start by telling your bosses that Max couldn't do this!"

"I've tried! The evidence shows a man that looks *exactly* like Maxim at the scene of the crime at the *exact* time the crime took place. What would you have me do with that?"

"Come up with some plausible alternatives!"

"Like what? This person had no changeling cuff like the one Sierra used on the *Galactic Dream*. Even if he had, he wouldn't have been able to look *exactly* like Maxim. It's impossible."

"What about a shifter?"

Matthias couldn't help rolling his eyes. "Do you know when the last reported sighting of a shifter was?"

"Does that go for Revashes too?" Shanta asked. "Hardly anyone has seen one, and we *have one in our crew!*"

"Yes, and the more you travel around, the more people see him. Take that total number of people and reduce it to far below one percent and you *may* come close to the number of shifter sightings."

"Clones?"

He folded his arms. "You tell me. Have you run into any rogue cloners lately?"

She paused for a beat. "Not that I'm aware of."

"Shanta, I've thought of all these possibilities. The best thing is for Max to come in and let me help him. If he didn't do thi—"

"*If?!*"

He stopped. "*If* he didn't do this, then the person who *did* either wants him dead or out of the way. I can protect him."

She stared at him incredulously. Considering how badly the locals had vecked everything up, he couldn't really blame her. "According to that news holo, the GAC's pegged him as galactic enemy number one. That means his bounty is at *least* ten million. If you let us leave, *I'll* bring him back to you for that kind of money."

She was clearly being sarcastic, but she had a point. The reward would bring out all types of lowlifes. "That classification wasn't my decision," Matthias said.

"Well, thanks for the heads up on this, Glintock."

"I'm not in a position to do things like that right now." He hated admitting that Brontin had him pinned.

"Maybe I should be talking to Blondie out there," Shanta said.

Before Matthias could react to Shanta's slight, the cell door snapped open and Dilton stormed inside. "You wanted Blondie? Well, here she is! Where is Ultra?"

Matthias stood up. "I told you, I would handle this!" he hissed.

"You're taking too long. She clearly knows something. Where is Ultra?"

"He's not here!" Shanta yelled.

"We already know that, but you *do* know where he is. Where is he?"

Shanta looked between Dilton and Matthias. "Lady, I don't *know* you!"

"I'm GAC! That's all you need to know!"

"Not when he's the only one of you I trust!"

"Fine. Put them all in solitary confinement as co-conspirators. We'll see how tight-lipped they'll be after a few days of that."

"We haven't *been* to Aval, lady!" Shanta yelled.

"Ultra could have easily hitched a ride himself."

"Then check our logs!"

"Oh, don't worry, we will!"

"ENOUGH!" Matthias cried. "We're getting nowhere here. Why won't you tell us where Maxim is?"

Shanta scowled. "Because, with this chick and her twin involved, we can't *trust* you, Glintock! Max told me what happened on the Memta job. Within five minutes of other GAC goons getting involved, he had Merthane on his ass! What's gonna happen this time?"

He had no answer for her. She was right.

Dilton opened her mouth, but Beattie entered the room before she could speak. "Varra, the field team has reported in."

"And?"

The bot's gaze fell on Shanta, who shifted uneasily. "The suspect is correct—no sign of Aval in the *Sequel*'s logs, nor any sign of being anywhere *near* Aval."

"*Thank you*," Shanta said with a matter-of-fact expression.

"However…"

"Oh, veck."

"The ship's last location prior to coming to Majis has been scrambled. We are running projected destinations based on the trajectory of their entrance into this system."

Matthias thought about everything he knew about Max and finally, it clicked. Max had gone to the *one* place the GAC *couldn't* keep him safe, but where every piece of scum could hunt him if they knew his location—Earth. "You can stop those scans," he said. "I know where he is."

Shanta's eyes went from knowing to terrified. "Glinto—"

He cut her off with a swipe of his hand and turned to Dilton. "Do you trust me?"

"I barely know you."

"All right, but given what you *do* know about me, do you trust that I'm equally or *more* invested in solving this case than protecting…." He paused. Just finishing his question could put him in line for another reprimand. "Protecting my friend?"

Her eyes narrowed. "Based on what I know about you, I'd have to say…yes."

"Then trust me now. Shut down their surveillance equipment, get these locals out of here, and send Beattie out for a hot drink."

"I do not drink, Agent," Beattie said coldly.

Dilton held her hand up to the bot. "And what happens if I do all this?"

"I can deliver Maxim. Safely. And we can get to the bottom of this."

"That's your guarantee?"

"Nothing in this galaxy is guaranteed, agent. But, this is the best way to do this, believe me."

Dilton looked into Matthias' eyes. "Beattie, go get us a couple of steaming caocas."

"Varra…." Beattie sounded unconvinced.

Dilton looked at the bot. "Beattie, please. I'm playing a hunch."

The bot stared right at Matthias for a moment and then toddled off to fulfill Dilton's request.

Dilton gave Matthias a slow nod and left. As he closed the door behind her, he heard Vantross protesting her orders.

Once the door was closed, he turned back to Shanta. "All right, Shanta, let's talk."

Two hours later, GAC security officers walked the *Sequel* crew out to the landing pad—single file and in chains. Matthias and Dilton stood with Vantross, looking on dispassionately, while Beattie prepped the shuttle for departure.

"What will you do with them?" Vantross asked, barely concealing a smile.

"We'll take them back to Central, see if our interrogators can get anything out of them," Matthias replied. Dilton kept her gaze on the shuttle.

"And what of Ultra?" Vantross asked. "Where does that investigation take you?"

"I'm not at liberty to say."

"Oh, come now, agent. Clearly I have proven that we are equals in this."

Matthias didn't consider Vantross his equal in *anything*, but before he could respond, a strange buzzing became audible. "Do you hear that?"

"Yes...it sounds like a...cloud-skipper!" As Vantross cried out the name, he hit the deck.

Two small flying vehicles piloted by two humanoids with tails swooped over the landing pad. The females piloting the vehicles buzzed the landing pad a few times. Everyone ducked. The women fired laser bolts wildly, scattering the security officers. Matthias huddled with Dilton and the cowering Vantross. He pulled his service weapon and fired a few errant bolts.

The party crashers were far more accurate, felling security team members left and right. Within moments, the women had collected the crew—the Glutob compacting himself to make room for Litning—and whisked them away toward the spaceport and the waiting *Sequel*—just as Matthias and Shanta had planned.

Vantross sputtered as Matthias helped Dilton to her feet. "You-you're letting them get away!"

"They got the drop on us," Matthias said with a shrug. "What can I say?"

As Vantross chastised his incapacitated officers, Dilton touched Matthias' arm.

"This had better work, Glintock."

CHAPTER II

Max sat at the kitchen table with his mother, sharing dinner before he headed off to meet Gina at the reunion. His mother had insisted. He'd been spending most of his free time with Gina. His mother wanted to ensure she had time with him. As much as he was enjoying being with Gina, he was happy to oblige.

"Are you excited for the reunion?" his mother asked.

"Not really. I mean, I'm looking forward to see Gina, but that's about it."

"I think you should loosen up a little bit," she said.

"Oh yeah? Why's that?"

"You're so worried about 'the big secrets.' I think if you go in with a relaxed attitude, you might actually enjoy yourself."

"Aside from Gina and Sam, I'm not really dying to see any of these people, Mom."

"You might be surprised."

He stuffed his mouth full of green beans, so that he could only offer an innocent shrug in reply.

"Sam told me that several of your old friends had been asking about you."

"When did you start hanging out with all of my friends?"

"It's the closest thing I've got to spending time with you."

He winced. His mother hadn't lost her talent for guilt-tripping. "I'm sorry I've been away so long. It wasn't *totally* my fault."

"I know, but you hadn't been back in some time before that, Max. Thank God Alesha and Roeger let me know what happened to you."

"I'm sorry."

"Your father used to take short trips. He was never gone for years on end." She paused. "Do you really hate it here that much?"

A pang of guilt lanced though him. "No, Mom. No. It's not that. It's just…."

She gave him an expectant look as he trailed off.

"It's just that…my life is out there."

She got very quiet. "Oh, I see."

He sighed. "You're taking it the wrong way, Mom."

"I really don't think I am, Max. Your father had no problem always returning to me. I don't know why you can't do the same; at least on a semi-regular basis."

"But, he was your husband. I'm your kid. Kids are supposed to leave the nest."

"To go live somewhere else *on Earth*, not across the *galaxy*."

"I don't know where this is coming from."

"You don't? Max, I lost your father to this life. I don't want to lose you too."

"But Mom, I could get hit by a truck tomorrow."

"At least I would know what had happened to you!"

He hadn't considered that. Max liked to think he was a considerate person, but clearly, he hadn't thought about how his lifestyle impacted his mother. Then, something clicked for him. "Is that why you've been pushing Gina so hard; so I'll stay?"

Her expression became bashful. "Is it so wrong for a mother to want her only son to live closer to her?"

"I wouldn't be happy on Earth, Mom."

"You don't know that! Your father died and you ran off to follow the same path, leaving me here, alone."

"That's not fair. Was I supposed to stay here forever after everything Dad had shown me?"

A silent moment passed. "No. I guess not. I don't know. I miss you, son. I want to be able to see you and you stay away longer and longer each time you leave. What you do is dangerous and I'm not going to be here forever. I don't want you coming back one day to find me gone."

Something else Max had never considered. He'd been wrapped up in his own problems for some time. Thinking about how his mother felt, alone on Earth, never really occurred to him. He was ashamed. "I…I don't know what to say. I wish I'd known you felt this way before. I probably should have asked. I'm sorry."

"I don't want you worrying about me all the time. I know you have a lot to deal with up there. But, I'd just like to see you now and again. I love you, honey. I miss you."

"I missed you too, Mom. But, I really doubt I'm going to move back to Earth any time soon."

"Not even for Gina?" Her smile was full of hope.

He chuckled. "We've been seeing each other less than a week."

She shrugged. "Still. A rekindled flame can burn brighter than a new one."

"You shouldn't be putting all your hopes on Gina keeping me here. The way she tells it, she wants to see what's out there."

"I can't believe she's known the truth, or at least part of it, all this time and never said anything."

"In her defense, I didn't give her much of an opportunity." The thought of her warmed his heart. "It's been…nice reconnecting with her."

"I'm glad. That's all I want for you. I'm sorry Alesha left."

"She…had a lot of things she needed to work out; things she wanted to do," he said. "They didn't necessarily include me."

"Do you think she'll come back?"

"I have no idea."

"What will you tell her about Gina?"

"I'll deal with that when the time comes." There was a slight lull in the conversation. He decided to consider his mother and shift to something she'd be delighted to discuss. "So…Billy."

She smiled broadly. "Yes?"

"How is that going? Roeger hasn't been too much of a damper, has he?"

"No, Roeger's fine. When Billy's here, he just stays in the basement. Billy's actually coming over later. I chose to spare you and keep dinner between us."

"I appreciate it and I'm sorry again for my initial reaction. I want you to be happy, Mom. I know Dad would have too."

"Thank you, honey. That means the world."

"What's his situation?"

"Happily retired. He stayed in the service when Jim left," she explained. "He made it his career."

"Where's he from?"

"Originally? Montana."

"And he came all the way across the country for you?"

"Don't act so surprised! I'm quite a catch!"

"Please, don't ever say that again. I just meant, you guys knew each other well enough for him to make that move?"

"I hate to keep mentioning it, Max, but you *have* been gone a long time."

"Fair enough."

Kate had a look in her eye he hadn't seen in years. She appeared to be truly happy. What more could he ask for? He tried to keep his suspicious nature in check and follow his mother's instincts. If Billy made her happy, he'd make the effort to accept him.

"What do you and Gina have planned for tonight?"

He shrugged. "Just going to the reunion and then we'll postgame with Sam and Cindy."

"Well, I hope you have a good time."

"I'm sure we will. I have to make sure I've got my cover story in place."

"It must be hard, having to lie all the time. That's the part I hated with your father."

"Did you ever want to go out there with him?"

"He took me once. That was enough for me. When he worked with Talon…let's just say Talon Merthane wasn't my favorite person."

"Something we have in common, Mom."

"Is he still making things difficult for you?"

He let out a humorless laugh. "That's quite the understatement."

"I wish you'd tell me more about it."

"You don't want to know. You'll just worry more. Believe me, I'm sparing you. I've got Litning around now. He keeps me safe."

"Am I going to get to meet the rest of the crew?"

"Sure, when they get back at the end of the week."

"I look forward to it. Well, not you leaving, but you know what I mean."

"I do. Thanks for dinner. This was nice."

"Well, I wanted to be sure to get time with you, but I am happy you and Gina are having fun."

"Thanks. I'm going to check on Roeger and get going."

"All right, honey."

He kissed his mother on her forehead and moved down to the basement. Roeger sat on the couch, cat in his lap. "How are we doing down here?"

"The kitty cat and I are enjoying the comedic stylings of Jerry Seinfeld," Roeger replied.

"We'll have to see if I can find my old DVDs before we leave—take 'em with us. Have you heard from the crew?"

"Not since they departed. I assume they are, as you say, 'living it up.'"

"Yeah, probably. Maybe try to hail them. Make sure we're still on schedule."

"Really? I thought that with the developments with Gina, you might want to stay?"

Max paused. The past several days with Gina had been extraordinary, but was he ready to change his life for her? "That's a conversation for later. I'll see you tomorrow."

"Enjoy your evening, Maxim."

"Later? Sure. The reunion? Highly doubtful."

"Do not plan for failure, for you shall surely find it."

"Who said that?"

"Roeger the Robot. Tell your friends."

Max chuckled and headed out to the Rover. He whipped out his communicator and sent Gina a message. *Dinner's done. OMW.*

OK. See U soon. ♥

His mother's house wasn't terribly far from the reunion venue, *The Manor*, so time wasn't a concern. All the housing developments in town were spread out, which made it all the more ridiculous that the reunion was being held in a manufactured section of town called *Main Street* which was central to nothing. *Main Street* was made up of overpriced housing and expensive boutiques. So, nothing like a traditional main street area. It was a crock.

As he drove, Max didn't notice the torpedo-like aircraft above the Rover until it was almost on top of him. He pulled back on the throttle, but not before the craft's underside opened and deposited a lithe, masked figure into the Rover's backseat. The aircraft peeled off into the night sky.

A car approached in the opposite lane. Max couldn't engage in any fancy driving maneuvers without risking an accident. He stopped short, sending his unwanted passenger ass-first into the front of the Rover. Max kept one hand on the wheel, while trying to dislodge the mask with the other.

The attacker yanked the steering wheel, forcing Max to cease grabbing at the mask. Then the attacker vaulted back into the rear seat and drew a sword from a scabbard. The blade crackled with electric energy.

"*Jesus, fuck!*"

The assailant drew back and thrust the sword at Max, who leaned against the steering wheel to dodge. The sword plunged into the Rover's door. More cars sped toward them. Headlights approached from behind. As the attacker struggled to dislodge the sword, Max had only one chance to gain the upper hand, consequences be damned. He pushed the throttle forward and pulled back on the steering column. The Rover rose higher in the air, allowing Max to tilt the vehicle side to side.

The attacker managed to yank the sword free as Max tilted the Rover to the right. In the glow of the streetlights, he could see the antagonist's curves. *A woman.* She lost balance and started to fall out of the vehicle. With a deft move, she thrust the sword into the rear floorboard.

As Max turned the Rover at a ninety-degree angle, the attacker dangled from the sword. He half-considered dragging her across the roof of one of the approaching cars, but he didn't want to harm any bystanders. At that moment, all the cars on the road had slowed to gawk and honk their horns at his flying car. He was about three miles from *Main Street*.

The dangling attacker drew a laser pistol and fired a bolt at Max. Clearly, she wasn't concerned about him crashing the Rover and killing them both. With Max jostling the vehicle, the attacker's aim was erratic. So, changing tactics, she aimed at a bigger target than Max—the engine.

Laser bolts drilled into the hood as Max tilted the Rover back and forth in a vain attempt to shake the attacker off. Metal chunks ripped from the hood as the laser bolts hit home. The Rover shuddered. Smoke poured from the engine as the steering column bucked in Max's grasp.

He descended toward the road as the first burst of flame erupted from the engine. The Rover pitched and buckled. Max struggled to control it. Sparing a glance behind him, he saw his assailant had vanished.

Hopefully, she fucking bought it. As much as he wished otherwise, he knew with someone that skilled, an accidental death was unlikely.

Max couldn't control the Rover's descent any longer. He had to bail or risk a fiery death on impact. He'd reached the outskirts of *Main Street*. It was as good a place as any to ditch. Unfastening his safety belt, he tried to guide the Rover in for the safest landing possible, away from any bystanders.

This is gonna fuckin' hurt. He leaped from the crashing hovercraft and hit the ground rolling.

The Rover smashed into and mangled a wrought iron fence. Luckily, there weren't any bodies underneath the smoldering wreck. Though the vehicle was salvageable, Max didn't have time for that. Many people had seen what the Rover could really do. He couldn't let the tech fall into the wrong hands. Reluctantly, he keyed the command on his wrist unit.

A small explosion rocked the front of the Rover, destroying the vital systems. Another controlled detonation knocked out the anti-gravity system. The vehicle was little more than melted slag, now. He lamented the loss, but it was the only way. Earth authorities could *not* possess the Rover.

Max looked to the *Main Street* complex. He was bruised and bloodied, but nothing felt broken. His pants had a hole in the knee and his jacket shoulder was torn. His knee throbbed.

The Manor was about half a mile away, so he started running as fast as his balky knee would carry him. The assassin had attacked him on the way to the reunion. Another attack could come there. He had to protect Gina and Sam, no matter what.

CHAPTER 12

"Do you think he's coming?"

"Who knows? I doubt it. He didn't come to the last reunion."

"He's not on social media, either. God, I hate to ask this, but, is he even still alive?"

Sam rolled his eyes. The explanations for Max's absences always left him amused. In this case, the latest theories were from their friends Paul and Mike, who stood at a table with him. It never occurred to any of these people that Max might not *want* to be there.

He checked his phone. Max and Gina were running late. He smiled; Max deserved a little happiness. It wasn't that Sam disliked Alesha—he loved her to death—she just wasn't the best choice for a stable relationship. She kind of had a wanderlust about her.

Two hundred classmates and their guests had turned up; everyone in the room was "dressed to impress." Throughout *The Manor*, friends reminisced about old times. A DJ played music from their high school days, but not so loudly that the guests had to shout to be heard.

"Well, let's ask the man himself," Paul said. "You're his best friend, Sam. Is he coming?"

"Why do you guys care so much?" Sam asked.

"Because, we haven't seen him in ages!" Mike said. "Max was always a fun guy. We can't even hit him up on social."

Again, Sam rolled his eyes. "Well, if you two dummies knew anything, you'd know you're talking to the wrong person."

"We are? What happened? You two have a falling out?" Paul asked.

"No, not at all. But, if you were in the know, you'd know the person you need to be talking to is Gina Rivio."

Mike balked. "*Really?* Max is dating Gina?"

"Yes, he is." Greg Wilson approached. Greg always seemed cool with Max, but Sam honestly found him to be kind of a jagoff. "I saw them out together the other night at *Rascals*. Kinda disappointed, not gonna lie. Was kinda hoping to bag Gina at this reunion."

Sam glared at Greg with disdain. "Hello, Greg."

"What's up, Samarino?"

God, Max was right about these things. Why did I even come?

Cindy brought drinks to the table and planted a kiss on Sam's cheek. "Here you go, hon. I swear, none of your classmates know how the nametags work. I've been called everything from Amy to Kimmy."

"But, you don't have a nametag," he said.

"My point exactly. Who's this?" she asked, sipping her gin and tonic.

Before Sam could introduce her, Greg jutted his hand out to Cindy. "Hi, Greg Wilson. Samarino, you didn't tell me you landed a stone cold fox."

Cindy clearly wasn't a fan of Greg either. "I'm also a lawyer, Mr. Wilson."

Sam caught sight of Gina moving through the crowd. "Gina? Where's Max?"

"We were meeting each other." She was obviously distressed. "He's not here already?"

"Hey, Gina," Greg said.

"Not now, Greg," was all she said in reply. Paul and Mike guffawed. "Did he text you?"

Sam looked at his phone again. "Nope. When did you last hear from him?"

"When he was on his way. His mom's place isn't far from here. Where could he be?"

Just as the question escaped her lips, two figures crashed through the glass doors and onto the dance floor. One was Max, bloody and struggling, and the other was a masked mystery.

This isn't good... Sam thought.

The assassin had ambushed Max outside *The Manor*. He'd tried to steer the fight toward one of the closed *Main Street* stores, but his assailant tackled him through the glass door and proceeded to beat the shit out of him.

Max covered his face with his forearm, warding off blows as his free hand groped around for anything he could use as a weapon. His fingers closed around a wooden shard from the door. With a swift motion, he stabbed her in the left side.

His attacker screamed—the first sound to emanate from behind the mask—and reeled back.

"Yeah, you keep that," he said as he rolled away. His body cursed him with every movement. He was deafened by his classmates' screams as he struggled to his feet. Sam and Gina stared in horror from across the room, while other familiar faces wore confused and excited looks. Apparently, some people wanted to see a fight no matter the circumstances.

He pulled his black box from his jacket and transformed it into his pistol. There was no need to keep a lid on his secret life, now. On the upside, this would trump any mundane stories of career, parenthood, and marriage.

The assassin pulled the wooden shard out. The bodysuit sealed almost instantly.

He leveled his pistol. "Okay, now that we've had a minute, who the fuck are you?"

"*I'm the last thing you'll ever see in this life,*" the woman replied.

Max snorted. "Yeah? Get in line. What did I do to you? Did I steal something from you?"

"*You stole the light from my world.*"

"That might be an even longer line. You're into the whole cryptic villain thing, huh?"

"*You see me as a villain? How ironic.*"

"Well, you're sure as shit not the hero." He fired off several shots, but each was met by her sword, which once again crackled with energy. Whoever she was, she was good—maybe too good.

"*A pistol in a melee fight? Coward.*"

"You jumped into my car and tried to *stab me* while I was *driving*. Maybe ease up on throwing around the C-word."

The assassin drew another sword. She charged at Max. He held his ground, firing his pistol at her. Normally, he'd have sought cover, but he wouldn't risk any of his gawking classmates, especially Gina and Sam. She deflected his shots and swung her sword, but he ducked. She knocked the pistol from his hand with a kick.

The weapon skittered across the floor. Instead of retrieving it, Max tackled the woman around her legs. They crashed to the floor. One of the swords fell from her grasp, but she used the hilt of the other to pound on Max's back. He returned the favor by punching her injured side. She screamed and released her hold. Scrambling to his feet, he moved for his pistol, but she grabbed his foot and brought him down.

"*Ooh!*" cried the assembled witnesses as Max's body smacked against the floor.

Why are these people still here?

"Max!" Sam's voice cut through the ringing in his ears. Sam stood about twenty feet away, holding Max's pistol. He was about to toss it to Max, but instead aimed and fired. Turning his head, Max saw the assassin bearing down on him, sword raised to strike. He rolled out of the way. The charged blade cut into the floor.

Sam fired more shots, but the assassin put a stop to that. As she yanked her sword out of the floor, she tossed a capsule from her belt at Sam. It exploded in a brilliant burst of light.

"Fuck!" Sam cried in chorus with the other blinded onlookers.

The assassin continued toward Max, brandishing her sword as she walked. He tried to get up, but his knee wasn't having it. "*It's fitting that you'll meet your end here, Ultra, in front of all your friends.*"

"I've got news for you, lady, most of these people aren't my friends."

"*You care about some of them.*" She glanced back toward Gina and Cindy.

"If you touch them, I'll fucking kill you."

A creepy chuckle echoed behind the mask. "*You'll try. I think we've proven that you're nothing compared to me. I can hardly fathom how you managed to kill her.*"

Ah, a peek into the window. "Her? I don't recall killing many women. Are you related to Sierra? Wait, your face is covered. Braneith? You're related to her?"

She stared down at him. Her sword crackled and hummed like a defective lightsaber. She raised the sword over her head with a battle cry and brought it down toward Max—right before a massive laser blast knocked her across the dance floor.

Max knew his pistol couldn't do *that*. He looked around and his chest seized with a mixture of panic and relief. Standing in the ruined patio doorway, massive laser cannon on her hip, was Alesha.

"Hi, Earth Boy. Miss me?"

CHAPTER 13

Alesha stood in *The Manor*'s demolished doorway like she
owned the place. The cannon resting on her hip was half her size,
but she carried it like she was born with it. Max's heart skipped a
beat. He told himself it was just the adrenaline wearing off.

A hulking, bald alien of indeterminate origin peered around
Alesha, as if looking for trouble. It had olive green skin and
wicked yellow claws. Its hands were about the size of Max's
head. The remaining reunion guests went into a screaming panic
at the sight. Whatever the alien was, it looked like a nasty
customer, despite its jumpsuit that looked like skin-tight overalls.

Alesha sauntered into the building sporting black pants,
boots, leather jacket, and loose-fitting white t-shirt. She'd
changed her hairstyle again. Her dark hair was cut in a pixie bob
combo, which made her look like a rock star. Her cool
detachment gave way to a broad smile. She handed the cannon to
her companion before bounding up to Max, burying him in kisses.
Gina walked over, looking none too pleased.

"'Lesha…'Lesha…" Max said as he tried to pry her off.

She responded by throwing her arms around his neck. "*Gods*, I missed you. If you weren't so squeamish about public affection, I'd take you right here."

"Rio not doing it for you anymore?"

She balked. "Ugh, no. He was good at his job, but a pervert. What was all that 'sweet baby' crap?" Alesha turned toward Gina, as if she'd only just seen her. "Hello, who's *this* gorgeous creature? Your name isn't Sierra is it?" Gina's mouth hung open.

"Alesha, this is, uh, this is Gina."

Alesha gasped. "Not...*the* Gina? Oh...he's told me *all* about you."

Gina's brow creased. She folded her arms. "Funny, he never mentioned you at all." She threw Max an angry look.

"That's because I'm his secret *space* girlfriend. He can't tell *anyone* on Earth about *me*. Well, except his mother." She started dropping the act. "And his best friend—both human *and* robot."

"Yes, we've met," Gina said.

"Really widening the circle of trust there, aren't we, Max?"

"It's a long story," he said. "Not that I don't appreciate the save, but what are you doing here?"

It was Alesha's turn to be shocked. "Gods, he was right—you haven't a clue."

His brow furrowed. "A clue about what?"

She looked at Gina and then back to him. "Max, you're the GAC's Enemy Number One."

He chuckled. "No, really. Why are you here?" When Alesha's expression didn't change, Max's stomach dropped. His body went hot. "What? H-how? Why?"

"There was a terrorist bombing on Aval. The man on the security vid had your face. Glintock sent me to collect you."

His mind reeled. Someone had framed him for a crime *on Aval*. If he was captured, his life was over. Then, something sliced through the fog of fear. *Glintock sent me to collect you.* Max immediately got into a defensive stance. "Gina, get behind me!"

Alesha's face twisted in confusion. "What the veck is wrong with you? Do you think I'm here to collect the *bounty?*"

"You said Glintock sent you. Why else would you be here?"

"To protect you, dummy! He sent me to protect you!" She looked to Gina. "Men, am I right?"

Gina didn't answer.

"This isn't funny!" Max cried. "None of this is funny!"

"Well, some of it's funny," Alesha said. She looked back to Gina. "You don't talk much, do you?"

"I'm, ah, a little overwhelmed right now." Gina's eyes stayed fixed on Alesha's companion.

Alesha gestured to the alien. "Jethan, give us some space. You're spooking the locals."

Jethan grunted and wandered back toward the hole in the wall. Gina visibly relaxed.

"Alesha!" Sam said as he greeted her with a warm embrace.

"Sam!" She returned the hug. When they parted, she waved. "Hi, Cindy."

"Hey, 'Lesha," Cindy said.

"I'm happy everyone is reconnecting, but can we get back to the fact that I'm about to have a thousand bounty hunters breathing down my neck?" Max's chest tightened.

"Don't forget, the GAC wants you too," Alesha said. She put a comforting hand on his shoulder. "Easy, Earth Boy. It's okay. Glintock sent me to keep you safe, not bring you in. He doesn't believe you did this. Of course, his bosses need a little more convincing."

Brontin. Glintock had told Max of the fallout he'd endured from the Memta case. It made sense to Max that the guy who tried to make Glintock's life hell before would do it again. Then, something clicked in his mind. "Wait, what exactly am I accused of?"

Alesha's face became solemn. "It was *The Gallant*, tallest residential tower on Aval."

His stomach heaved. "How many victims?"

She swallowed hard. "Thousands," her voice was barely audible. Gina gasped.

The room spun. *Thousands.* The horrific nature was unfathomable. His heart rate spiked.

Alesha squeezed his arm. "Hey, Max, we'll beat this."

He forced a smile. "I really appreciate that, 'Lesha. But, I'm not that confident."

"Why not?"

He pointed to the unconscious assassin. "She's the first of many. If bounty hunters aren't afraid to come to Earth, where will I be safe?" Alesha, Sam, and Gina stared beyond Max. He spun around. The assassin was gone. "Where'd she go? Did anyone see where she went?"

Then, a pair of familiar faces peered through the hole in the wall. Shanta led the way, pistol drawn, followed by Litning, who carried a rifle.

Max ran his hand down his face. "Yeah, that's not conspicuous at all," he muttered.

"We were only concerned for your safety, Maxim," Litning said. Max should have known that nothing escaped his finely tuned hearing.

"Thank the gods you're all right," Shanta said as she crossed to Max.

"I'm glad to see you guys. Truly," Max said.

"We called ahead," Shanta said. "Roeger told us you were here. Your communicator sent him a signal that you were in trouble."

"Did you go to the house? Is my mom okay?"

"No, we came straight here. We're picking Roeger up on the way out of here. What the veck happened?"

"Bounty hunter paid me a visit," he replied. Despite complaining about his crew's lack of discretion, he was happy and relieved to see them.

Shanta's eyebrow shot up. "Here on Earth? That's…not great."

"No, it's not." He looked at Sam. "Sam. I hate to ask…."

"No need to ask at all, buddy. We'll pick up your mom on the way home. She'll be safe with us."

"In fact, we should go now," Cindy said. "With all of this, I want to get back to the kids as soon as we can."

"That's my cue," Sam said. He and Max embraced. "You take care of yourself, brother. Don't be a stranger."

"Thanks, Sam. I'll reach out once we've gotten this all figured out."

Sam nodded. He hugged Gina and then turned to Alesha. He kissed her cheek. "I wish it could have been under better circumstances, Alesha."

"Me too, Sam. Me too."

Sam turned to Shanta and Litning. "Take care of my friend, please."

"He's our friend too," Shanta said. "We've got this."

Sam nodded again and took Cindy's hand. They stopped in front of Litning. Sam looked up at him. "You're actually bigger than I imagined."

"All the more to protect the ones we love," Litning replied.

"Thanks."

As Sam and Cindy departed, Max dialed his mother. She picked up on the first ring.

"*Max, what is going on?*"

"Uh, some bad people came looking for me, so Sam is coming to take you to his house. You'll need to pack a bag."

There was a brief pause. "*No.*"

"What? Mom, I need you safe. You're going with Sam."

"*Maxim, your father did this for decades. I know how to take care of myself. I'm not leaving my home.*"

"Mom, please."

"*Max, no one is running me out of my house. I'll be fine. Be careful. I love you.*"

He gritted his teeth. Why wouldn't she listen? "I love you too, Mom."

"*Let me know you're safe.*"

"You too."

She ended the call; her way of letting Max get on with it. She was right. How many times had she gone through something like this with Dad? He didn't doubt his mother could take care of herself, but going to Sam's couldn't hurt.

He looked at Gina; her panicked eyes focused on him. He took her in his arms. She shuddered in his embrace. "It'll be okay," he whispered.

"No, it won't. You're a fugitive, Max!"

"Well, at least I have the FBI on my side."

She chuckled, but it ended with a sob.

He kissed the top of her head and turned to Shanta. "Okay, let's get moving."

Shanta's mouth opened, but Alesha spoke up. "You're not going anywhere with them."

"What? Of course I am. I'm getting on the *Sequel* and finding out who's trying to fuck me."

"And how easy do you think that'll be flying around in a marked ship?" Alesha asked. "I don't think you get what's happening here. You are galactic enemy number one, Max. That means the GAC and every bounty hunter in the galaxy will be gunning for you. You're not safe on the *Sequel*."

"Glintock can keep the GAC off of us and—"

"No, boss, he can't," Shanta cut in. "That's why he called us in. The *Sequel* will be his eyes and ears in trying to clear you. Alesha will keep you safe in some hidey-hole, while we sort this out."

"You can't expect me to sit on the sidelines while everyone is out risking their lives for me." Max felt control of the situation slipping through his fingers.

"*Yes*, we can," Shanta said. "Look, Cap, we've already sorted this out with Glintock. We came here to warn you and collect Roeger. If this bounty hunter hadn't hit you here, I'd suggest staying on Earth, but now…. Where is he anyway?"

"*She* slipped away in the confusion," Max replied, the sour taste of bile rising in his throat.

"That's…a problem," Shanta said.

"And even more reason for Max to stay away from the *Sequel*," Alesha added.

"Just what I was thinking," Shanta said.

"Great minds, I guess," Alesha replied with a smile.

He couldn't believe that his former and current first mates were flirting at a time like this. "Have you two met before?"

Alesha shook her head. "Ah, no. Only by reputation."

"And you *know* you can't stop talking about Alesha," Shanta said.

Max looked to a visibly disappointed Gina, but before he could reassure her, a low growl arrested his attention. He looked over to see Litning and Jethan standing nose-to-nose. "What's the problem, Fuzzy?"

"I do not like the smell of this one," Litning rumbled.

"Perhaps it is all your musty fur that fills your nostrils, Revash," Jethan hit back.

The two of them bared their teeth until Alesha marched up to them. "That's enough of this nakra! Litning, Jethan's with me, so relax. And Jethan, Litning is a friend—treat him accordingly."

Both aliens continued their stare down for another moment. "Very well, Alesha," Litning said, moving toward Max. "I do not trust him," he said under his breath.

"You just met him. How can you be sure?"

"Something…does not smell right about him. If you are going with Alesha, I am coming with you."

"The crew needs you m—"

"I offered to stay with you here on Earth and look at the consequences of your refusal. Human, if you take a photograph, I will crush both your arms," Litning said as he turned his head toward one of the reunion's stragglers.

It was Greg Wilson. He'd been setting up for a selfie with Litning in the background, but deflated under Litning's glare. "Max. Gina. Good to see you guys," he managed as he scurried away.

"Okay," Alesha said. "So, the *Sequel* gang will run errands for Glintock, while Max comes with me."

"I will stay with Max," Litning said, daring Max to contradict him.

"That just leaves you, darling," Alesha said, turning to Gina. "You got a ride here or do you need us to drop you somewhere?"

Gina shuffled her feet. "No, I can get a ride home, but…." She sighed. "Can I talk to Max for a minute? Privately?"

Alesha got a funny little smile on her face before gesturing to Max. "Be my guest, but make it quick. Law enforcement can't be far."

Gina grabbed Max's arm and led him to a corner.

"What's up?" He asked. "I'm really sorry about all this."

Gina took a deep breath. "I want to come with you."

He shook his head. "Gina, *no*. This," he said, gesturing around, "is nothing compared to what's out there. I can't risk you getting hurt."

"Will you listen to yourself? I work for the *FBI*, Max—I can handle myself."

"But, what about your job, your friends and family, your *life?*"

"No offense, Max, but the risk is mine. Ever since I discovered your secret, I've wondered about what's out there. This is my only chance to find out!"

He wanted to protect Gina. With bounty hunters invading their hometown, having her close by might be the best way to do that. "All right. But you have to stay close to me or Litning."

"I intend to stay close to you. And it's sweet that you want to protect me." She kissed his cheek.

They approached Alesha, Litning, and Jethan—Shanta had departed to collect Roeger. "Yes, she can come," Alesha said. "But, we've got to run."

Sirens sounded in the distance. "Right, let's go," Max said.

The group left through the hole in the wall. Alesha touched Max's arm. "Despite the circumstances, I *am* happy to see you, Max. I missed you."

He smiled. "I missed you too."

She leaned in and whispered in his ear. "And Gina is adorable. Can't wait to see what she and I get up to."

"Uh…nothing."

"Well, I think that's her decision," she replied with a wink.

As they hustled into the night, he asked, "So, what's the plan?"

"Glintock wants me to stash you away somewhere, but I can tell you won't go for that."

"No way."

"So, I thought I'd mention some rumors I've heard."

The back of his brain itched. "What rumors?"

"Of a woman leading high volume heists—a woman with glowing blue eyes."

A shudder ran through him. "Sierra."

"Exactly. And I thought to myself, 'Self, who would try and frame Max?'"

If it *was* Sierra, he was both surprised and not that she was alive. And yes, she definitely would have wanted to frame him. "Let's get her."

CHAPTER 14

Earth.

Talon Merthane had never planned to return to the backwater planet, but life was full of little surprises. He had also been sure he'd never be a parent again, but here they were.

Alexis lay unconscious in front of him on a rooftop not far from Maxim Ultra's little party. Talon wasn't sure what they'd hit her with, but it was enough to put her on her ass for an extended period. Finally, she jerked awake. Sitting bolt upright, she flailed her arms, lashing out at potential attackers.

Talon sat on his haunches at a safe distance. "Peace, Alexis. Peace. You're safe here."

She looked at him through the lifeless lenses of her mask. "*Father.*"

"That's the greeting I get after pulling you out of that mess?"

Alexis pulled the mask off, revealing her short blonde hair and soft blue eyes. "What do you want? My gratitude? My admiration? I had that under control."

He couldn't help smirking. "Yes, it definitely looked that way with you flat on your back."

"I didn't count on the Cabal woman," Alexis said, getting to her feet.

"You're hunting Maxim Ultra. You *always* prepare for Alesha Cabal."

"My information said they were no longer partnered. I *do* know how to research my targets."

"Oh, really? Have you been keeping up with current events since your little jaunt to Iswat? That world is devolving into planet-wide war thanks to your visit."

"I had a job. I completed it. That's where my involvement ends. *You* taught me that."

"Who were the clients?"

"Anonymous. You know the majority of assassination contracts are done through third parties. Why are you giving me all this grief?"

"Because, plunging a planet into civil war is a little more than an incidental result of an assassination. Yes, a job is a job is a job, but with political hits, you have to weigh the consequences."

She was quiet for a moment. "You're just mad that I ignored you on this Maxim Ultra business."

"Oh, no argument there." He gave her a stern stare. "I told you to wait to hit Maxim."

"I'm done waiting. *He killed Dayna*. I still can't believe you let him walk away from that."

Talon's face did not betray his thoughts. It was Sierra Numani, possessed by the goddess Memta, who had murdered his partner and Alexis' surrogate mother, Dayna. However, since Maxim had found the statue that imprisoned the goddess, Talon foisted the blame onto him. It served his purposes with Alexis.

"Like you predicted, Ultra got himself into trouble again and there's a clear bounty on his head. I don't see where the problem is."

"Alexis, you're very good at what you do, but that doesn't mean you're totally ready to be on your own."

She snorted. "You don't think I can handle Ultra?"

"No, love, I don't think you're ready for a blood vendetta." He softened his tone.

"Oh, I'm fine on that score."

"Did you kill him? Is he tied up somewhere waiting for you to pick him up?" She didn't offer an answer. "Not only could you not corral Maxim, you've let him know we're onto him, and you're about to have a mountain of competition in trying to capture him."

"I chose to go with the element of surpr—"

"And you failed!" He stopped himself. His goal was to guide her, not crush her spirit. "If you'd just done what I asked, you and I would be counting that reward now."

She gestured down to the street. "Well, stop lecturing me and let's go! He's still down there!"

He put a gentle hand on her shoulder. "With layers of protection and the knowledge that you're still lurking out here."

In the distance, a ship lifted off. A device on Alexis' belt beeped.

"It's the *Sequel!* He's escaping!" She started to head off on the chase, but Talon grabbed her arm.

"Your enthusiasm is admirable, but wait."

"For what? He's leaving!"

"*Wait.*"

She struggled in his grip another moment, but he held her fast. Finally, she relented. "When he gets away, you'll be to blame."

"He's not getting away," Talon said.

Several minutes passed in silence. The local authorities arrived and swarmed the street below. Their emergency lights painted the night red and blue. Talon found the witness accounts that floated up to his ears to be highly amusing.

Finally, distant movement caught his eye. Another ship took off in the distance. He pointed. "Look."

Alexis followed his finger and pointed her transponder reader toward the vehicle. "Cabal's ship?"

"The most wanted man in the galaxy isn't going to fly around in his own ship," Talon said. "And hers is the ship I tagged on the way to help you. Now, let's go."

Alexis fell in beside him, an expression of quiet amusement on her face.

"You can say it, you know," he said with a tight smile.

"You...*may* have more to teach me."

"Never smash a door when you can go in quietly through a window."

"Noted." They worked their way across the rooftops away from the ruined party. "Do you think Ultra blew up that building on Aval?"

"No, of course not. But, who cares?" He chuckled, prompting her to do the same. The *Claw* and the pursuit of Maxim Ultra awaited.

CHAPTER 15

Sierra laughed as she piled into the repurposed military dropship with her comrades. Another successful heist; she reveled in a job well done. The target had been another of Zeth's own facilities, one specializing in blast-enforced metal. She and her team had cleaned out the warehouses and relieved many of the security personnel of their lives.

Sierra remained in awe of Lady Zeth's ruthlessness. She'd order the deaths of her own employees at a moment's notice if it meant keeping her plan on course. The families were well-compensated, but Zeth made no illusions about what was most important. In that way, she was much like Memta.

Sierra's heart ached at the thought of her goddess. She wanted nothing more in the galaxy than to commune with her again. Memta's absence left a black hole in her soul. All the random killing and vecking in the universe could never fill it. She knew what she needed and was convinced she'd never find it again.

Pushing Memta from her mind, Sierra plopped down into an empty seat; the rest of the seats were filled by her team of soldiers. The woman beside her removed her mask. Her short spiky hair was drenched with sweat, camouflaging her crimson highlights throughout her dark locks. There was an eagerness in the young woman's eyes that made Sierra's blood burn.

"Ma'am?" the soldier asked haltingly.

Sierra waved her off. "Please, call me Sierra."

The young woman smiled. "All right, Sierra."

Hearing the soldier say Sierra's name sent a thrill through her. "And who are you?"

"Petra."

"What a beautiful name for a tough lady. Where does it come from?"

"It's a family name. We're from the Arerea Province on Modan."

"Ah, the heart of the GAC. Kind of ironic that you're here then, no?"

Petra arched her eyebrow. "Not sure what you mean."

Sierra's eyes narrowed in confusion. Had Zeth compartmentalized her operations so much that the soldiers didn't even know what they were fighting for? "It's nothing. How did you come into our service?"

"Years ago, I hooked up with a merc group—the Saviors. We were hired for this job through our broker. What about you? With that power you were throwing around, you can't be some standard grunt."

"Is that what prompted you to talk to me?"

"Sure, but you're also the only thing worth looking at around here."

Sierra blushed. "Flatterer. You clearly haven't looked into a mirror for some time. It's a shame you keep your face covered so much."

Now it was Petra's turn to look away bashfully. "Yeah, I'm sure I look amazing with all this battle grime all over me."

"I'm imagining you without it. In fact, I'm imagining you without a lot of things right now."

Petra balked. "You're bad!"

A sultry look took hold in Sierra's eyes. "I'm the best you'll ever have, Petra. *That*, I can promise."

Petra's eyes narrowed. "*Really?*"

Hours later, Sierra and her new friend were tangled in Sierra's satin sheets, their naked bodies entwined. They breathed heavily, sweat coating their bodies.

"You're right," Petra gasped. "That *might* be the best I've ever had."

Sierra raised her eyebrows. "Only *might?*"

"Well, let's say I'd be hard-pressed to remember any better."

"That's good enough—for now." She kissed Petra tenderly. Their hands linked together.

"Where does that…energy you use come from?" Petra asked.

"It's a long story, but it's inside me." Sierra bit her lip, a bitter expression on her face. "To my dismay, it's been fading on these missions. I'm using it too much." The hole in her soul grew a little bit more. Without the statue, there was no way to replenish her power. Or was there? If there was one thing Memta desired, it was souls. Her lustful eyes turned back to Petra.

"You looked so beautiful out there," Petra said. "Like an angel."

"Was this your first mission with us?"

"Yes. Believe me, I would have remembered seeing you before."

"And they didn't tell you anything about what we were doing there?"

"The job was light on details, but high on pay. They said we needed to support some other mercs, but I think there's much more going on than just a simple support operation."

"I can't really talk about it." She playfully pressed her finger to her lips. "I'm sworn to secrecy."

"Oooh, mysterious. I can do mysterious."

Sierra took Petra in her arms and kissed her deeply. She finally had an idea as to how Zeth got her soldiers to so casually kill her own people—none of them knew they were working for her, nor did they owe her any loyalty.

Her sexual needs sated, Sierra concentrated on what she believed Memta needed. As she kissed Petra, she took the woman's head in her hands. She started to squeeze.

"Hey, ow, you-you're hurting me," Petra said with a note of concern.

"Hush, Petra. You're about to become one with the goddess Memta." Sierra had no idea if that was even true, but it sounded good.

"Get off of me!" Petra struggled, but to no avail. Sierra's hands glowed bright turquoise, giving her increased strength.

Petra started to scream as Sierra's hands flared with blue fire. A wicked grin took hold of Sierra's face as Memta's energy flowed through her body, incinerating Petra. After several moments, Sierra fell back onto her bed, spent. All that remained of her most recent lover was ash. She felt a pang of regret, as she'd really liked Petra, but the hole inside her felt slightly smaller with her sacrifice. That brought a warm smile to Sierra's lips as she hugged one of her pillows and fell into blissful sleep.

CHAPTER 16

"I can't believe I let you talk me into this," Dilton said as Matthias stood behind her studying a terminal in his quarters on their ship.

He couldn't believe he'd been able to separate Dilton from her doppelganger. For the most part, they'd left Beattie out of their plans, but the bot wasn't stupid. She'd figure it out sooner or later.

"Ultra was supposed to stay secure on Earth. That's the *only* reason why I agreed to this," Dilton said. "That way, we could collect him at our leisure. Now you're telling me that he and Cabal are *leaving* Earth?"

"The attack on Earth shows the bounty hunters are no longer playing by the rules. Alesha will take Maxim somewhere safe and stash him away."

Her blank face showed what she thought about that plan. "You really think she'll stick to that?"

"I can only hope."

"So, you've risked both our reputations and careers on...a hunch?" She did *not* sound happy.

"He didn't do this, Dilton. I'd bet my life on it."

"That's a lot of faith, Glintock. What makes you so sure?"

"I know this man. Is he without fault? No, but could he commit a crime *this* horrific? No. It's just not in his nature. The *last* thing Maxim Ultra is, is a cold-blooded murderer."

"You *hope*."

"I *know*."

"So, why did we let his friends run free?"

He leaned over her and tapped a few keys on the terminal. *Gods, she smells good.* He tamped down those thoughts. That's not who Matthias Glintock was. He didn't mix work and pleasure. *Never again.*

A still from *The Gallant*'s surveillance footage appeared on the terminal. "Here's the bomber. Through other various surveillance sources, we tracked him to the nearest spaceport. Within a few hours of his entering the port, twelve ships left Aval."

"And you have the *Sequel* tracking down those ships," Dilton said. "It's a good plan." Something in her voice didn't ring true.

"What's wrong?"

"I'm just worried that *if* this guy *isn't* Ultra—and I'm still maintaining that I'm not fully convinced—then he achieved an amazing likeness."

Matthias thought for a moment. "You're afraid he wasn't on any of those ships."

"I think we should be looking at the perpetrator. If Ultra's innocent, how did this person recreate his face?"

"Well, we've already ruled out a change band. This is an exact match for Maxim. You can't achieve that effect with a change band. Hologram?"

She shook her head. "No, we'd see some shimmer on the video."

"Shanta couldn't recall them running into any rogue cloners recently, so it's probably not that. Most illicit cloning operations have been shut down since the GAC ban. Life mask?"

She squinted. "I can't see that. There's still a level of fakeness to a mask that I'm not seeing here. I mean, a scan would at least pick it up." A brief moment of silence hung between them. She turned her chair and faced him. "I know you discounted it with Morrico, but what about a shifter?"

"I can't even remember the last time there was a confirmed sighting." Before the Memta case, Matthias never considered he'd ever lay eyes on a Revash either, much less meet one. Was it possible to encounter another rare species in a relative short order? Improbable, maybe, but not impossible.

"Still, shifter or not, tracking his possible destinations is a good start," Dilton said.

"Thank you," he replied, taking a seat across from her.

"The only question is now, what do *we* do? I mean, we *are* supposed to be solving this crime." He couldn't tell if her smile was genuine or not.

"We follow the *Sequel*. They escaped our custody, so it makes sense that we would try to track them down. Plus, if people like, say, Brontin, think Maxim is aboard, so much the better."

"That's a dangerous game, Glintock. Brontin could ruin you."

"Only if he has help," he replied, looking at her squarely.

Her humorless smile was inscrutable. "I see what you're getting at. I have no love for Brontin."

"But, do you owe him your loyalty?"

She returned his even gaze. "I respect his position in the GAC, but not the man himself."

"Not exactly answering my question. What about your bot?"

"What about her?"

"Can she be trusted to keep her mouth shut?"

"Beattie is her own individual. If you're asking if I can influence her thinking—yes. But, why would I? I'm still not completely convinced Ultra's not our man."

His brow furrowed. "Then why—"

"Why am I going along with your plan? I *want* you to be right. You're a little unorthodox, but you get results. I want you to be right for *your* sake, not Ultra's."

"Then what do you want to do?"

"I want to scoop Ultra up and end this."

"Even if he's not the culprit?"

"*Especially* if he's not the culprit. Who can keep him safer than the GAC?"

Matthias held his tongue. He still wasn't sure how far he could trust her. Maxim was most definitely *not* safer with the GAC.

"But, if he stays put with Cabal and out of the way, he'll keep—for now," she said.

"On that point, we can agree." All he wanted was for Max to stay safe until he could figure out what happened on Aval. For the time being, he needed to feel out Dilton to see how much faith he could put in her. "So, tell me, Agent, how did you pull this case?"

"Just dumb luck, I guess. Or, depending on how it all pans out, lack of luck."

"What were you doing before this?"

"Mostly homicide. Before that, I was an iniquity agent."

"How did you like that?"

She shrugged. "It was highly misogynistic, especially with an exact duplicate running around with me."

"Double the lewd comments?"

"You got it. Beattie came in handy playing scantily-clad bait, but it was beneath both of us. We both much enjoy being fully clothed."

"I can imagine. So, what led you to become a GAC agent?"

She said nothing for a moment. "My father was a doctor. My mother was a doctor. I was supposed to be a doctor. However, growing up, I realized that I had a strong sense of justice. I wasn't raised with it. It just seemed...ingrained in me." She paused, appearing as though she wasn't sure whether to continue or not. "In my teens, my father was put on trial for...taking liberties with the access his physician's license afforded him. He was guilty—I knew it. He and my mother fought about it often. I loved my father, but I felt a deep satisfaction when he was convicted and sent to prison. I knew then what path my life would take."

"That's where I knew your name from. I remember your father's case." He paused, wondering how his next statement would be received. "I'm sorry for your loss."

"My father got what he deserved. Again, I loved him dearly, but he had to pay for his crimes."

"So, your life path led you to law enforcement. When did the bot enter the picture?"

Her expression became quizzical. "You really don't like androids, do you?"

He shifted in his chair. "Is it that obvious?"

"Yes. What happened?"

He looked away. The pain was still as fresh as the day it happened. Not even the rapport he'd developed with Roeger had been enough to dull it. Also, his wariness with Dilton made him reluctant to reveal the truth. However, how could he expect to trust her if she couldn't trust him? "I...cared for someone."

"Wife?"

"Yes. My wife, Fiona. We'd started out as colleagues at the GAC, broke all the unspoken rules about romance in the workplace. We didn't care. All we were filled with was…passion for each other."

"You? Passionate? *That's* interesting," Dilton said with a sultry smile.

Is she…flirting with me? "I know it doesn't seem like me at all, but Fiona just did something to me. I couldn't control myself with her. But, it was more than that. She was the most intelligent person I'd ever met. We connected in ways that I never had with another partner."

"That sounds nice. So, what happened?"

"We were very happy for a time, but my career intervened in a…tragic way. I was paired with a bot. All of us were back then. V7 was one of the first emote models."

"*Really?* You're older than you look."

He answered her interruption with a deadpan stare. "Thank you. V7 was devoted to justice. Overly devoted. It got into its head that my family life was hindering our pursuit of that justice."

Dilton's face changed, as if she knew where the story was heading. "Oh, no…."

"It was a beautiful day. Fiona and I had been in a little rut, but we made an effort and had made love that morning. It was…so sweet. As a result, I was running a little late. It wasn't until I reached headquarters that I got the call. V7 had burst into our home and brutally murdered Fiona. When I arrived, there was blood all over the apartment. Fiona knew how to fight. I know she didn't go quietly. I found her in the bedroom." His chest tightened. The memory was so clear in his mind, it was like looking at a picture of it. "Her face was…completely smashed.

I…I barely recognized her. Her arms and legs were broken, misshapen." He drew a shuddering breath. "Despite the horror of all that, the part that has stuck with me all these years was that while I stood over the broken body of my murdered wife, V7 sat in the corner nonchalantly, waiting for me to arrive. When I came in, it said, 'Now we can get to work,' like it was doing me a *favor!*" He spat the last word out like poison.

"And that's why you hate bots. I researched you pretty thoroughly, Glintock. I didn't find any of this."

"I had the records sealed. V7 was deactivated and the matter closed."

"Did anything come from V7's crime?" she asked.

Matthias paused, recalling the bitterness he felt in the immediate aftermath of Fiona's murder. "Not right away. It was treated as an anomaly until the same model behaved violently again…and again…*and again.*"

"Gods…" she whispered as she took his hand.

A connection had been formed. He didn't know if he could count on her to back his play with Max, but he felt he could at least trust her. For the first time in a long time with the GAC, that was enough.

CHAPTER 17

The *Sequel* exited the Cardon Lane near the fourth moon of the planet Kenota. Going from the multi-colored swirl of the Cardon Lanes to the stark darkness of space always left Shanta disoriented. She watched from the co-pilot's seat as Robert piloted the ship toward the dark side of the moon.

"We should be all right here for a few minutes," he said.

"Let's get down to the others," Shanta replied, rising from her seat.

Roeger, Gerry, and the holographic Christi waited in the common area. Shanta and Robert took seats at the table.

"Okay, so we're just outside Kenota," Shanta said.

"The first planet to which the imposter may have fled?" Roeger asked.

"You've got it," she replied.

"How many worlds are on our list?" Gerry asked.

Robert sighed. "Twenty."

"Exactly," Shanta said. "Based on the time the imposter hit the spaceport on Aval, twelve ships left before the authorities locked everything down."

"Then why is our list twenty?" Gerry asked.

"*Because some of our ships made multiple stops*," Christi replied.

"Right," Shanta said. "Kenota is just the first one we picked."

"How will we find the culprit on a world of billions?" Gerry asked.

Robert pointed to Christi. "We're going to get her into the destination spaceport's surveillance system."

"Unfortunately, that means we have to get down to the surface," Shanta said.

Gerry's squishy brow furrowed. "But, Maxim is the one who is wanted, not us."

"The ship's flagged," Robert said. "And we're known associates—wait a minute, weren't you *in* prison? Why am I explaining this to you?"

Gerry's expression shifted to surprise. "Robert, I was innocent."

Roeger turned to Gerry. "That is a humorous joke. May I use that?

"*Anyway*, we're going to have people looking for us too. And while Glintock will try and cover for us as best he can, the GAC is bound to figure out the line of investigation soon enough. So, we can expect to run into them as well as asshole bounty hunters," Shanta said.

"*Shanta, I must point out that, sometimes, we are the bounty hunters*," Christi said.

Shanta gave her a look. "Well, we're not assholes."

"How do we get down to the planet undetected?" Gerry asked.

"That's where our good friend Roeger comes into play," Robert said with a smile.

"Yes, I will hack into the spaceport's system and disguise the *Sequel*'s identity."

"Something you have clearly done in the past," Gerry said. "You have committed more crime than I ever have."

"Perhaps, but I did not get caught," Roeger shot back.

Shanta had to stifle her laughter. Roeger was getting better as a comedian. "As I was saying, once we get down to the surface, we have to move quickly and quietly to get this done. Now, Gerry, with Litning out, that means you're our muscle. Can you handle that?" Shanta asked.

"While I am not nearly as intimidating as Litning, I will do my best to fill his role." Shanta wasn't sure if Gerry could sweat, but it looked like he was sweating.

"Okay, good. So, Roeger will cover our tracks, we'll dock the ship, and then make our way to the control center where we'll put Christi to work. If everything works out, we'll walk out and nab our guy. Ready?" The rest of the crew all exchanged a solemn look and nodded at each other.

Robert's eyes touched each of them. "All right, let's do this."

"Fuck! Fuck! Fuck! Fuck!" Robert cried as he and Shanta raced down a corridor in the control building, laser fire at their backs.

"What about Roeger?!" Shanta screamed, firing her pistol back at their pursuers.

"He can take care of himself! He's got Gerry!" Robert yelled.

The whole plan had gone to nakra. Roeger had successfully masked the *Sequel*'s identity as they docked, but nothing else had gone right. The control building was more heavily-defended than they thought it'd be, so it took some doing to get inside. Then, as soon as Roeger plugged Christi into the system, the alarms went off.

The rest was a blur. Shanta and Robert agreed to lure the security teams away, leaving Gerry to defend Roeger in the control center. That plan seemed to have worked *too* well; it felt like every guard in the building chased after them. It was a *bit* much.

Shanta and Robert took cover in a pair of opposing doorways, the sunken alcoves providing adequate protection from the incoming laser fire. They fired back, but there were too many of them. The orange-suited guards were both garish and inaccurate, but that made escape *more* impossible. An errant shot could easily find its mark.

"This was a terrible plan!" Robert yelled across the hall.

"It was good to start!" she shot back. "*This* is where we went wrong!"

"We have to put some distance between us and them! Get back to the *Sequel*—extract the others off the roof or something!" Robert yelled between laser volleys.

Shanta glanced down the hallway. She lost count at fifteen officers—how they weren't shooting each other, she couldn't say. Also, their dark visors protected against flash weapons. Checking her belt, she saw that there wasn't anything else she could use to incapacitate the guards. All the incoming laser bolts made it clear that running wasn't an option.

Then, a strange sound echoed over the constant laser fire—screams. Shanta poked her head out as the torrent of laser bolts slowed to a trickle. The guards now faced the way they'd come, firing their weapons in that direction. A great roar reverberated down the hall. More screams. Shanta shared a frightened look with Robert. She gripped her weapon tighter.

Finally, after several anxiety-riddled moments, the source of the mystery moved around the corner. Gerry emerged, twice his normal size! Shanta had never seen the Glutob like that. She hadn't even known he could do such a thing.

Gerry's amorphous body absorbed the guards' laser bolts as he advanced on them like a relentless tide of gooey flesh. When he'd reach a helpless opponent, he'd form an appendage and whack the guard in the head. Each blow appeared to render the victim lifeless, but Shanta believed he was simply knocking them out.

With the guards fully focused on Gerry, Shanta and Robert resumed firing. Some had the good sense to return fire, but most appeared too horrified with their gelatinous tormentor.

Within a few moments, the guards were incapacitated and Shanta fell back against the wall, breathless. Gerry slinked down the hall, back to his normal size, looking as if nothing were amiss, followed by a tentative Roeger.

"When were you going to tell us you could do that?" Robert asked the Glutob.

"No one ever asked," Gerry responded good-naturedly. "I have been working on my forms to be of more use to the crew."

"We have to work on your assertiveness, Gerry," Shanta said before turning to Roeger. "What did Christi find out?"

"Unfortunately, the perpetrator did not come to Kenota."

"Motherfucker!" Robert exclaimed.

Shanta covered her face. "So, this was all for nothing."

"We must be prepared for that result," Roeger said.

Shanta glared at him. "I know that, Roeger. I don't need it spelled out for me. I'm just venting, because…look at this vecking nakra!"

"Simply preparing you against future disappointment."

She shook her head. Max had been right about Roeger—it was impossible to stay mad at him. "All right, let's get back to the ship."

The alarm klaxons blared, but the corridors remained conspicuously empty. The crewmates exchanged uneasy glances. If they were going to let the crew walk unimpeded to the ship, Shanta wasn't going to talk them out of it.

Proceeding cautiously, the crew encountered no resistance. They reached the *Sequel*. Still nothing. Robert and Roeger went aboard, while Shanta and Gerry hung back. She scanned for anything out of place, but the only thing amiss was the lack of *any* other living beings.

"I don't like this," she said, turning back and forth, unease creeping in.

"It is quite odd that they have not sent any further guards," Gerry said, mimicking her movements.

"*We're good to go here,*" Robert chimed in on the communicator as the *Sequel*'s engine whine pierced the silence.

Shanta and Gerry boarded the ship. She headed up to the cockpit, while Gerry retreated to the engine room. As she took a seat in the co-pilot's chair, Robert lifted off.

He grinned at her. "Easy breezy, right?"

"If you don't think there's anything supremely vecked up about this whole situation, I'm going to have to discuss your employment with Max."

Robert laughed as the *Sequel* soared into the sky. His laughter ceased once they reached orbit. A flotilla of ships blocked the *Sequel*'s path. Whoever commanded the blockade knew what they were doing as the ships were stacked to prevent the *Sequel* from going above or below them.

"This doesn't look good," Robert said.

Christi appeared, miniaturized on the control console. "*Transmission coming through.*"

"Let 'em have their say," Shanta said.

The comms system crackled to life. "*This is GAC Captain Binez,*" said a female voice. "*Shut down your engines and prepare to be boarded.*"

"Fuck," Robert muttered. "Open a channel, Christi." The comms system beeped. "Uh, he's not here."

There was a brief pause. "*Excuse me?*"

"Max isn't here."

"*Well, considering you are also fugitives, we're boarding you. Shut down your engines.*"

Robert turned to Shanta, but she was already climbing out of her seat to head for the gunner's pod. "Looks like Glintock wasn't able to cover for us."

"We knew this might happen," Shanta called back, racing down the stairs.

At the bottom of the stairs, she met Roeger, who held his palm up to her. "Shanta, please return to the cockpit. I will handle the weapons."

"But, Roeg—"

"Shanta, we do not want to kill any GAC personnel. I am a far more accurate gunner," he said.

She couldn't argue with him. "Fine. Get in there." She scrambled back up to the cockpit.

"What happened?" Robert asked as she strapped in.

"Roeger's got the weapons handled. Are we just going to sit here?"

"*Roeger is in place, Robert,*" Christi said.

"That's all I needed to hear," Robert said. The *Sequel* went into a dive before streaking to starboard.

"Sequel, *don't do this. You can't win!*" Binez' voice came through.

Shanta hit the comms button. "Sorry, no time for prison today!" She swiped her hand across her throat.

"*Connection has been terminated*," Christi said.

Several craft broke from the flotilla to pursue them while the others adjusted their formation to cut down on the *Sequel*'s options.

"Plot in a course for the nearest Cardon Lane!" Robert called out as warning shots came from the approaching ships. "I'll try to keep them off us."

"Let Roeger worry about that! Just concentrate on getting us the veck out of here!" Shanta said, scanning her terminal for the nearest escape route.

The approaching GAC ships swooped toward the *Sequel* and Robert put the ship into another dive. Shanta gripped the arms of her seat as her stomach lurched. The ship leveled out and immediately started rocking as the GAC fired on it.

"Sequel *captain, stand down! I repeat, stand down!*" Binez' cut in on the comms system.

"I thought we shut her off!" Robert cried as he piloted the ship amidst the hail of cannon fire.

"*The GAC Emergency Channel can cut through an—*" Christi tried to explain.

"Who gives a veck?! Just fly the ship!" Shanta hit the intercom. "Roeger, shoot back any time!"

"*Shanta, I want to target their engines, but they are currently pursuing us.*"

"Then shoot at their weapons!"

After a brief pause, Roeger came back. "*A sound course of action.*"

Shanta's panel showed that Roeger fired back. He connected with one of the four pursuing ships and caused another to peel off. Two remained, but the rest of the flotilla maneuvered to keep the *Sequel* hemmed in.

"Where's that Cardon Lane, Shanta?" Robbie asked, twisting the yoke to the right. The pursuit ships stayed with them as Kenota loomed in the starboard side of the viewport.

"I'm working on it! Those ships are putting out a lot of interference. Christi, see if you can cut through!" Again, she slapped the intercom. "Gerry, we need as much engine power as you can give us!"

"*Understood, Shanta.*"

"*Shanta, I am attempting to send a spike through the sensor disruption,*" Christi said. "*Stand by.*"

A moment passed. Two more ships joined the chase. Shanta's scanners were nothing but scrambled nonsense. The *Sequel* shook again from GAC cannon fire. Roeger fired back. No effect. The ship rocked with a direct hit. Shields dropped to fifty percent. Robert did his best to dodge, but they were vastly outnumbered.

Then, Shanta's panel lit up and beeped. The sensors had found a nearby Cardon Lane—on the other side of the planet. *Nothing we can do about it*, she thought with a shrug. She sent the coordinates to Robert.

"Fuck! The other side of the planet?"

"Unless you want to fly through *that*," she replied with a gesture to the flotilla.

"*Shanta, it is possible the GAC scanned our sensors,*" Christi said. "*Look.*"

The flotilla began breaking up. Half moved like it was heading to the other side of Kenota. "Nakra," she muttered as the ship shook again. Roeger kept their pursuers honest, but he couldn't shake them.

"No, this could work for us," Robert said. He looked over the control panel. "Okay. Okay, Shanta pull up the coordinates of the tunnel that got us here."

"I don't know if this is the best idea," Shanta said as she sent Robert the coordinates.

The ship rocked again. "*Shields at forty percent*," Christi said.

"Just trust me," Robert said. He glanced at the control panel. "Got 'em, thanks. Roeger, get ready."

"*Of course, Robert.*"

Without warning, Robert pulled up, flipping the ship upside-down and flying over and away from their pursuers. Roeger struck with frightening accuracy at three of the four engines, immobilizing those ships. The fourth tried to do a U-turn, but the *Sequel* was already streaking toward the broken flotilla.

"Sequel, *stand down!*"

"Yeah, fuck that, Captain Binez," Robert muttered. "Gerry, give me everything you've got!"

"*You have it, Robert!*"

Robert piloted the ship toward the gap between the two halves of the flotilla. The half on the port side sent volleys the *Sequel*'s way, while the starboard half tried to come back around to engage.

More pursuit ships launched. They appeared to be little fighters—highly maneuverable, but light on weapon power. Roeger had already adjusted his aim to incapacitate the new arrivals. He wasn't having much luck, though—the fighters were too agile.

"Just keep them off us, Roeger," Shanta said. "We're almost there!"

Robert swept through the cannon fire.

"Sequel, *stop now or risk destruction*," Binez' voice broke through.

Shanta's blood burned. She switched on the communicator. "For what? Fleeing questioning? Who's giving you your orders, Captain?"

No answer came. The portside cannon fire increased. The starboard side group had almost come about. Robert hit a few buttons and went into a stomach-churning dive before immediately pulling back up. When he did, the *Sequel* was through the gap. Shanta wasted no time keying in the Cardon code. The tunnel opened. The *Sequel* streaked through.

A few moments of silence passed. No one pursued them into the Cardon Lane. Finally, Shanta and Robert let out a shared breath.

"Okay, where to next?" he asked with a weary smile.

CHAPTER 18

Alesha's pilot, Grandy, brought the *Heartbreaker* in for a soft landing on their assigned docking pad on the planet Vicot. The spaceport was thirty miles from the crime scene where Sierra had been spotted. Max and the others would have to secure transport out to the site.

"I think my crew should stay put," Alesha said as she, Max, Gina, and Litning sat in the *Heartbreaker*'s common area. "We'll be ready if we need to make a quick getaway."

Max nodded. "Makes sense." While he hoped for the best, the area would be crawling with law enforcement; anyone catching a whiff of Maxim Ultra would ruin the whole excursion.

"I also think, for her own safety..." Alesha started.

"No way," Gina cut in. "Uh-uh, no way."

Alesha folded her arms. "What was I about to say?"

"That I should stay on the ship too, and that is *not* happening."

"Gina, I'm not trying to sideline you, I promise," Alesha said in a surprisingly gentle tone. "I just think you'll be safer here."

"I appreciate that, Alesha, but I'm FBI back home."

Alesha looked at her blankly and turned to Max. "I don't know what that means."

Max smiled. "It means she can handle herself. Plus, I'm not going anywhere without Litning and she's his number one priority. So, she comes with."

"Is stubbornness an Earth thing or just where you're both from?" Alesha asked.

"Probably a little of both," Max replied.

"Litning is the most conspicuous of us all!" Alesha argued.

"I can also take care of myself," Litning said.

"Yeah, I know, Fuzzy. But, you're not the best when it comes to sneaking around."

While Litning grumbled at the nickname, Max tried to smooth Alesha's ruffled feathers. "Alesha, come on. This isn't our first lay low job. We know what we're doing."

"I wonder sometimes. Don't forget, this is *my* ship and *I* make the rules."

Max rolled his eyes. It had only been the tenth time she'd reminded him. "Are we going or not?"

Alesha paused. "Well, you're looking a little shabby."

Max looked down at himself. She wasn't wrong. The fight with the female assassin had left both his jacket and pants torn. "I guess I can stop at a shop in town."

"Nonsense," Alesha said. "Follow me."

He squeezed Gina's hand and got up from the table to follow Alesha. As she walked in front of him, all the old feelings and memories came rushing back. His mind snapped back to the present. He wouldn't do that to Gina—he couldn't. Alesha left. She'd been true to her word. She had helped him kick the rimi and then left. Now, he was with Gina. He wouldn't flush what they had to rekindle his romance with Alesha. Being stuck on a ship with her wouldn't make it easy, though.

She opened the door to her cabin. As he followed her through the hatch, he was greeted by Vanga, Alesha's gray cat. Vanga rubbed his body against Max's legs.

"Hey, Vanga," he said, crouching down to scratch the cat behind his ear. "Before we hit orbit, Gina managed to get a neighbor to watch her cat."

"That was lucky," Alesha said, beaming at Max playing with Vanga.

After a couple of moments of loving the affection, Vanga walked away from Max, rose up on his hind legs, and continued strutting around the cabin like a biped. Max could only look on in shock.

"Oh, come on, Max, you had to know that Vanga wasn't a regular Earth cat. He's a Bucklan. Eventually, he'll grow some more and become a pretty formidable little fur ball," Alesha said.

"I had no idea." He couldn't take his eyes off the cat walking around like a toddler.

"It's like I always say, no matter how long you're out here, you still have a lot to learn." She handed him a small stack of clothes.

He was taken aback. "Did you steal these from my room?"

She blushed. "I packed you a set just in case you ever wanted to come aboard."

He smiled at her warmly. "Thanks, 'Lesha. This is…really sweet."

"You're welcome. I'll let Gina borrow some of my clothes." She tossed him a black mask as well. "You'll need this too."

About an hour later, the four moved through the port city of Trinton. Max's head was concealed in the black mask, which sported glowing green lenses. They didn't even attempt to disguise Litning. While Revashes were definitely rare, he wasn't the *only* one traipsing around the galaxy.

"Doesn't this mask draw *more* attention to me?" Max asked, leaning into Alesha.

"And then they'll instantly dismiss you. Trust me, Max, I've lived out here longer than you," she reminded him.

He said nothing, wanting to avoid an argument. The mask was hot and sweaty. The glowing lenses were a bit of a nuisance. Everything he saw had a green tint; disorienting to say the least.

Trinton was a modest port city on one of Vicot's vast plains regions. There was little humidity, but plenty of green where technology hadn't encroached. Max guessed Trinton wasn't a popular destination. With its proximity to an active crime scene, the local law could've been diverting ships from the area.

Alesha led the way through the streets with Litning bringing up the rear. Gina stayed close to Max, her eyes wide. Despite whatever training she'd received from the FBI, she looked like a tourist. Max couldn't blame her. He remembered having the exact expression when his father took him to space the first time.

"We'll pick up a hover sled and head out to the site," Alesha said.

"Just like that?" Max asked. "We'll just roll up, no questions asked?"

"Of course not. We'll have to sneak out there." She abruptly changed course, leading them to the other side of the street.

Max looked along their original route. A trio of law officers loitered at the end of the block.

"Those guys are crawling all over the place," Alesha said in a low whisper.

Max picked out at least seven more officers. "This isn't going to be easy. But, these people look local. Where's the GAC?"

"They're busy hunting you down. Why would they be here? It's a local matter," Alesha said.

"You said there were multiple sites reporting someone looking like Sierra," Max said. "That wouldn't garner GAC attention?"

"Not if they're not looking for a connection," Gina said, as she continued looking around. She ceased gawking and found everyone looking at her. "At least…that's how it is on Earth. No one talks to anyone else. The different jurisdictions pretend to work together, but they don't. Law enforcement is very territorial. If it's the same out here, then Alesha's probably right—for now, it's a bunch of locals stumbling around in the dark. Can't we do some intel gathering here? Y'know, ask some people what happened, so we're not walking in blind?"

Alesha gave her a thoughtful look. "I told you it was a good idea to bring her along." She winked at Gina. "My only fear with talking to people is that it might tip off the law. They may not be actively looking for us, but once they figure out who we are…. That said, it would be nice to not be in the dark."

"I'm assuming you have news in space," Gina said. "What did they say about the crime?"

Max shook his head. "The Information Network is kind of unreliable. There are no real regulations on it and even reputable news agencies will run with complete bullshit without corroborating it just to be first with a story. It's like the Internet on steroids *and* cocaine."

"That doesn't sound very enlightened," Gina said.

"Even with all the civilization around, it really is the frontier out here," Max said. "Look, I'm not saying that all the news is a pack of lies, but trying to get information about an active crime investigation requires a little more groundwork than just flipping open a laptop."

"Got it. Now I *really* think we need some personal intel," Gina said.

"But, who do we ask? Asking every random stranger will draw unwanted attention," Litning said.

Max scanned the area. Vicot was not a regular stomping ground for him.

A flickering electronic sign pointed the way to a dingy drinking establishment with some less-than-savory characters hanging around out front. Max touched Alesha's arm and gestured.

"That place could be a good start," she said. She turned to the others. "You three go check it out. I'll keep looking for a vehicle to get us out to the site."

"You sure?" he asked.

"Oh, definitely. We need to do this quickly, and talking to everyone in that bar will take too long. I'll let you know when I'm ready." Alesha walked off deeper into Trinton's sprawl.

The bar was poorly lit and filled with all manner of beings. Loud, pulsing music bombarded them. Many of the tables were filled with small parties, but the majority of the traffic centered on the bar top. A few bartenders filled drink orders.

"Which one looks the chattiest?" Max asked.

Gina's gaze followed his, while Litning's wary eyes scanned the establishment. After a few moments of observation, Gina pointed. "Her."

She indicated a female bartender with light blue skin and oval-shaped eyes, who slung drinks as freely as she engaged in cheerful banter. Her white blouse was stained.

Gina strode forward. Max could only follow along after his determined partner. The bar's warm, dank interior made sweat pool inside his mask. Uncomfortable didn't begin to describe it. He stayed on course behind Gina, but itched to take off the mask.

"Hey there," Gina said to the bartender, with a dazzling smile. "What's good here?"

"Hi!" The bartender was just as cheery as she appeared from afar. "I would recommend our Vicot Brew—a big seller across the quadrant."

"I'll take one," Gina said, extending a credit chit to the bartender.

"And for your friends?" the bartender asked; her eyes widened at the sight of Litning.

"Staunch non-drinkers, I'm afraid," Gina said before Max or Litning could respond. She leaned closer to the bartender. "The one with the mask can't even remove it in public."

"Got it," the bartender said with a wink. She went off to prepare the drink and Gina turned to Max.

"Having fun?" he asked.

"Oh, I'm right in my element. Can you two crowd around me to keep other customers away?"

He smiled, impressed. He and Litning did as Gina asked, protecting their bar top real estate.

The bartender returned. "One Vicot Brew for the beautiful woman with the very odd companions."

Gina laughed. "They are definitely that. So, tell me, what's with all the law enforcement spookiness?"

The bartender glanced around before lowering her voice. "Apparently, there was some big attack over at the Zeth facility east of here."

Max's ears pricked at the name "Zeth." Looking around the bar, he noticed a trio of patrons—two men and a woman—taking an interest in them. As he inhaled, sweat went up his nose. The mask had to go—at least for a minute. He nudged Litning. "Keep an eye out. I'm hitting the can."

"Be careful," Litning growled softly, his eyes searching.

Max walked to the back of the establishment where the relief stations were located, resisting the urge to see if anyone followed him. He stepped into one of the three unisex stations. They weren't all that different from restrooms on Earth; public restroom design was universal.

He couldn't take it anymore. After a quick search of the restroom, he stopped at the mirror and yanked the mask off. Sweat drenched his face. "This thing sucks," he muttered, splashing water on his face.

He saw a woman had entered the room. She stared at him in the mirror. Her mouth hung open and Max quickly saw why. Hanging on the wall by the doorway was a wanted poster with Max's face on it. The poster was a digital device, complete with a red button to alert local law enforcement. The woman's eyes flicked to the poster.

"Come on…I didn't do that," Max said. Even to his ears, the plea sounded pathetic.

She smashed the button. The poster emitted a deafening, high-pitched wail that could be heard throughout the bar. She drew a small pistol from her shoulder bag and trained it on Max. Her hand trembled. "You're not going anywhere," she said in a shaky voice. "I need that money."

"So do I. Maybe I'll turn myself in," he replied, raising his arms. Instead of surrendering, he closed the short distance between them and snatched the pistol from the woman, reversing their roles.

"P-please, don't kill me," she said, cringing.

"Lady, why the fuck would I do that?" He knocked her to the side on his way out the door.

Every eye in the bar was on him. That's when he realized the mask was in his hand and not on his head. The people that had been giving him the eyeball were *indeed* plainclothes law enforcement. Two of them had Gina and Litning at gunpoint, while the third approached him with a smarmy smile.

"I knew it was you," the male lawman said. "When I spotted a Revash coming in here with Alesha Cabal, I knew you had to be my masked man."

"Oh, he thinks I look like Alesha? How flattering. I'd kill for her skin," Gina gushed.

Her comment put some doubt on the talkative agent's face. "So, you three are coming with us until the GAC task force gets here to take over. And the three of us are all getting promotions."

"Buddy, don't do this," Max said. "Just let us walk away." He felt compelled to add, "I didn't do it."

The agent gave a short, harsh laugh. "Spoken like a true criminal, Ultra. But, all that's for the task force to determine."

"This is your last warning—let us go."

"Or what?"

"Or my friend will make a scene."

"Wh—" Before the leader could get the word out of his mouth, Litning roared and grabbed the guy covering him. In one deft motion, the Revash snatched his pistol away and threw him into his female companion, who'd been keeping Gina under gunpoint. Litning scooped Gina up and barreled through the patrons crowded around the scene.

Max made a break for the exit. Unfortunately, with his identity revealed, everyone along his path tried to help the lawmen apprehend him. Dodging the grabbing hands, he pushed through, threatening his assailants with the pistol. That kept most of the other patrons at bay, but some managed to grab hold. He shrugged the first couple off, but others held him fast. Someone kept his arm in check, leaving him unable to aim.

"Hold him tight!" one of the men grappling him yelled. "We'll split the reward!"

Max kicked out with his feet to keep others at a distance, but it was no use. They had him.

As the law officers crossed the floor toward him, another great roar rang out from the front of the establishment. Litning crashed through the entrance and flung people out of his way as he rumbled over to Max.

"Oh, *veck* this!" The officer Litning had used as a blunt instrument made a bee-line for the exit.

To Max's surprise, his captors still held him fast in the face of a snarling Revash. At the same time, he felt them quaking in fear as Litning drew nearer.

"Let my friend *go*," Litning growled, staring down at Max's captors.

They all released him at once. "Yeah, sure, of course," the man who had been keen to split the bounty said. "We was just keepin' him safe."

"Of course," was all Litning replied as he directed Max to the exit like an incensed parent preparing to discipline his child.

The remaining officers did nothing to try and stop them. That didn't prevent the leader from calling out to them. "You won't be able to go to a civilized planet after this!"

That threat *did* worry Max. All the guy had to do was put out an alert and the search for Max would intensify. *Everyone* would be looking for them, if they hadn't been already. Outside, Alesha pulled up in a hover sled. Gina was already aboard.

"Well, I guess this rental was a waste of credits. What the veck happened?" Alesha asked.

"Someone made me in the relief station," Max said as he and Litning climbed aboard the sled.

"Gods damn it, Max! You couldn't keep that thing on for more than five minutes? Veck!" she fumed as they headed off toward the spaceport. "I don't think you know how serious this is."

"He does now," Litning rumbled.

Another klaxon rang out over the city. "*Alert. Alert. A fugitive is at large. Be on the lookout for a human male traveling with a Revash and a human female.*"

"Well, that guy didn't waste any fucking time, did he?" Max said.

"We're completely vecked now," Alesha said. "How are we going to get the intel?"

"I've got that," Gina spoke up. "The bartender was quite helpful."

"What'd she say?" Max asked.

"The rumors are that a woman with extraordinary powers led a group of soldiers on a robbery of the nearby Zeth facility." Gina paused. "Of course, I don't know what any of that means."

"It's Sierra. It's got to be," Alesha said. "Any idea what they stole?"

"The bartender wasn't sure. She heard they made some kind of reinforced metal there," Gina said.

"I did some digging of my own," Alesha said. "The other Sierra sightings? All Zeth facilities or subsidiaries."

"What does she have against *Zeth?*" Litning asked.

"I don't know," Max said. "But, Baron Zeth owns, like, half the galaxy."

"An exaggeration, but yes," Alesha said.

"My point is, we could be chasing our tails on this forever. We need solid information."

Alesha winced. "Oh honey, no…."

"Yeah. We have to go see Murrall."

CHAPTER 19

Dilton hurled a data pad across the shuttle, just missing Matthias. As it hit the wall, the pad's screen cracked in several places.

"I hope there wasn't anything important on that," he said calmly.

"Oh, are we making jokes now, Glintock? Here's a good one—this investigation!"

"I think you may be—"

"I swear to all the known gods, Glintock, if you say, 'overreacting,' I will shoot you."

Matthias paused. "Exaggerating."

"Am I, Glintock? Am I? Your pals Cabal and Ultra only had to do one thing. *One!* Go lay low and wait for us to give them the all clear. Instead, they decide to go to Vicot and trigger an agency-wide alert! Now, there's *nowhere* for them to go. So, call your little friends and tell them to turn themselves in."

"You think I haven't tried? They're not answering my hails."

"I *knew* this was going to blow up in our faces! *Why* did I listen to you?"

Matthias took another moment to let Dilton fume. "Are you finished?"

She glared at him. "I can't believe you're so calm right now. Ultra took this vecking *gift* we handed him and spat in our faces!"

"You're taking my demeanor as an indication that I'm not angry. I'm furious. But, yelling about the situation isn't going to fix it."

Her eyes continued to bore into him.

"The real question here is, why Vicot?" he asked. "Why not Modan—back home?"

She shook her head with a sour look. "Glintock, they'd never be that stupid. We have agents waiting for them in Marina. They'd know that."

"Correct. But, they were spotted in Trinton, where there just so happens to be a major criminal investigation going on. Why leave the relative safety of Earth, avoid Modan because of the GAC, only to land smack dab into a nest of vigilant law enforcement?"

"Bad luck?" She looked bored with his rundown, but at least she'd sat back down.

"No one is that unlucky, especially not two seasoned spacers like Ultra and Cabal."

"Then what's your theory?"

"They were looking for something."

"What in the galaxy could they want on Vicot?"

"There was a large-scale robbery near Trinton—a Zeth facility. Several hundred meters of blast-enforced metal were stolen by a cadre of black-uniformed soldiers and they were led by a woman with glowing blue eyes."

Dilton looked at him blankly for a moment. Then, recognition lit in her eyes. "Sierra Numani?"

"So, you *have* read the file."

"But, I thought Ultra told you she'd died?"

"No, her fate was undetermined. She rolled off a roof with Talon Merthane and he's certainly not dead. It stands to reason that they escaped Ventu together. And, it appears that Numani joined up with the same mercs who attacked the *Galactic Dream*."

"That's a stretch."

"The eyewitness reports of these people are *very* similar to what I saw with my own eyes on that cruise ship."

"Whatever, fine. Numani is potentially running with the people who wanted the Memta artifact. So what? What does this have to do with Ultra and Cabal?"

"I looked into it. This isn't the only crime perpetrated by this particular band of criminals."

Dilton cocked an eyebrow. "Oh?"

"Multiple crimes, all of a similar nature. All Zeth companies or subsidiaries."

"Okay, Numani has it in for Zeth—again, what does that have to do with Ultra?"

"Clearly, Ultra thinks someone framed him. No better suspect than Sierra Numani." Memories of Memta sent a shiver down his spine.

He must have been wearing it on his face. Dilton looked at him with an expression of deep empathy. "What was it like?"

"It was…terrifying. I'd never seen such…unbridled malevolence. She roasted her victims alive, laughing as she did so."

"I thought Ultra drained the Memta entity from Numani?"

Matthias took another moment to let the waking nightmare leave his mind's eye. "He did, but who knows with things like this. Maybe there was still some left over."

"And you only saw it when it was in Cabal, right?"

"Yes. And *she* was fighting it. I'd hate to see someone who actually *embraced* that monster." Matthias' terminal trilled with an incoming call. "Veck."

The screen filled with the bloated visage of Brynden Brontin. "*I am assuming that you two are on your way to Vicot.*"

"Captain Brontin, we were just discussing that," Matthias said.

"*You shouldn't be discussing anything. This is a fresh lead. The* only *lead you've had since the case began*," Brontin said with the condescending tone that Matthias detested.

"Just because he was sighted there, doesn't mean he's still there," he said.

"*Are you questioning my investigative acumen, Agent?*" Brontin asked with a sinister edge.

Matthias resisted the urge to sigh in frustration. "No, of course not, but—"

"'*Of course not,* Captain.'"

"What?"

"'*Of course not,* Captain.' *You've been forgetting that more often than I should allow.*"

Matthias' blood became magma. Dilton's continued silence was maddening. He gave her a pleading look, but still she said nothing. The mystery of her true allegiance haunted him. Was she reporting back to Brontin? That might have even prompted his call. Then, she surprised him.

She turned the terminal screen to her. "Captain Brontin, let me assure you, we're pursuing every lead diligently. We've gathered all the intel we need from Vicot and there's no reason for us to go there."

"*Oh, really, Agent Dilton? And why is that?*"

"Because, we know where Maxim Ultra is headed next." She terminated the connection.

Matthias' mouth dropped open. He'd never seen anyone handle Brontin like that since he'd gotten his promotion to Captain. "*Do* we know where Max is going?"

"Oh, yes. I do at least. And we're doing things my way, now."

CHAPTER 20

Open space.

The *Claw* drifted lazily in an unoccupied corner of space, hovering before a gorgeous nebula. Its vibrant colors swirled and danced in a silent ballet of beauty. Talon Merthane watched it all from the *Claw*'s darkened cockpit, melancholy on his mind. Dayna had loved coming out here.

His eyes flicked to his terminal screen. Green letters flashed before him. Maxim had been spotted on Vicot. If the boy was that clumsy, the GAC would pick him up in no time. How they'd botched it on Vicot, he had no clue. That meant no bounty for Talon and worse, denial of being the one to bring Maxim in. Was one man really worth all the work he was passing up? His mind said, "No," but his heart couldn't let go.

If Maxim hadn't gotten involved with Sierra Numani, the word Memta never would have entered Talon's lexicon and his sweet Dayna would still be alive. He looked to his left. Affixed to the inner hull was a photograph of Talon and his son, Gage. The photo had been taken by Maxim's father, Jimmy, in happier times.

It had been years since Maxim had gotten Gage killed, but the ache remained. He'd hold onto it forever. Gage deserved nothing less. If Talon lost his grief, Gage would cease to exist.

A steady chime interrupted his musings. Someone was calling on his video comm unit. He sighed at the name scrolling across the top of the screen. "What can I do for you, Klothir?" he asked.

The gruesome visage of Klothir Winsnap, a fellow bounty hunter, stared back at him. Of course, Talon would never want to be associated with the likes of him. Talon could definitely be underhanded—it came with the territory—but he at least had a code. Klothir had nothing like that. He was a bottom-feeder, a petch that would stick a knife in your back as soon as shake your hand.

Klothir was a Yandit with craggy maroon skin and two deep, garish scars on his face—one where his right eye used to be. In its place was a fancy, high-tech eyepatch that plugged directly into his brain. So, he could see, but he looked like an ugly cyborg. His lone, bulging eyeball darted around before it focused on his camera.

"What's wrong, Merthane? Can't friends call each other?" Klothir asked, his voice like rocks scraping against each other.

Talon gave him a tight smile. "We're not friends."

"Fine. Work associates. Is that more appealing to you?"

Talon wanted to tell Klothir how little he wanted to deal with him, but he didn't need one more vecker out to get him. "What's on your mind, Klothir?"

"Thought you might be interested in a proposition."

Talon had an idea where this was going. "I'm listening."

"The reward for your favorite pet project keeps going up."

"Really? What's it up to now?"

"Twenty million."

Talon didn't react to the large figure. "So, what are you calling me for? I doubt you'd want to share that reward with anyone."

"Everyone knows you're the Maxim Ultra expert, Merthane. I'm talking about a partnership with you and a couple of other hunters to bring this kid in."

Talon couldn't hide his distaste. "Why so many extra hands?"

Klothir chuckled. *"Well, you know better than anyone what a handful that Revash is."*

Yes, Talon knew all too well, which made him even *more* inclined to turn Klothir down. Litning had ripped his last compatriot, Elkeith, apart with his claws. "I'm really not interested, Klothir."

Klothir's silence unnerved Talon. *"Merthane, this is twenty million credits we're talking about. That's a lot of money for any hunter. Are you telling me you don't want a piece of it?"*

"No, I'm telling you I want *all* of it. As you alluded to, my last team up didn't go so well, so I'll be running solo on this one." Certainly he'd have Alexis with him, but there was no need for him to tip his hand to the likes of Klothir.

"But...you're the expert on Maxim Ultra. We need you."

"You're right. I am. All the more reason *not* to join you and keep those millions in one place."

Another few moments of silence followed Talon's brutal, but calm, rejection of Klothir's plan. *"All I can say is, you've made a terrible mistake, Merthane. That money is* ours *and if you're not with us, then you are an obstacle and will be treated thusly."*

Talon tried to not burst out laughing. "Consider me duly warned."

"I'm serious, Merthane. There's blood in the water and I won't be able to call the hunters back once they smell it."

Klothir didn't scare Talon, but there were other hunters that turned his blood to ice. Not everyone was as efficient as he. Some hunters were in the game to be as brutal and cruel as possible. Talon was excellent at his job and that made others envious. In his experience, envy never led to anything but pain.

"I appreciate the offer, Klothir. But, again, I'll have to pass." Before Klothir could interject, Talon severed the connection. *Probably pay for that later.* Klothir wasn't an overly forgiving individual. He'd have to watch himself. Luckily, he had a secret weapon.

As if she'd read his mind, Alexis entered the cockpit. She looked at the nebula. Talon saw no warmth in her eyes. "What are we doing here? Do we have a lead on Ultra?"

"You need to take a moment to be in the present. Look at that nebula out there. Appreciate its beauty for a bit."

"This isn't getting us closer to Maxim Ultra."

She hadn't even hesitated. Straight to business for her. As a fellow hunter, he had to respect it. As a mentor and father figure, it saddened him. "Dayna loved coming out here." He hoped that tugging on her heartstrings might melt her icy demeanor.

"It's beautiful, but how is this getting us on Ultra's trail?"

He shook his head. There was no getting through to her. "Ultra isn't going anywhere I can't find him."

"Well, according to that GAC alert that came in, he's on Vicot. Why aren't we heading there?"

"Because, he won't be there once we arrive."

"Then what are we doing? We're just sitting here!"

"Have I really taught you nothing about patience? We know where he was. *I* know where he's *going* and I know how long it will take us to get there. So, enjoy the nebula." There was a pause in their talk. Talon took in the nebula, but Alexis fidgeted. "And I thought *I* hated Maxim Ultra."

"Of course I hate him. I've always been curious what *your* obsession was with him."

"You already know that. He killed Dayna." Though his version of the truth was skewed, he hadn't forgotten about Sierra. Powerful interests protected her; she would have to wait.

"Right, but this goes beyond that. *I* can take him out for *that*. But, you've had it in for this guy since I was a kid—"

"Not so long ago, I'll remind you."

"You're deflecting."

He was. His gaze fell back to Gage's picture. "Maxim is responsible for Gage's death." He couldn't bring himself to say he'd murdered his son, but like with Dayna, Maxim had set the conditions.

"You've never told me much about him," Alexis said.

"He was the light of my life until he was snuffed out. And then, you came into my life." It was the most honest thing he'd ever said to her.

"Thank you, but that doesn't really tell me anything about *who* Gage was."

Talon kept his life compartmentalized, never wanting any one person to know too much about him, even those closest to him. Dayna hadn't known all his secrets either. "He was intelligent, brave, strong...."

"Was he a big guy?"

"Hmph. Bigger than Maxim, if that's what you're asking. Maxim seems drawn to large crewmembers."

"That explains the Revash. I'd never seen one before."

"Few have. But, the most important thing Gage was, was loyal. *That's* what put him on Maxim's ship and Maxim *knew* he'd never say no."

"How did he die?"

Talon held his tongue. To say he was generally stoic was an understatement. Whenever he thought about Gage and his death, his emotions spiraled. "He…went on a job to Pentave Six with Maxim, Alesha, and their old pilot, Sam. From what I understand, they were ambushed. It was ugly. Sam lost his legs. Gage wasn't as lucky."

"What happened after?"

"They brought me his body. Seeing Maxim and Alesha unscathed almost drove me to homicide. They escaped with their lives twice on that job. I hoped Maxim wouldn't follow in his father's footsteps, but he ended up disappointing me."

"Who was his father to you?"

"A lifetime ago, he was my best friend in the galaxy."

"What happened?"

"He betrayed me. Later he died."

"Did you have anything to do with that?"

"No, no. Though I would have happily taken part, no. He contracted an illness and died."

"How old was Ultra?"

"A teenager? Maybe early twenties?"

She said nothing for a moment. "Just like me."

There was an ache in Talon's heart. "Yes. Though she wasn't your mother, Dayna loved you as her own."

"I know. Did…did Ultra's father know my mother?"

"Yes."

"So, she was in your crew?"

"For a time, yes. But, then she had you and walked away from the life."

She sighed. "I wish I had more memories of her."

"Well, you can't help that. You were fairly young when she passed."

"Still…now I have *no* mother."

"Sadly, no."

"And the man who took my last is getting away, so where is he going?"

"There's only one place he *can* go. The real question is, what were they doing on Vicot?" He turned his pilot's seat to a terminal on the left. "Let's find out."

The terminal launched a holographic display as Talon scanned the info net for any standout news about Vicot. He clicked a few keys, his eyes searching. "The only reason he'd go there is to find some way to clear his name…" he said as he skimmed different articles.

"Is there any write-up on how they found him?" Alexis asked. "Maybe the information is there."

"Could be. Good thinking." He was pleased that she wasn't only exercising her physical muscles. The story popped up and Talon laughed. "What a vat of nakra this turned out to be." A passage of the article caught his eye. "Might have something here."

Alexis leaned in. "What is it?"

"Something about some big robbery at a…Zeth facility nearby." He did another search. "Metalwork?"

"Why would Ultra be looking into a robbery? Does he have Zeth stock or something?"

Before he could theorize, Talon came to the pertinent part of the article. "*Witnesses said the black-uniformed perpetrators were led by a woman with glowing blue eyes and 'magic powers.'*" Talon's eyes narrowed. "No vecking way...."

"What?" Alexis said as her focus shifted to the article.

Talon switched off the display.

"Hey! I was reading that!"

He barely registered her voice. Sierra Numani. *That* was why Maxim went to Vicot. Could Sierra have pulled off such a frame? He'd seen the pictures from *The Gallant* surveillance video. Whoever impersonated Maxim was an *exact* double. Zeth might have been able to pull it off, but then why have Sierra attack a Zeth facility? Just the thought of Sierra's face made Talon see red.

"Talon?" Alexis asked gently. "What is it?"

"Despite how you and I feel about him, Maxim Ultra didn't bomb that building, but I think I know who did."

"Not that it should matter to us, but who?"

He'd embellished Maxim's level of responsibility in Dayna's murder, but he didn't ignore Sierra's involvement. Zeth was supposed to keep Sierra in check, but now that she was operating in the open, she was fair game. However, he needed to keep Alexis on task and running off after Sierra Numani wasn't part of the plan.

After another moment of reflection, he gave her a sad smile. "Nothing you need to worry about, princess. Let's get moving." He set a course away from his peaceful nebula. He'd made a promise to Dayna and himself that he'd kill Sierra. Now, he had a chance to bag Maxim *and* sate his thirst for revenge.

CHAPTER 21

The *Sequel* emerged from the Cardon Lane near the planet
Wychev. After the debacle on Kenota, Shanta had decided to play
a hunch. An old girlfriend of hers, Hara, worked on Wychev's
space station, *MD07*.

The locals weren't fans of visitors, so the station served as a
waypoint for ships to check in before their passengers
disembarked to the planet below. Hara assured Shanta that a ship
that had arrived from Aval after the bombing remained docked at
the station. Shanta only hoped the perpetrator hadn't gone planet
side.

"So, your ex couldn't divulge the heavy GAC presence out
here?" Robert asked as they sailed toward Wychev and *MD07*.

"What the veck?" was all Shanta could reply, leaning forward
in the co-pilot seat. Outside the viewport, in the distance, a group
of GAC ships patrolled the area. "Can you get us to the station?"

"Get to the station? Yes. Without being seen? Probably not."

"*Veck.*" Anger rose in Shanta's blood. "Just get us over there,
Robbie. I have a call to make."

"Yeah, you probably do. Better get Roeger on weapons, just in case."

"We can't get into another firefight with the GAC."

"It's not the GAC I'm worried about, Shanta."

She nodded. "Gotcha. Right. Will do." She scrambled down from the cockpit and found Roeger and Gerry conversing in the common area. "Battle stations, boys. Or…whatever. There might be trouble."

The pair nodded and went their separate ways—Roeger to the weapons pod and Gerry to the engine room. Once alone, Shanta whipped out her communicator. Hara answered immediately.

"What the *veck*, Hara?" Shanta hissed.

"Shan, I am so sorry," Hara replied, downcast.

"What happened?"

"The GAC showed up not long after we spoke, as well as some other more…unsavory characters." She meant bounty hunters. "I tried to call you."

Shanta sighed. "We were in the Lane." While Cardon Lanes were good for getting travelers around the galaxy quickly, they were nakra for communications. It wasn't impossible, but only reserved for commercial accounts and high rollers; the *Sequel* was neither. "Is our ship still there?"

Hara smiled. "It is."

"Any chance you can keep him on the station?"

"Afraid not, love. I *can*, however, set you up in a nearby docking bay."

Shanta finally had reason to smile. "You're the best, Hara. The closer the better, please."

"I'll do what I can. The ship you're looking for is in bay twelve."

"Thanks again, Hara."

"Don't be such a stranger, Shanta. I miss you."

She paused, wondering why she'd let this woman get away. Hara's cascading blonde hair contrasted beautifully with her lavender skin. "I miss you too." Shanta raced back to the cockpit. "Have they spotted us yet?"

"Not yet," Robert replied. "The third moon here is giving us some decent cover, but if their patrols are orbiting the planet, it could get dicey."

"My contact will set us up with a docking bay near the target."

"Great, as long as we can get to the station without being seen. God only knows what's waiting for us in there."

Shanta hadn't considered that the GAC had a cozy welcome planned on the station. "They'll probably have no problem with us docking."

"A lot easier to scoop us up when we're *not* in a flying tin can."

Second thoughts multiplied in her mind. "Are we making the right move here?"

Robert turned in his seat, his expression thoughtful. "Yes. They're here because of you."

"Come again?"

"No, you're mistaking my meaning. You figured out how to track this guy and the GAC is using your method to track us. Honestly, I'm impressed and you should be at least a little proud of it. But, it's also making our lives difficult. So, I wouldn't get too inflated an ego over it."

Shanta smiled as her communicator chimed. "Okay, Hara has us set up in docking bay nine."

"Gotcha." Robert clicked the ship's intercom. "Stay ready, Roeger. This could get tricky."

"*I am always ready, Robert.*"

Shanta rolled her eyes. She loved the bot, but he always had to have the last word.

"Hold on tight," Robert said.

Without warning, he brought the *Sequel* around in a stomach-churning turn. As soon as he had a clear line around the moon, he slammed the throttle forward. The ship practically buckled as it shot toward the space station.

Christi's holographic form appeared. "*This is a highly dangerous maneuver, Robert.*"

"Just show me docking bay nine on the schematic!"

Christi dissolved into an exterior map of the space station. A box on the near side of the structure flashed yellow. In the distance, Shanta could see the GAC ships breaking formation. They'd spotted them. Robert kept the *Sequel* at an impossible speed.

"Are you going to ram the thing?!" Shanta cried as she braced herself against the co-pilot's panel.

"Just another few seconds…" was all Robert muttered before throwing the engines in reverse.

The *Sequel* came to a brutally hard stop. Shanta was sure she'd either soiled herself, vomited in her mouth, or both. Robert had a happy little smile on his face as the *Sequel* slowly moved into the docking bay, guided by the station's tractor beam.

From the intercom, the cockpit filled with Gerry's guttural laugh. "*It worked!*"

"How are the engines?" Robert asked as his smile broadened.

"*They seem all right. I will have to do a full diagnostic to be sure.*"

"You two have been *working* on that vomit-inducing maneuver?" Shanta asked.

Robert shrugged. "With all the heat on us, I figured we'd need some high speed precision. Gerry agreed. This was the first time we were able to test it."

"A little warning next time, maybe?"

"How was I to know the GAC would be waiting for us?"

She narrowed her eyes, but said nothing. Robert had gotten them inside the station with no GAC entanglements. A green light blinked on the console, indicating that the docking bay blast doors had closed and the bay had pressurized. "Let's get down there."

"Wait, what's the plan?" Robert asked.

"We go down there and confront him."

"Just like that? What if this isn't our guy? What about the GAC?"

She moved to the stairs. Robert followed. "If it's not our guy, then we leave. A waste of time, yes, but we can cross one more off our list. As for the GAC, the longer we dawdle, the more time they have to trap us."

"Good point."

"Christi?"

"*Yes, Shanta?*"

"Keep the ship primed. We may have to blast our way out of here."

"*Of course, Shanta.*" Gerry and a wobbly-looking Roeger entered the common area.

"You all right, Roeger?" Shanta asked.

"Just recalibrating, Shanta. I was not prepared for Robert's high-flying acrobatics."

Robert's brow scrunched. "You don't get sick."

"Nevertheless, the sudden stop was…unexpected."

"Time's wasting, boys. Let's go." Shanta led the way down to the cargo hold, where Christi had the loading ramp descending. *Love that girl.*

The docking bay doors leading into the station remained sealed. Shanta wasn't sure what that meant for them. The GAC could have been on the other side, ready to pounce. She looked to Roeger. "Any chance you can patch into the security system and see what's waiting for us?"

Roeger glanced up at the conspicuous surveillance pod on the hangar wall. "It would take some time and we are not exactly alone."

Shanta nodded. They'd be going in blind. There was only one choice to lead the way. "How much punishment can you take?" she asked Gerry.

"Physical or energy?"

"Laser fire."

"It depends. If they shoot to kill, not much. If they are only trying to stun, quite a bit."

"There's no way they'll shoot to kill," Robert said. "They want Max, not us."

"Well, I'm not interested in spending another minute in a holding cell," Shanta replied. She really wished Litning hadn't gone with Max. They could've used the extra muscle. "All right. Gerry, you're out front."

Gerry's body morphed into a large rectangle with feet, which would provide them with excellent cover. "The shield?"

"That'll work great. Robbie, I want you bringing up the rear. This place feels ripe for an ambush. Roeger and I will stay in the middle, helping where we can."

Robert slung a rifle across his chest and hefted his burst blaster, a shotgun-type weapon. "Let's get rolling."

In the time she'd been running with Max, Shanta had been surprised how easily Robert had accepted her leadership. She had figured he'd want to be Max's second after Alesha left. She appreciated his support. Hopefully if they got through all this, she'd have a chance to buy him a drink and tell him.

"Okay, Gerry. Open the door," she said, gripping her pistol tighter.

Gerry extended an appendage and hit the door release. The massive metal doors unlocked and squealed as they opened. No one waited on the other side.

Shanta had expected a cadre of GAC agents. A whole lotta nothing was not on her menu. After a moment, she nodded firmly. "They're at the bomber's ship."

"*Alleged* bomber, Shanta," Roeger said.

"Whatever. They're waiting for us there."

"What's the play?" Robert asked.

"Wouldn't want to disappoint them. To the right, Gerry."

"Of course, Shanta."

The crew marched behind Gerry down the brightly-lit corridor. For a population that didn't want any visitors, they certainly made their waypoint bright and cheery. The walls were shades of yellow—light at the top, dark on the bottom. The floor panels clanked under their boots. Shanta wondered if anyone might be lying in wait beneath them. Clearly displayed docking bay numbers above and beside the doors showed they'd passed docking bay ten.

"Two more to go," Shanta whispered.

"Nobody around," Robert said. "I don't like this."

"Neither do I. They have to be waiting for us—sealed off the hallway or something." The station had a clear dividing line between each docking pod. Each was set up with a force field generator. *Is that their play?* "Roeger, how long would it take you to breach their security system?"

"Too long if I am not at a dedicated security terminal," Roeger replied. "Might…I make a suggestion?"

"All ears."

"It may be more effective for Miss Hara to lend us some assistance."

Shanta looked to Robert, who shrugged. "Couldn't hurt," he said.

She grimaced. "I'm not keen on that. She's exposed herself enough. I don't want her to lose her job, or worse, get arrested. What about Christi?"

"Again, it may take her some time to breach the system remotely," Roeger said. "If you can get me to a terminal, I can try my best, but I believe the clearest solution is Hara."

"We'll try it ourselves," Shanta said after another moment of contemplation. "I don't want to hem Hara up if at all possible."

"Fair enough," Robert said. "Let's keep moving."

Soon, the crew reached docking by twelve. The door remained sealed—the GAC nowhere to be found.

"Now what?" Robert asked.

Shanta had the same question. None of this was going the way she'd envisioned. "Can you at least open the door?" she asked Roeger.

The bot looked up and down the corridor. "That, I can do." Roeger looked at the door pad for a moment and the tip of his right index finger flipped open. He plugged his appendage into a socket just below the digital security pad. Roeger moved his head back and forth, scanning thousands of lines of code that raced up the screen. The satisfying *THUNK* of the doors unlocking echoed down the hall.

"Good work, Roeger," Shanta said as the doors squealed open.

"If they didn't know we were here before, they do now," Robert muttered.

"Let's stay optimistic." Shanta grit her teeth against the noise.

Docking bay twelve opened to reveal a small, beat-up freighter, but still, the *Sequel* crew members were the only lifeforms around. Leading the way with a shrug, Shanta took a step into the docking bay. That was the moment the neighboring docking bays opened up.

"*Veck*," Shanta swore as her ears filled with the clatter of boots.

The crew turned to find two squads of GAC soldiers decked out in battle gear—their weapons trained on the crew. The leader held a scruffy-looking gentleman by his jacket collar.

"Here we are, Mr. Ultra," the leader said down his nose. "Finally reunited with your crew."

Shanta gave the others a confused look before they all burst out laughing, even Roeger.

"What's so funny?" the leader asked.

"Don't know where you got your information from, friend, but that is *not* Maxim Ultra," Shanta said. Were these people serious?

"That's what I've been tryin' to tell 'em!" the victim of mistaken identity cried as he struggled against the leader's grip. Maybe from far away and if she was squinting, he looked like Max with a scruffy beard—maybe.

"If this isn't Maxim Ultra, then why are you here?" the squad leader asked.

"Trying to clear him," Robert said.

"Difficult to do when that video of him is plastered all over the galaxy," the leader said.

"Then, why do you have the wrong man?" Roeger asked.

The leader shrugged. "Wishful thinking. You're here and surprise, surprise, you all are wanted too." He released Scruffy, who blew past the *Sequel* crew on his way to his ship.

"Did you even bother to question that guy?" Shanta asked.

"Of course. He claimed to have been unaware of the terrorist attack until after he'd left Aval."

"That…seems hard to believe," Robert said. "Considering we tracked him here."

"Ah, so you *are* tracking the trajectories of the ships Ultra may have taken. Our analysis teams were correct."

Shanta clenched her jaw. "Maxim didn't *take* any ship, because he was with *us* when that building blew."

"So you say. And I agree with Mr. Land here that the pilot's story *is* hard to believe, until you confirmed he's not with you. My thanks for clearing that up."

"You're welcome," Shanta deadpanned. "Can we go now?"

"Oh, gods no. You're all under arrest. Take them," the leader said with a motion to his troops.

The squads advanced. Gerry popped back into shield mode. Shanta gripped her weapon. She didn't want to kill any GAC agents, but her crew was not being taken again.

An explosion sounded from the hallway. The GAC troops turned to face the new potential threat. Shanta leaned out of the docking bay to see what was happening. Five shadowy figures emerged out of the haze of smoke, rappelling through a hole in the ceiling to face off with the GAC. The smoke thinned as the figures reached the floor; five beefy Inwains stood with mismatched armor pieces and some wicked-looking weapons. *Bounty hunters.*

The Inwain at the head of the pack snorted through his bulbous snout. "Out of our way, *skrags.* This bounty belongs to us."

"We're GAC, hog-man. We move for no one," the GAC leader said.

"Welp, we warned ya," the lead Inwain said as he pulled his laser rifle. His cronies followed suit. Apparently, the bounty hunters weren't as averse to shooting the GAC.

The hallway erupted in laser fire and smoke from concealment grenades. Shanta pulled back into the docking bay. The GAC soldiers pounded on Gerry's belly like he was an obstinate door. Gerry simply bulged out his middle and bounced them back into the hallway.

"This is an unexpected turn of events," Shanta said. "How ya doing, Gerry?" Shanta called to the Glutob, who absorbed laser fire as some of the GAC troops ignored the bounty hunters.

"It tickles, but is starting to burn," Gerry replied. Despite his discomfort, he still maintained his cheerful tone.

"Okay, options," Shanta said.

"Hop on this guy's ship, fly over to the *Sequel*, get the fuck out of here," Robert suggested.

She shook her head. "Too risky. We don't know this guy's story. He could try to space us as soon as we step on board."

"We could...make a run for it," Roeger suggested.

They turned to witness the punishment Gerry endured. "Really? You are all going to stand and stare?" If Gerry's good-natured personality was cracking, he was clearly in trouble.

"Okay, we go with Roeger's plan. Robbie, you and I will bring up the rear to give these veckers something to think about,"

Shanta said as she walked back over to the trembling Gerry. "Christi, spin up the drives. We're leaving."

"*Of course, Shanta,*" Christi replied over comms.

"All right, boys—" Deafening klaxons cut Shanta off. Her stomach fell into her feet. The alarms meant one thing—Scruffy was leaving. *He* is *going to space us!* The ship's engines powered up and the docking bay doors began to close. "*Veck!* We've gotta go! Shrink, Gerry!"

Gerry snapped back to his regular size and dodged most of the incoming laser volley. Shanta and the others leaped out of the way, but returned fire to keep the GAC honest. Even Roeger aimed just over their heads to make them think twice.

Robert fired his burst blaster, which sent the troops scrambling for cover, but pushed them into the fight with the Inwains. Roeger hustled Gerry away from the action, while Shanta and Robert followed, keeping the GAC at bay.

The doors to docking bay twelve slammed shut. Shanta and the others retreated down the hall, but their pursuers would not be denied. The Inwain leader charged through the smoke and laser fire. "Bring me ULTRA!!!" he screamed as he cut through a swath of GAC troops with a serrated sword.

"He's not here, moron!" Shanta called back as she ran from the monstrous bounty hunter. She fired her pistol over her shoulder, but failed to connect. The Inwain's fingertips grazed her as he tried to make a grab. Suddenly, there was a low hum and the sounds of battle became muted. The Inwain wasn't feasting on her arm, so Shanta chanced to look over her shoulder.

The bounty hunter thrashed and screamed as he pounded on the newly established force field that separated them. Shanta could barely hear him thanks to the field's sound dampening. Another force field activated down the hall, trapping the lead

Inwain with a bunch of GAC troops that had survived his assault. They opened fire and cut him down.

The last thing Shanta saw as she turned to race to the *Sequel* was the bloody streak the Inwain's handprint left on the force field. She scrambled on board the ship and raised the loading ramp.

"What kept you?" Robert called down from the cockpit as she crossed into the common area.

"The final moments of that Inwain's life," she replied, climbing into the co-pilot's chair.

"Roeger's at weapons and Gerry's resting in the med area. Christi's got us all set," Robert said.

"Then let's hit it!"

The outer docking bay doors opened to a group of GAC ships heading their way. The *Sequel* flew out of the station and banked to starboard, away from the GAC.

"Where to?" Robert asked as his hands danced over the controls.

Shanta finished a thank you message to Hara for the force fields, then she pulled up the planet list on her terminal. "I think we've been going about this the wrong way."

"Well, please pick somewhere, because those GAC ships are coming this way." There was a hint of panic in his voice.

She scanned the list. "Got it." She punched in the coordinates.

Robert glanced down at his display. "Really? It's kind of dicey there."

"It's also the only non-GAC planet in the list. I think it's time to step out of the GAC's shadow."

He shrugged. "All right. Iswat it is." He hit the throttle and the *Sequel* sped away from the lumbering GAC ships toward the unknown.

CHAPTER 22

Max and Alesha stood in the docking tunnel at the gun metal door that led into the Marina Spaceport. Behind them, Litning and Gina departed the *Heartbreaker* to join them. They all wore dark gray cloaks. Alesha's crew had been directed to stay put in case things went south, but a few members were set to disembark, including Jethan. Litning wouldn't stop giving the alien side-eye.

"You're sure I can't convince you to wear the mask?" Alesha asked.

"Everyone in this city knows your ship," Max replied. "If the GAC's here, they know we are too."

"Then *why* are we here?" Gina asked.

"A valid question," Litning rumbled.

"We're here, because if we try to hunt down all of Sierra's heists or investigate all of Zeth's holdings, we'll be looking forever," Max said. "We have to see Murrall. If there's some kind of conspiracy or something, Murrall's sure to know about it."

"You hope," Litning said.

"Yes, I'm putting a bit of faith on the line here."

"What about you guys?" Alesha asked her crew members.

"We have been cooped up on the ship for this entire voyage," Jethan said. "We need a break." He was joined by Vinx and Grathell. Max hadn't seen much of them as they usually toiled in the bowels of the ship.

"Fair enough. Just be ready to dust off at a moment's notice. In the unlikely event you get left behin—" Her crew members balked and moaned at the possibility. "Hey, we're dealing with the GAC *and* bounty hunters. I'm planning for every eventuality."

"Why not simply hand him over to the GAC for the reward?" Jethan asked with a cold glare at Max.

Litning stepped between them with his own menacing glower. "Over my corpse, perhaps."

"That can be arranged, Revash," Jethan replied.

"All right, that's enough!" Alesha yelled. "What the veck's gotten into you, Jethan? If any of you get stranded, just go to the safe house. I'll swing back and collect you later."

"Understood, Captain."

Max began to share Litning's distrust of Jethan.

Alesha turned Max to face her. "Are you sure you want to do this? I don't think you want to be owing Murrall any favors."

"I already do. This bit of information isn't going to change that." He glanced at an uneasy Gina. "You all right?"

"Yeah." Her reply was less than convincing. "No."

"I've got this, Gina. Don't worry."

"How can I *not* worry, Max? I'm on an alien world and you're talking about dealing with a criminal!"

"You know, I don't know for sure if Murrall has done any time. We've had regular dealings in the past, though."

"You *do* know that with my career of choice, I'm a little uncomfortable with all this, right?"

"Did you ever deal with confidential informants? Same thing."

"Thank you for explaining my job to me, manly man."

"We must go," Litning growled. "Modan is not a sanctuary for us now."

Max's expression grew solemn. "No. No, probably not." The quartet pulled their hoods up. He didn't think it would do much good, especially in Litning's case, but attempting anonymity was better than nothing.

Alesha hit the door release to enter the spaceport. A bustling concourse crowded with all sorts of beings greeted them. The Marina Spaceport was a giant tower of circular levels built on top of one another. The *Heartbreaker* was docked in the middle of the stack, so the tower extended equally upward as downward. Everything looked cutting edge, which given the city's history, was surprising. Marina had originally been a sleepy lakeside town. The lake had dried up and the town became a bustling city with one of the largest spaceports on Modan. The shops had colorful, electronic displays designed to lure patrons. Residential areas were mixed throughout, so the spaceport was a self-contained city of its own. Each level had a central hole in the floor and ceiling that allowed natural light from the outside in.

"Murrall's in the upper levels," Max said. "Let's get a lift."

"Do you need us, Captain?" Jethan asked.

Alesha looked at her departing crew members. "No. Go do what you need to do."

"Watch out for GAC," Max said. "They know who you are too."

"Thank you for that, Ultra," was all Jethan said as he and his crewmates shoved off.

"Charming fellow," Max said.

"He's…an acquired taste," Alesha said. "Let's go."

She walked on ahead with Gina, who looked dazzled. Litning hung back. Max looked up at his friend. "What's up?"

Litning's eyes remained locked on Jethan's back. "I do not trust him."

"That makes two of us. What's got your hackles up?"

Litning shook his head. "I cannot say for sure. He simply…doesn't smell right."

"Yeah, you said that on Earth."

"Why do *you* mistrust him?" Litning asked.

"I just think he's an asshole. Come on, Murrall's waiting."

The two of them joined Alesha and Gina, who had halted their progress to wait. "About time," Alesha said. "You having second thoughts?"

"Not at all. Fuzzy was just admiring that guy's mumu," Max replied pointing to a random passerby.

Litning grumbled under his breath, but purred when Alesha reached up and scratched his neck. "Poor Fuzzy…."

He glared at her and Gina chuckled.

The four of them entered a lift with transparent walls. As the lift rose, the clear walls afforded the passengers a panoramic view of the spaceport. The multitude of colors from the storefronts speeding by reminded Max of a Cardon Lane. The kaleidoscopic effect made him a little queasy. Glancing at Gina, he squeezed her hand. She gave him a little smile, but soon closed her eyes against the rushing scenery.

The lift slowed to a stop on the eighty-second level. Max grabbed Alesha's arm and ushered all four of them behind a merchant's cart in the middle of the concourse. Alesha was about to protest, but Max pointed out a trio of well-dressed humans clustered outside a bar. None of them appeared inebriated.

"GAC," he said. His eyes darted around. "They're probably everywhere."

"We knew this was a possibility," Alesha said. "Do you want to make the correct decision and abort?"

"No. Murrall will know what's going on. We *have* to do this."

"Then how do we get there?" Litning asked.

"Murrall's place is down that street. We'll approach it from different angles," Max replied.

Gina tapped his arm. "More of them over there."

Max followed her finger and saw three more agents perusing another merchant's cart. "Your law enforcement instincts kicking in?"

"When you know what to look for, they stick out like beacons."

"Are you people going to buy anything?" the cart owner demanded with an annoyed expression on his orange face, framed by a shock of purple hair and matching muttonchops.

Max smiled desperately. "Please give us a minute. We're talking."

"Well, you're standing by my cart, so either purchase something or get gone."

Litning gave a low growl.

"Of course, I could simply alert those obvious GAC agents that you're hiding from—poorly."

"All right, all right! We're leaving!" Max hissed. He took Gina's arm. "We'll go left. You and Litning go right. Meet at Murrall's."

"If you say so." Alesha did *not* sound confident.

They split up.

"Max, slow down," Gina said. "If you try to hide from them, they'll spot you. Do like Alesha and Litning. Easy. Casual. We're just going for a stroll."

He stopped. His eyes flicked between the two GAC groups, sweat breaking out on his brow. He exhaled heavily. Gina gripped his hand. Coolness flowed from her touch, calming him. He closed his eyes.

"That's right," she said softly. "Relax. We're going to walk to Murrall's and no one is going to trouble us."

He turned to Gina and kissed her. As he drew away, he spotted Alesha; she had a funny little smile on her face. "Thank you," he said to Gina. "I feel much better." They continued walking.

"Glad I could help."

Max relaxed a bit more. "So, how are you enjoying space?"

She beamed. "It's amazing. Everywhere I look, I see something new that NO one I know has ever seen before—well, except you of course."

"No, I get it. It's awesome—and pretty overwhelming."

"When does that go away?"

"After about a year." He paused. "It's not weird for you with Alesha around, is it?"

"It's…not ideal, but I really do like her. I don't feel like I'm jealous. I'm just intimidated. She's *so* impressive. Why, is it weird for you?"

"A little. More embarrassing, I think. She and I have a lot of history. There's ample opportunity to make me look like a jackass in front of you."

"Oh, you do that fine on your own," she said with a wide smile. "You know what I think? I think you've kept secrets for so long, you're uncomfortable showing so much of yourself. I doubt your mom knows about half the stuff I've seen. I feel honored. Thank you for bringing me."

"Well, luckily for you, a bounty hunter showed up to try and punch my ticket." He'd meant it as a joke—a dark joke, to be sure—but Gina became very quiet.

"Why would you joke about that? She could have killed you."

He gave her a little shrug. "I'm not going to say she didn't rattle me, but this is my life, Gina. Whatever I do, I end up pissing *somebody* off."

"Except you didn't do this."

His mood darkened. "No, this I did not do."

They continued their walk in silence. As much as space thrilled Gina, Max had an inkling that she would never completely understand or accept what he did for a living. That nagging question popped up in his head again—was he willing to chuck it all for her? He cared for her, sure, but spacefaring had been his entire life for nearly twenty years. Once the crisis passed, they'd have a conversation. At the end of all this, he might *want* to return to Earth.

They arrived at a large building face—bigger than any of the others they'd seen thus far. A metal sheet hung horizontally over a set of ornate double doors. Emblazoned on the sheet in gold was: *Murrall's*.

"This Murrall doesn't skimp on grandeur, huh?" Gina asked, gazing up at the building.

"Not at all." Max had seen it several times before, but it was no less impressive.

Torches hung on either side of the entrance. Two bruising guards dressed in fine suits stood in front of the doors. The two were Daramwus, bipedal rhinos, except there were two bone horns jutting out of their foreheads as opposed to one. They didn't look happy to see Max.

Alesha and Litning joined Max and Gina several yards away from *Murrall's*. "I see you made it unscathed," Alesha said.

"The GAC didn't bother us," Max replied. "You?"

"We sidestepped them altogether. However, we *did* see some shady individuals that might also have an interest in you," Alesha said.

"Bounty hunters. Fantastic."

"Won't we be safe in *Murrall's?*" Gina asked.

Even Litning joined in on the ensuing laughter. Max explained. "Sorry, but there are probably more bounty hunters in there than in this whole port."

"Again, I'm not seeing why we need to see this person," Gina said, embarrassed.

"Thank *you*," Alesha said.

"Murrall has connections all over the galaxy. Any information we need, we'll find here."

The four of them approached the entrance. One of the bouncers held up a gnarled hand. "Welcome back, Mr. Ultra," he said with a low, creaking voice. "What can we do for you?"

"We're here to see Murrall."

Both bouncers looked them over. The first continued. "You and Miss Cabal may enter, but the Revash must wait outside. So must this female that is unknown to us."

"Why do we have to wait outside?" Gina asked. "This is a business, isn't it? Doesn't a business require patrons?"

The bouncers chuckled. The first one looked to Max. "You haven't told her?"

Max shrugged innocently and tried to ignore Gina's accusing glare.

The first bouncer saved him from any further knotty explanations. "The Revash is banned and we do not allow unknowns to see the boss."

Max crossed to Gina and Litning. "Keep an eye out for her, Fuzzy, and for yourself too. We have no idea what's waiting for us in this city."

"Understood."

Max moved to Gina, who pouted. His attempt to kiss her was rebuffed, leading to catcalls from the two bouncers. "What's wrong?"

"You're not giving me all the facts and it's making me look foolish."

"That wasn't my intent. I'm sorry."

"What is this place, Max?"

"It's a high-end sex club." Before Gina could properly react to Max's revelation, he and Alesha were ushered through the front doors by the second bouncer.

"You didn't tell her anything about this place, did you?" Alesha asked with a lopsided smile.

"No. It…must have slipped my mind."

"Wrong. You didn't want to tell her what Murrall actually was, because you knew she wouldn't be all right with it. Hey, no judgment from me. This is the last place I'd bring a girlfriend."

"Fair." The two of them stood in a dimly-lit anteroom. Another set of double doors awaited them. The color scheme was dark—lots of burgundy and navy blue.

The second bouncer stood at the doors. "Someone will take you to the boss. Enjoy your stay."

Max and Alesha stood waiting with the bouncer a few silent moments. She nudged him. "I *am* happy for you, Max. She's great for you."

He smiled. "Thanks." However, something nagged at him. "Greater than you?"

She chuckled. "Max, you'll always have me. I'm not going anywhere. I just think an Earth girl like Gina is probably more your speed."

It was nice to have Alesha's blessing, but he wasn't sure how to feel about the whole situation. Yes, the rekindled romance with Gina was sweet, but he'd loved Alesha since he was seventeen years old.

She laced her fingers through his. He looked at her quizzically. "So, they'll leave us alone."

He nodded. If they looked like a couple, they wouldn't be propositioned by every Jane and Tom in the place.

The doors opened and they were smacked in the face with the sounds and smells of sex. The second bouncer extended his arm to welcome them and they walked into the next room as the doors closed behind them. The color scheme was different from the anteroom. The floor appeared to be made of amber, while every other wall panel provided dim, golden light through a thin latticework of wooden coverings. Several sunken pits populated the room. In each shallow pit, there were pillows and cushions topped with writhing, sweating, and heaving bodies.

Most were men with women. Others were men with men or women with women. Most participants made noises of ecstasy, while other individuals were content to simply watch.

Alesha tightened her grip on Max's hand. "This room makes my skin crawl," she whispered. "Despite how hot Murrall's employees are." It was all very titillating, but neither of them had ever been huge fans of Murrall's sex-capades. Despite Alesha's propensity to find varied sexual partners, she was not into the group thing. A trio at most, and never on public display, like Murrall's clients.

The opening sex room was designed to put people at ease, but it only set Max on edge. Yes, Alesha was correct, Murrall's ladies were all fantastically beautiful and sexy, but public sex didn't appeal to him. He was too much of an Earth prude.

The escorts were of every species and race. Most were humanoids, but there were a few more…exotic servers. The water tank in the far corner was built explicitly for Murrall's Yantean twins. They were a squid-like race. Watching them have sex was like enduring bad Japanese hentai.

A woman approached them. She had dark skin, slicked bleach-blonde hair, and a charcoal suit. "Mr. Ultra, Miss Cabal, would you like to participate in the festivities? I'm sure one of our groups can make room for you."

"Not in a million years, Jhantra, thanks," Max replied. "We're here to see Murrall."

"Are you expected?"

"Probably not, but I have some business."

"According to the news net, it may be a little more than that, hm?" Jhantra looked them up and down. "I'll see what I can do. Wait here, please."

"Do we have to?" Max asked after her.

Alesha gave him a disgusted look. "She did that on purpose." She glanced around. "Recognize anyone?" she asked under her breath.

Max nodded. There were a few known bounty hunters here and there enjoying Murrall's staff. "Keep on guard. We may have to make a run for it."

A moment later, Jhantra returned. She'd been gone such a short time, Max was convinced she hadn't spoken to Murrall at all. She'd probably been watching the two of them on a video feed, waiting for them to tip their hand. "Right this way, friends." Her smile was positively wolfish.

Max had a bad feeling, but this was Murrall's turf. Jhantra led them into a hallway that had the same golden décor as the sex room. The floor sloped downward and the hall turned a corner.

Once out of the sight of the sex workers, Alesha took her hand back from Max. He gave her a reassuring smile, but everything she'd said since they arrived on Modan confirmed that she did not share his optimism. If he had to be honest, he was putting up a front.

The hallway ended in another set of double doors. Jhantra turned to the two of them. "I am afraid you'll have to leave your weapons here." Two bots emerged from either side of the hallway, as if they were a part of the walls themselves. Their chests opened like mailboxes waiting for Max and Alesha's weapons.

"Why would we want to kill Murrall?" Alesha asked.

"Merely a precaution, given…current events," Jhantra said, her eyes settling on Max.

"We've worked together a long time. I'm no threat to Murrall. You know I didn't do this."

"I only know what is official knowledge, Mr. Ultra. Weapons. Now."

Both of them reluctantly placed their pistols in the bots. Their chests snapped shut and they melted back into the walls. Max hoped his pistol hadn't melted as well.

Jhantra was all smiles again. "Right this way."

The double doors opened for her. The three of them entered a raucous party. Gambling, drinking, dancing, narcotics, and yes, screwing from every variety of being was happening in the spacious room. The party room had more light than the sex room, but it felt like all the partygoers had their faces turned away from Max and Alesha.

"Maxim! *And* Alesha! So nice to see you two working together again!" the sharp voice of Murrall cut through the din of the party.

She moved through the crowd slowly, more for dramatic effect than because she wasn't spry. Her usual outfit of a bright white fur coat with matching wide-brimmed hat made it appear as though a spotlight was constantly trained on her. Murrall—Max had no idea if it was her first or last name—usually wore her graying hair up in a tight bun and her round glasses changed color with the shifting light. She was an imposing figure and known to go to the mat for the girls and boys in her employ. No one Max knew would go against her either mentally *or* physically. She took Max and Alesha in with a sly smile.

"I was sorry to hear about my friend—vecked to death by a sex cult. Probably the way he wanted to go, but I'm sure he'd rather be alive. Thank you for trying to find him," Murrall said.

"We did our best. How did you hear about that? Did Shanta send you a report?"

"Maxim," she purred from behind a large wine glass. "You of all people should know that I know almost everything."

"Funny you should say that, because that's why we're here."

"Oh? Do tell." She drew away slightly so Jhantra could whisper something in her ear.

"Yes, we've been tracking some crimes perpetrated by Sierra Numani against the Zeth Corporation," Alesha said. "We have no idea what all she's done and we were hoping you knew something." She glanced at Max before looking back at Murrall.

"We also think she may have had something to do with framing Max for Aval."

Murrall raised her eyebrows. "Really? I wasn't aware that Max was the victim of a frame job."

"Really, Murrall? *Really?*" Max didn't hide his anger.

She shrugged. "I only know what I hear, my boy, and I haven't heard anything about anyone else being behind the bombing on Aval. In fact, it's strange that I haven't heard anything else. It's almost as if someone is actively suppressing that narrative. If so, you have some powerful enemies, Maxim." She looked at Alesha. "This woman is becoming a bit of an obsession for you, Alesha, no?"

Max looked to Alesha and then back to Murrall. "What does that mean?"

"It means that this isn't the first time Alesha's come to me searching for Miss Numani."

"Why didn't you tell me?" Max whispered to Alesha.

"Not now, Max," she hissed.

"I can tell you two probably have much to discuss, but unfortunately, our meeting has to come to a quick end."

"What? Why?" Max asked. Some of the revelers began turning their way.

"Well, as I said, I only know the information that is available to me. Your Sierra has been hitting several Zeth businesses with a cadre of black-uniformed soldiers, but the ultimate goal is unclear."

"Black uniforms?" Max asked. His mind reeled back to the *Galactic Dream* and Ventu. Sierra was working *with* the guys that hit the cruise ship? How? Why?

"The other thing I know," Murrall continued. "Is that the price on Maxim's head is up to twenty million—no small amount, even for someone of my considerable means. There are several GAC agents in this city as we speak and I'm afraid I'm going to have to turn Max over to them."

"Wow. That's really fucked up, Murrall, given our history."

"I appreciate that, dear, but this is business."

"Well then, we'll just be going," Alesha said, taking Max's hand.

"I think my party guests would have something to say about that, Alesha."

All the partygoers drew weapons and trained them on Max and Alesha. Finally seeing their faces, he could see that they were all bounty hunters. He and Alesha were trapped.

CHAPTER 23

Gina stood outside the doors to *Murrall's* with Litning, perturbed to say the least. She was annoyed with Max for not telling her that *Murrall's* was a whorehouse, but she was also furious with the bouncers for barring her from said whorehouse.

"Why aren't you allowed inside?" she asked Litning, folding her arms.

The Revash growled softly. "The females inside do not know how to...*match* the affections of a Revash. There was...a misunderstanding and...some property damage."

Her jaw set. "You didn't hurt any of the women in there, did you?" Her opinion of Litning hinged on his answer.

"No, no, never. My experience was...frustrating and I took those frustrations out on Murrall's establishment. She banned me."

"*She?* I have to say, not the image I conjured in my mind."

"Most do not, but she is a formidable human. She should never be underestimated. For that reason, we should remain close."

"Makes sense."

Litning sniffed the air. For a moment, his body went rigid. He was quickly all smiles. "Come, allow me to show you the port."

"Sure." He led the way and Gina followed. "Is everything okay? You seem distracted."

He sniffed the air again. "Everything is fine, Gina. Mind the GAC agents we saw earlier."

"Oh, I remember them." She actually expected to spot some more on their little jaunt around the concourse.

Keeping to the edges in order to avoid the GAC, Litning led Gina around to the various shop stalls. Her eyes stayed peeled for any other agents. The pair of trios they'd seen earlier were still in position. Either they had Max right where they wanted him or they were terrible at their jobs.

Though there didn't seem to be any more obvious law enforcement agents around, some other beings looked in their direction as they made their way through the mall. Being unfamiliar with the local flavor, she couldn't tell if they were hunters, curious onlookers, or Litning's friends. She was still getting her footing in space. Things usually came easily to her, so it was awkward to be struggling.

Litning continued sniffing at the air. Clearly, he was on some*thing*'s trail. The walking mountain cleaved a wide path through the bustling crowd of various alien beings. He had seemingly forgotten all about Gina. His hooded head jerked here and there, his snout pointed in the air.

While Litning searched for whatever he was looking for, Gina's head swam with all the different smells and dazzling visuals before her. How Litning could follow *one* scent through all of it was beyond her. Sweet spices, fragrant perfumes, and savory foods all combined into a wave of dizzying aromas.

Her eyes fell on one of the vendor stalls set up on the street, separate from the storefronts. The mobile cart had a glittering array of different gems and jewelry. The various colors and polished metals sparkled in her eyes. The vendor was a short man with pale blue skin and a potbelly unsuccessfully hidden beneath a multi-colored silk robe. He spoke with a taller man with orange skin and didn't seem to pay Gina much mind. Litning stood about twenty yards away, scanning the crowd, but he wasn't moving on any farther. Gina decided to steal a moment to admire the vendor's wares.

If Gina was a sucker for anything, it was jewelry. Ever since childhood, she'd been drawn to the elegance and beauty of fine craftsmanship. The vendor's pieces were stunning, containing intricate latticework and detail. The gems he had embedded in each piece glittered and sparkled in the spaceport's artificial light.

However, Gina found her focus landing on the more alien-looking metals than the familiar silvers and golds. On Earth, the multi-colored metals would appear to be painted, but these were clearly some type of metal she'd never seen before. Metals of purple, blue, and green consumed her imagination.

"There!" she heard Litning call out.

Looking up, she found that he'd wandered off a little farther into the crowd than where she'd marked him previously. She followed his eyes across the concourse and her gaze fell on....

"Jethan!" she said the name in a hushed whisper. She knew Litning wasn't a fan, but wondered why he stalked Alesha's crewmember. As she watched, her hand absent-mindedly drifted down to one of the pieces on the vendor's stall.

Jethan moved from his position. Litning moved to counter. As Gina stepped forward to follow Litning, she was stopped by hot, rough flesh on her wrist. She whipped her head around to see the vendor holding her fast.

"You touch, you buy! You touch, you buy!" the vendor yelled in a heavily-accented voice.

"No, I have to go," Gina tried talking to the man, but she wasn't even sure if he understood her. "I-I'll come back later!"

"You touch, you buy! *You touch, you buy!*" The vendor was furious.

Gina attempted to free herself, but to no avail. The man's grip belied his small stature. On Earth, she'd tossed men three times his size, but he possessed a strength that shocked her. "Let go of me!"

The vendor called out something in an alien language and two additional short, blue men arose from a café table nearby. Worse, a couple of the GAC agents took notice of the developing scene.

Again, Gina attempted to wrench her arm away, but it was no use. The little man wasn't giving up. Despite drawing the attention of the GAC, as well as several onlookers, Gina had no choice but to call out to the *one* person completely oblivious to her plight. "*Litning!*"

The Revash spun around instantly. His eyes widened in shock, but quickly narrowed in anger as he bared his teeth. The vendor didn't appear to notice the cloaked figure barreling toward the jewelry cart, but the GAC agents and the vendor's friends sure did. As the vendor continued tugging on Gina's arm, his friends balked and went back to their drinks, while the GAC agents hollered into their communication devices for backup.

"Please, let go! I don't want you to get hurt!" Gina pleaded with the vendor, who clearly had no qualms about hurting her.

"You touch, you buy! *AIIIIEE!*" Finally, the vendor caught sight of Litning and released Gina's wrist. She snatched her arm back and the vendor abandoned his stall. Litning halted his charge just short of plowing through the structure.

"Are you all right?" he asked.

"I am now. I just touched one of these bracelets and he lost his mind."

"Yes. Some of these vendors are very…strict."

"We've got bigger problems, though," she said, pointing to the approaching GAC agents.

"Let us move elsewhere," Litning said as he led Gina in the opposite direction. He stopped short at the sight of a group of armed and armored beings heading their way. Of the four individuals approaching them, two wore masks, while the other two had such scarred faces, they might as well have been wearing masks. Their skin was a dark purple. "Bounty hunters."

"Looks like we're stuck," Gina said. "What was so important about Jethan?"

"I was curious why he came to this level of the spaceport. Why did he not ride up with us? I do not trust him."

"You think he's responsible for these jokers?"

"He is no longer here, so I cannot ask him."

"Then, we'll have to ask them," she said, getting into a defensive posture.

"I hope you are trained to fight," Litning said, squaring up to face their attackers.

"I do all right," Gina replied. A male GAC agent reached for her and she decked him, sending him reeling.

Litning grinned at her before unleashing a soul-rattling roar that gave all their opponents pause. Bystanders fled the concourse, screaming. Shops sealed their blast doors to protect their premises. The GAC goons and bounty hunters left on the concourse were more than enough to keep Gina and Litning busy. Gina's hopes faded a bit.

"Are we all right here?" she asked Litning.

"We are well-armed. My weapon is my strength."

She made a face. "No offense, but…"

He sighed. "Please, do not continue."

Their opponents closed in on all sides. Gina wondered if they might be able to turn the factions against each other. There was no time to find out. Three of the bounty hunters charged in with bludgeoning weapons.

Litning slashed at the approaching hunters with his long reach and razor-sharp claws. He didn't tag any of the hunters, but kept them at bay. More GAC agents arrived on the scene. Litning snarled.

"Don't kill any of the GAC agents," she said. "They're law enforcement. It'll just complicate matters." Of course, that wasn't the only reason for her hesitation. She felt a kinship with the law even if, at that moment, it wasn't on their side.

"You are severely hampering my effectiveness in battle," Litning growled as he took another swipe at the bounty hunters.

"You know Max would tell you the same thing."

An alarm sounded throughout the concourse. "*Security to Level Eighty-Two, Sector Nine!*"

"Is that us?" Gina asked.

"No. *Murrall's.*"

She looked back the way they'd come. "Max…."

CHAPTER 24

Max and Alesha stared down the barrels of several guns. "This isn't the way I saw this going," he said.

"You know I don't like to say, 'I told you so,' but..." Alesha replied.

"What? You're *always* telling me that! You love it!"

"Enough!" Murrall cried with a pained expression. "I swear to all the gods in the known universe, you two can be the most insufferable...."

"Hey, hey, no need for name-calling," Max said.

"So, what are we doing, Murrall?" Alesha asked. "Only one of these filthy petches can bring Max in."

"Very astute, Alesha, as always. I have gathered all these hunters as a precautionary measure," Murrall answered.

Max gestured around. "Quite a bit of precaution."

Again, Murrall flashed her sly grin. "Well, one can never be sure if Litning will follow directions."

"That's fair."

"I had a feeling you'd seek me out sooner rather than later," Murrall said. "Given our past professional relationship, and your current predicament, I knew you'd come to me for help. I'm surprised that you're only seeking information about Sierra, though. I thought for sure you'd come to me for fake identities or to hide you."

"I'm not running from this," Max said. "I'm trying to clear my name."

"Yes. Well, I counted on the fact that you'd need help. The end result is the same. *I* will be collecting the substantial bounty on your head."

"*What?*" one of the bounty hunters roared. He was called Torfan, a pink-skinned humanoid with three legs and a wicked scar across his neck. "What do *we* get?"

Murrall gave him a withering look. "We discussed this. Whomever helps me bring him in gets a finders fee fo—"

"But, we're doing all the work!" Torfan exclaimed. "This is vecking nakra!"

Arguing immediately broke out, with Murrall and Jhantra trying to get a word in edgewise. It was no use. In trying to turn Max's situation to her favor, Murrall had broken the cardinal rule—never get between a bounty hunter and their money. Her assembled flunkies were *not* happy.

"They're mine!" Torfan bellowed as he got a hold of Max's arm. The bounty hunter cuffed him on the head with his pistol. The room spun, but Max had the wherewithal to stomp on one of Torfan's three feet—*hard*. Torfan screamed in pain, loosening his grip.

Still woozy, Max grabbed Alesha's arm and swung her at Torfan. The hunter, still nursing his injured foot, failed to see Alesha's fist sailing toward his jaw. It was a maneuver they had used in the past with success. Torfan dropped his pistol. Alesha scooped it up and fired it at another bounty hunter. The hunter fell to the floor, unconscious.

Max picked up the second hunter's pistol as the room devolved into an all-out brawl. The hunters pummeled each other for the right to claim the bounty. Luckily for everyone in the room, they observed a modicum of professional courtesy by keeping everything to fisticuffs. If anyone stunned Max and Alesha, another competitor could easily cart off the prize.

Max and Alesha didn't follow such precautions. If any of the hunters got too close, they were quickly dispatched by the pair's newfound weapons. The two of them had amassed a small pile of unconscious bodies by the time Max motioned for Alesha to head for the exit.

Amidst the chaos, Murrall and Jhantra withdrew down a concealed ramp that led to a lower level. As she backed down the ramp, Murrall caught Max's eye. She gave him a knowing smile and a nod before they vanished from the room. Max nodded back and led Alesha to the exit.

"So, she was on our side the whole time," Alesha said.

"Looks like it." He smiled. "I guess she really does love me best. Lured a mess of bounty hunters here to keep them off of me. Ballsy."

"Well, she's always been that."

The two of them exited the party room and the robots holding their weapons emerged from the walls. They retrieved their own guns, while holding on to their newly-acquired weapons. "Is there any way to bar these doors?" Max asked his robot. The automaton said nothing and the two of them merged again with the walls. "So much for that."

"We've gotta go," Alesha said, tugging on his arm.

They raced up the corridor that led back to the sex room. The pair didn't even pause at the threshold. They sprinted into the room and many of the bounty hunters lost in the throes of passion looked their way. Some scrambled to find their clothing, while others were guided back to lust by Murrall's highly competent staff. More moaning than angry swearing could be heard.

"Can you believe this?" Max asked, grinning. "We got our info and we're going to get away scot-free!"

They crashed through the exit to find…pandemonium. Station security clashed with bounty hunters in a free-for-all melee. The screaming echoed around them. Even Murrall's bouncers maintained defensive stances. In the center of the scrum, Litning tossed bounty hunters left and right. Gina gave as good as she got, decking any hunters that got past Litning's defense.

Alesha gave Max a sardonic look. "I need you to stop jinxing us with all your early celebrating."

"Noted."

Before he could say anything else, a bounty hunter wearing what looked like a hockey helmet with a red visor over his eyes pointed in their direction. "*Hey! Ultra's over there!*" he cried in his digitally-amplified voice.

The participants in the melee fell silent and turned to Max and Alesha. Though the pause in the action creeped Max out, he chuckled nervously and waved at the hunters. A great roar filled the square. The bounty hunters lost all interest in Litning and Gina as they rushed toward *Murrall's*.

"*Jesus fuck!*" Max exclaimed. He grabbed Alesha's hand and ran to the left. The mob pursued them.

As they dashed down a corridor to Level Eighty-Two's main concourse, Alesha fired her weapon wildly behind them. "Will you stop pulling my arm?!"

"We've gotta get to the ship!" he cried. He waved pedestrians out of their way with his pistol.

"Yes, but they're after *you*. We should split up."

That stung. "Thanks for your deep concern."

"I *am* concerned—that they'll catch us both and there'll be no escape. If we split up, we have a chance."

He hated when she was right. They passed into Sector Eight of the main concourse, which was curiously devoid of people. The storefronts were sealed up. "What the hell happened here?" He saw some bounty hunters and their GAC tails slowly getting up off the ground. *Litning.*

One of the agents spotted them. "There they are!"

"Shit," Max muttered as they ran through the mostly empty sector. Sector Seven was packed with people—half of them probably fleeing Sector Eight. As they entered the sector, Max pushed Alesha into the crowd and split to the right. The screaming mob of bounty hunters and station security largely ignored Alesha and followed him. They chased Max deeper into the spaceport. He was able to thread through the mass of people more easily than his pursuers, but they nipped at his heels.

Max kept his eyes up, scanning the storefronts to get his bearings. He needed a safe haven, then he could get to the ship. *I've gotta get to the* Con-3. Pepper would help him, or at least give him a place to lay low. The problem was, the *Con-3* was located clear on the other end of the spaceport.

The crowd in front of him became less fluid. He peered over their heads and saw a line of port security officers marching toward him. *Now I'm getting screwed at both ends!* He cut right, staying parallel with the security line. The bounty hunter horde drew closer. He tried to melt into the crowd, but it was useless. The hunters angled to intercept him. Who knew what kind of tracking tech they had zeroed in on him?

One of the hunters reached for Max's arm through the crowd. Max pulled away, drew his weapon, and hit him in the gut with a stun blast. Max grabbed him by the front of his jacket and pushed his unconscious frame into oncoming bounty hunters.

More hunters caught up and grabbed at him, knocking away the weapon he'd stolen at *Murrall's*. A female with bulging yellow eyes reached out with a shock glove. Max dodged the attack and redirected the glove to one of her competitors and shocked the shit out of him instead.

As the electroshock patient fell away, Max pushed Ms. Shock Glove into another pair of approaching hunters. Two more hunters moved in from the right. The big one, Max recognized—a hulking Yandit called Klothir.

"Well, hello there, Ultra!" Klothir called over the general commotion. "Mind if I borrow you for a trip to Aval?"

"Go fuck yourself, Klothir," Max replied. His defiance didn't stop Klothir from grabbing his arm, while another hunter, a Corthlan with mottled gray skin, went to work on Max's mid-section. The pain of the Corthlan's strikes at least made Max close his eyes so he wouldn't have to look at Klothir's ugly face or his creepy eyepatch.

With his free hand, Max pulled his collapsible pistol from his jacket and shot the Corthlan in the chest. The unconscious hunter fell back into the, now, stampeding crowd. The panicked mob jostled Klothir enough for him to loosen his grip on Max's arm. Max twisted his body around and gave Klothir two blasts from his pistol. To Max's surprise, Klothir's grip tightened as he fell,

taking Max with him. As they hit the deck, Klothir's hand finally
came free, but Max didn't immediately get back to his feet. Due
to the Yandit's size, the fleeing crowd flowed around him, and, as
a result, Max. So, Max dragged Klothir on top of him, hiding
himself from view.

Klothir…didn't smell great. Max gagged. The heat Klothir
gave off was ridiculous. After a few moments, Max was drenched
in sweat. He heard the clanking of marching boots. They stopped
nearby. Then, the clatter of boots went in all directions.

"*So, we're just waiting for these two to wake up?*" a female
voice asked. Her voice was digitized and amplified.

"*Yeah,*" replied her male companion. "*They might be able to
give us some information. Ultra seemed to just up and
disappear.*"

As quietly as he could, Max wriggled out from under Klothir.
Two port security officers stood by the unconscious bounty
hunters, their backs to Max. While the crowds had dissipated on
the concourse, there was plenty of ambient noise to mask his
movements. Slowly, he pulled out his pistol. He felt a twinge of
guilt at shooting them in the back, but he soothed himself with the
knowledge that at least he was only stunning them. He fired. The
laser bolt hit the female officer square in the back…and was
completely absorbed by her armor.

"Jesus, *fuck!*"

The officers spun around and drew their shock batons. "*Nice
try, you vecking petch,*" the woman said.

Max fired wildly at both officers. The laser bolts went wide
of their marks, but they forced the pair to back off. The bolts
drew the attention of the other security officers in the sector, who
had been busy corralling the errant bounty hunters.

Footsteps pounded in Max's head as he struggled to pull his foot out from under the meaty Klothir. The other security officers charged in his direction. The two security officers looming over him poked at him with their shock batons.

The first shock ripped through him. The second went straight to his head. Grogginess clouded his mind, but clearly the batons weren't on the highest setting. He had the presence of mind to fire his pistol. One bolt clipped the male's helmet and knocked him on his ass. That allowed Max to concentrate all his fire on the female, who attempted to deliver another blow with her shock baton. Max took careful aim and unloaded six shots into her torso, finally overpowering her armor. The officer fell to the deck and Max pushed the groaning Klothir off his trapped leg.

He struggled to his feet and lurched through the sparse foot traffic. Unfortunately, the suddenly open lanes made it that much easier for his pursuers to give chase. Though still woozy from the shock treatment, Max kept his feet moving. He *had* to get to the *Con-3*. The bounty hunters would never stop and until he cleared his name, neither would port security. But, this was Marina, his *home*. He had to make it right.

Glancing behind him, he saw that bounty hunters and security officers were in a mad stampede to claim him. As the hunters took the lead, Max felt more comfortable firing at them. His aim was shit as usual, but it kept them at bay.

He saw the blinking blue neon of the *Con-3*'s marquee ahead. A bounty hunter's fingertips brushed against his back and Max threw a vicious elbow behind him, catching the hunter in the head.

Max crashed through the front door. Every head inside the *Con-3* turned to face him. All sorts of alien beings populated the dimly lit restaurant. The large, oval bar was packed. Pepper stood at the center.

Pepper was a pot-bellied, dark-skinned man with a fluffy salt and pepper beard. He dressed smartly, with the flour smears of the kitchen on his sleeves. Despite all the paying patrons surrounding him, Pepper's eyes locked on Max. Pep moved from behind the bar, faster than his heft would imply. He waved Max into the restaurant. Max wasted no time.

"In here, my boy! In here!" Pep hissed as he ushered Max through the swinging door into the kitchen. He snapped at two of his busboys and they rushed to secure the front door.

Max squinted against the kitchen's bright lights. Pep pushed him out of the way to take the lead.

"*Max!*" came the collective cry from Pepper's kitchen staff. Every member of the team was a Larth—squat creatures with tan fur, no necks, and long arms. Max could only offer the friendly aliens a weak smile and wave as he followed Pep to the rear of the restaurant.

Pep hustled Max into the walk-in freezer. He moved several boxes and revealed a trap door. Beneath it, a staircase descended into darkness. "Take the stairs all the way down. Push on the wall. You'll come out on Level Eighty," Pepper said.

Gratitude swelled in Max's chest. "Pep…thank you."

Pepper smiled "Always, my boy. You know that." He squeezed Max's arm. "Now, get going!"

He closed the hatch behind Max. Tiny running lights illuminated the stairway, but not much else. Everything in the passage was the same dark blue metal as the rest of the spaceport. Max moved carefully down the long staircase.

He had to get to the *Heartbreaker*; he hoped that Litning and Alesha were safe. A pang of guilt shot through him. *Gina.* He reminded himself that she was a trained FBI agent and he should stop thinking of her as defenseless. Nonetheless, he moved with renewed urgency.

Finally, he reached the bottom of the staircase. Taking a moment to catch his breath and tuck his pistol into his jacket, he listened. Nothing—not a sound. Pep had successfully stymied his pursuers. He pushed on the wall panel. The secret door popped open, but before he could even step outside, he was greeted with the familiar scowl of Matthias Glintock. It was accompanied by a pistol pointed right in Max's face.

"Maxim Ultra, you are under arrest."

CHAPTER 25

Max raised his hands above his head. Glintock glared at him, his aim unwavering. "You know I didn't do this thing, right?"

Glintock kept his aim on Max another moment before relenting. "Of course."

Max let out a slow breath. "Then, can you tell those guys upstairs?"

Glintock didn't crack a smile. "Do you understand how serious this is?"

"The greedy mob upstairs was a pretty good giveaway."

"Then why are you vecking here?" Glintock asked as he holstered his pistol. "*Why* would you come to the *one* planet that *every* bounty hunter in the galaxy would be *looking* for you?"

"I had to. I needed information and no one knows more than Murrall. There's something else going on besides the bombing."

"You were supposed to stay hidden." Glintock paused, looking uncomfortable. "I'm glad you're in one piece. I've been worried."

The sentiment touched Max, but he responded to sincere emotions the same way he always did—with humor. "Thanks,

Dad." Glintock's stern glare returned. "Look, Matthias, I couldn't cower in the corner while everyone tried to bail my ass out. If Earth isn't safe for me, where can I go? How'd you even find me here?"

"Are you really asking me that? Did you think that Pepper was able to build this escape route without the knowledge of the spaceport? We know who your allies are, Maxim, and the staircase is in the schematics. It was a simple deduction."

"Well, thanks for the heads up." Max felt his face get hot. What good was a secret escape hatch if anyone could find out about it? He intended to have a word with Pepper once he was out of danger.

"The bounty hunter on Earth, who was he?" Glintock asked.

"No idea. *She* wore a mask and escaped before we could question her."

From his expression, Max could see Glintock's mind working. "Exactly where did this fight take place?"

Max winced. He'd hoped to avoid that question. "Ah, at my high school reunion."

"In full view of *how* many people?"

Max shrugged. "Couple hundred…maybe."

"*Veck!*"

"Yeah, you may need a big cleanup crew down there."

"Why?" Glintock looked wary. "This assassin wasn't human?"

"No, no, she was—I think. But, that was before Alesha showed up…then Shanta and Litning." Mass alien sightings on non-GAC planets were a no-no, especially if the individuals involved were part of the GAC. Since Max was kind of a dual citizen, any alien sighting in his presence would fall on him. It was one of the reasons why his return trips to Earth were frowned upon.

"Nakra! Veck!" Clearly, Glintock wasn't happy. "Did *anyone* on Earth *not* see an alien while you were there?"

"Uh…my mom?"

"Gods, what a mess." Glintock paused. "However, that could go a long way to proving you were on Earth at the time of the bombing."

"I'm assuming Brontin is really pushing this narrative?"

Glintock grimaced. "Among others."

As if on cue, a woman who appeared to be Asian with a blonde pixie cut entered the corridor, pistol drawn. "Get on the ground, Ultra!"

Max ignored her order and looked to Glintock. "I'm guessing this is to whom you were referring?"

"She's only the half of it. Maxim Ultra, meet Agent Varra Dilton. Dilton, this is the incorrigible Maxim Ultra."

"I know who he is, Glintock. I gave you an order, you vecking petch! Get on the ground!"

"Dilton, nice to meet you. I'm innocent."

"Fascinating. So was every other perp I've ever caught. Get. On. The. Ground."

He looked to Glintock for help. "Are you going to pull rank here, or…?"

"Oh, no. She's in charge of this investigation."

"And now that we have our man, we can sort out this vecking mess of a case. Beattie!" At Dilton's command, her exact double approached, pistol drawn. The newcomer was Dilton's twin, but she walked with a more precise gait.

Robot. "Must be nice to have an android duplicate."

"It's very nice. It allows me to get rough with perpetrators without dirtying my hands." Beattie slugged Max in the stomach, dropping him to his knees.

"What the *veck* is this, Dilton?" Glintock exclaimed, positioning himself between his partners and Max.

She shrugged. "He wouldn't get on the ground. I told you we were going to start doing things my way. Plus, he broke your agreement by coming here. The sooner we take him into custody, the sooner we can get him safe."

"Right," Max gasped. "Because, bounty hunters have *never* taken someone out of GAC custody."

"This wasn't the plan, Varra!" Glintock hissed.

"He clearly can't be trusted to follow simple commands. If we want to take him into custody, we just have to do it!"

"If you take me into custody, I'm just going to end up dead," Max said.

"How do you figure that?" Dilton asked.

"*Accidents* happen," he replied. "I'm accused of murdering thousands of beings. That tends to stir up some emotions."

"Then do not murder thousands of beings," the bot replied.

"News flash, I didn't," he said, getting back to his feet. "How could I have blown up a building on Aval while I was on Earth? It's impossible!"

"Save it, Ultra. We know you were on Earth. I'm just expressing my disappointment that you don't know how to follow directions," Dilton said.

"Not all of us are convinced," Beattie said.

"We also know what you've been up to since you failed to follow our instructions," Glintock said. "You think Sierra's on the loose."

"Very good, Agent. The question is, what are we going to do about it?"

"Local law enforcement departments are working those cases," Dilton said. "What else do you want us to do about it?"

Max gave her an incredulous look. "Are you serious? Sierra is clearly working with the people that stormed the *Galactic Dream* last year—an independent, well-equipped, well-funded army. I'd think that would warrant the GAC's attention."

"I said, people are looking into it," Dilton said, crossing her arms.

"Murrall said she heard I was the only suspect for Aval, that there wasn't any other chatter. Isn't that a little odd?"

"As far as the GAC is concerned, you *are* the only suspect," Glintock said.

"So, the biggest corporation in the galaxy is getting hit in big jobs and no one knows anything about it?" Max asked. "That doesn't seem weird to you?"

"Zeth could be concealing the information," Glintock said.

"But, why?" Max asked. "Wouldn't he want the culprits caught?"

"Bad publicity?" Glintock offered.

"Maybe," Max conceded. "I guess it wouldn't do to have people lose confidence in the corporation that controls the galaxy. No offense."

"What does any of this have to do with anything?" Dilton asked. "They're separate cases and you're coming with us."

"What I'm getting at is, if the entire GAC is busy chasing me around the galaxy, it's real easy for an unknown player to pull off something big. It helps that they have someone working for them who would have no qualms about framing me. You guys have all the information—what is she stealing? What could she do with it?"

Dilton and Glintock looked at each other and then turned to Beattie. The bot stood motionless for a moment before coming out of her processing trance. "The most logical result would be a facility. Based on the quantities stolen, it would be a *large* facility."

The other three shared a sobering look. "A fringe military unit building a home base with a living weapon in their midst? Yeah, it seems like they'd have good reason to have the GAC distracted with a flashy, high profile crime," Max said.

Glintock looked at Dilton. "Not so unbelievable when it's framed like that, is it?"

"No, that's…but, who's behind it?"

"That's the only part I haven't worked out," Max said. "Does Zeth have any rivals?"

Beattie emitted a terrifying, mechanical laugh. The others looked at her with confused looks. "Oh, I am sorry. I believed you were being facetious."

"That's her way of saying Zeth's enemies are too numerous to list. It would take time to dig through the whole list," Dilton said.

"Time we don't have," Glintock said.

Dilton paused, as if weighing her options. "You've given us a lot to think about, Ultra, but you're still the most wanted man in the galaxy. We need to take you in to keep you safe. Then we can sort all this out."

Max didn't like it. He wasn't a fan of being taken into custody, friendly or otherwise. His mind shifted to his friends. Didn't *they* have a right to be safe and free from harm? A deal with Dilton and Glintock would protect them.

"All right, you've got yourself a de—" A high-tensile cord wrapped around Max and jerked him into the air, cutting off his response. The spaceport spun around him until he came to a stop on a rooftop fifty yards away. A rough hand grabbed him and turned him around. "*Merthane*."

"Hello, Maxim. You didn't think I'd let you climb to the top of the most wanted list and *not* try to catch you, did you?"

"After we kicked your ass last year? Yeah, I had my doubts."

"We remember that day quite differently, you and I. The day you took her away from me."

"Wait a minu—" Before Max could get the words out, Merthane threw him off the roof, onto a not-so-soft vendor cart on the Level Eighty concourse. No matter how bad Max's day had been so far, it was about to get worse.

CHAPTER 26

Alesha, Gina, and Litning escaped the mob and raced to the docking bay where the *Heartbreaker* waited. Alesha held up her hand. The trio stood across from the docking bay, hidden in an alcove.

"Why are we waiting?" Gina asked.

Alesha resisted rolling her eyes. She liked Gina a lot, but the Earth girl had a few things to learn about space. "I want to make sure no one is staking out the ship. I thought Max said you were law enforcement on Earth?"

"I am, but usually we do the chasing, not the other way around."

Alesha shrugged. "Makes sense." She looked to Litning. "You smell anything, Fuzzy?"

He grumbled. "The air is too fragrant from all the food vendors. However, I do not hear anything out of the ordinary."

"Perfect," Alesha said. She took a small black remote from her belt and pressed the lone button twice. "Okay, let's go."

The three of them crossed over to the docking bay. Alesha held them at the entrance, poking her head in for one more scan.

There was no one. Even the docking staff was missing. Her body tensed. She waved the others in. The *Heartbreaker* sat, undisturbed, with no evidence that GAC agents had visited. That didn't sit right with her. Everything felt off. The ship's landing ramp was lowered.

"Let's get on board," she said.

"What about Max and your crew?" Litning asked.

Before Alesha could get a word out, a shadow fell over them. She looked up just in time to jump back as the assassin from Earth finished her flip. She landed in the middle of the trio, sword drawn.

"Shit, her again?" Gina said, drawing the pistol Alesha had given her.

The mystery woman kicked the weapon out of her hand, but Earth Girl didn't miss a step—she responded with a kick. The assassin brought her sword down toward Gina's leg, but Gina pulled back before it could connect.

Alesha shot the floor at the assassin's feet, forcing her backwards into Litning's waiting arms. The Revash wrapped the assassin up and squeezed. She grunted as he pinned her arms to her sides.

"Who are you?" Litning growled as the assassin squirmed in his grip. "Speak!"

The assassin's answer came in the form of an electric pulse that emanated from her armor. The attack knocked Litning to the floor, his body wracked with spasms. The assassin stood over his fallen body, unharmed.

In the time they'd worked together, Alesha had seen Litning take a lot of punishment, so she was sure he was still alive. "That wasn't very nice. He asked you a question."

The tight-lipped assassin moved into a defensive posture. She held her sword horizontally. It crackled with energy.

Alesha kept her aim on the assassin, while Gina took up a fighting stance. She was impressed—she'd figured Earth Girl would run and cower in a corner. Her eyes flicked back to the assassin. "So, why are you so hot for Max?"

"*He murdered thousands of people on Aval. That isn't enough?*" the assassin asked, her voice digitized by her mask.

"Yeah, I know why the mob upstairs is out to get him, but you went to Earth, breaking a well-established GAC neutrality law. That's a major no-no. You must have it in for him something fierce."

If it were possible, the assassin's tone became even colder. "*You were there, so you should know.*"

Alesha's brow furrowed. *When did we wrong a female assassin?*

The masked woman didn't give her any time to ponder. She lashed out with her sword. Alesha fired, but it was no use. The assassin deflected the bolts. Gina came in on her flank with a flurry of kicks. Earth Girl definitely had skills.

The assassin turned to counter Gina, but that left her open for Alesha to shoot her in the side. The skilled fighter deflected Alesha's bolts, while keeping Gina at bay with her other sword. Alesha holstered her pistol and whipped out an expandable baton, hoping to get in close. She went for the assassin's knee, but her baton clanged against the sword. However, she distracted the masked woman enough for Gina to land a kick.

The kick knocked the assassin back. She flourished her swords, which kept Alesha from making a move. The energy buzzing around the blades was more fearsome than the possibility of being cut. The masked warrior was formidable.

Movement in her periphery sent a flood of relief through Alesha. Keeping her eye on the assassin, she crouched to pick up Gina's pistol, which she tossed to her. "Shoot her," Alesha said.

Both fired at the assassin. As Alesha expected, the assassin blocked their bolts. She nodded to Gina, and the two pressed forward, keeping up the pressure. The assassin backed away from their offensive…right into Litning's hands.

The Revash's clawed hand closed around the assassin's ankle. Before she could react, he threw her against the nearest wall. Her swords clattered to the floor as her limp form hit the ground.

Gina charged forward and scooped up the first sword she encountered. She brought the blade down in an overhead strike, but the assassin blocked her with the other sword.

Both the assassin and Litning rose to their feet. He kept his distance, while she faced off with Gina, blades at the ready. Neither emitted any energy—Gina's probably because she didn't know how to activate it. The assassin struck first, but Gina easily parried. The two crossed swords to another stalemate. That was about the time Alesha's crew members arrived in the hangar with one notable exception. "Where's Jethan?" she asked.

Grathell shrugged. "No idea. Maybe he didn't get your signal?"

"Not likely. We'll wait as long as we can, but we have to get out of here as soon as possible."

"But, we'll wait for Ultra, won't we?" Grathell asked.

"If you don't like your captain's orders, then you can stay here and deal with the GAC. Clear?"

He hesitated for a moment. "Yes, Captain."

The final two members of Alesha's crew, Plim and Grandy, raced down the boarding ramp carrying laser rifles. Alesha directed them to keep their distance and lock down the perimeter. Gina and the assassin crossed swords a final time and Gina disarmed the masked woman, flipping her blade to the opposite side of the hangar.

"Oh, yes, baby, yes!" Alesha exclaimed. She motioned for Vinx and Grathell to surround the antagonist. Gina blushed, but kept her blade pointed at the assassin. "Where did you learn that fancy sword work?" Alesha asked.

"I spent a few years in Japan." She caught herself. "I'm sorry. I know that probably doesn't mean anything to you."

"Nope. But, I get it. You did great!" She then turned to the assassin. "All right, you tricky horvorka, we've got you now."

Though she couldn't see the assassin's face, Alesha had the distinct feeling that she was sneering at her. The woman's only response was a snort. "*Hmph.*"

CHAPTER 27

Max groaned as he struggled to get up. Merthane's attack left him discombobulated. He needed to get his bearings. There was no telling when Glintock and Dilton would get back to the concourse to help. He was on his own.

The clatter of multiple boots drew his attention. A group of eight, dressed in matching maroon tactical uniforms, headed his way. They all wore faceless masks, so he couldn't tell who or what he was about to deal with. His heart sank when he saw the flag patches on their sleeves—Aval.

The lead soldier motioned for the others to halt in front of the sitting Max. The leader's faceplate shimmered to reveal a hard, feminine face. Her mask instantly reminded him of the assassin on Earth. *"Mr. Ultra, my name is Londa. Aval will have justice for the five thousand ninety-seven souls you stole."* She said it as if taking his order at a restaurant. He knew they meant business as soon as they drew their laser rifles.

He couldn't outrun their lasers, so instead, he launched himself at them, closing the gap. If they wanted to shoot him, they'd have to shoot each other. They immediately drew energy daggers as Max struggled with Londa for her rifle.

"There's no escape, Ultra. Your journey ends here," Londa said. The soldiers closed in, brandishing their knives.

Max's very public murder was interrupted by the arrival of Merthane, who rocketed into the center of the circle with jets attached to his boots. He slapped a metal disc on Londa's shoulder and in the same motion, tackled Max to the deck. A high-pitched, electronic whine pierced Max's ears, followed by a soundwave that pulsed twice. It knocked all the Avalians to the deck.

Merthane hauled him to his feet. "Poachers. Can't vecking stand them."

"No, they're here to kill me. They're from Aval."

"Fantastic." Merthane pulled out a set of cuffs. "Here. Let's go."

Max looked to the cuffs, to Merthane, and repeated that cycle. "Ha, yeah, no."

"I just saved your life!"

"So you can cart me off to prison? I don't think so." He started walking away.

Merthane grabbed his arm. "It's hilarious that you think you're not in custody."

The Avalians stirred.

Max feared the kill squad, but the more immediate threat was Merthane. He could *not* set foot on Aval until he'd proven his innocence. "Get the fuck off me," he said, yanking his arm away.

Merthane grabbed at him. Max parried. "Maxim, stop vecking around! You're coming with me."

The Avalians started rising.

"The fuck I am!" Max kicked his rival in his left knee. Merthane cried out and crumpled to the deck. Max turned and ran in the direction of the *Heartbreaker*, twenty-nine levels down. It didn't take long for the laser bolts to follow. Sparing a glance behind him, he saw the kill squad in hot pursuit. The odds were daunting, but Marina was Max's home. He could lose them.

Other pedestrians cleared the way as Max bolted through the spaceport, waving his arms wildly. He only *looked* like a madman. What he really did was scan the storefronts. It didn't take long to find what he needed—*Cictros*.

A cacophony of sound and a kaleidoscope of color, *Cictros* was a bustling arcade, filled with games of chance and entertainment designed to suck away patrons' credits. Usually, when he was in town, Max was a frequent visitor. Aside from the adult beverage bar, the place took him back to Earth and the video game palaces of his youth. Several years earlier, Max had donated a *Ms. Pac-Man*. It had been quite the hit.

He pushed his way through the crowd of revelers, the kill squad hot on his heels. Meeja was behind the bar, her dirty blonde hair up in a tall topknot. The place was so busy, she didn't see him coming.

"Meeja!" he yelled at the top of his lungs.

She looked at Max and behind him. She ducked behind the bar and popped back up with a burst blaster. She tossed it to Max, who caught it in his outstretched hands. He spun and fired the weapon at his nearest pursuer. The non-lethal energy blast blew the kill squad member back about thirty feet. Max pulled the recharge lever and fired at the next soldier in line.

A panic ensued. The crowd clearly had no idea the weapon was non-lethal—like a shotgun, the burst blaster was *loud*. People pushed and scrambled for the front door, slowing the advance of the rest of Londa's crew. Max tossed Meeja's burst blaster back to her and blew her a kiss, high-tailing it for the back door. There were still plenty of people to push through, as the panic spread to the rear of the arcade.

As Max managed to bust through the back door into a dimly-lit corridor, his chin met with a hard wallop. He crashed to the deck. Londa loomed over him with a few of her goons.

"*Goodbye, Mr. Ultra.*" She raised a gleaming longsword over her head.

Max kicked out at Londa's legs, throwing off her strike. He then drew his pistol and fired wildly, keeping the kill squad at bay. One of his bolts hit the faceplate of one of Londa's men, knocking him to the floor. Max kept firing as he wormed his way to the hole in the kill squad's circle.

As he got to his feet, a hail of laser bolts screamed down the corridor. A hobbled Merthane, bracing himself against the corner of *Cictros*, fired his pistol at Londa's squad.

Max used the distraction to get a few point blank shots in on the other squad members before scooping up an unattended laser rifle and taking off in the opposite direction of the approaching Merthane.

"Gods dammit, Maxim! Come back here!" Merthane called after him as he struggled down the corridor.

Max tucked his pistol away and gripped the rifle tightly as he raced around to the front of *Cictros*. Three more of Londa's people spotted him and gave chase. Max bobbed and weaved through the spaceport crowds, keeping the innocents between him and certain death. The kill squad showed *some* restraint, curbing their fire during the foot chase. Londa's screams carried over the general din of the port crowds. Max wondered if they'd killed Merthane or if he still limped after them.

Finally, a break in the clouds—a pair of lift doors opened to reveal ten port security agents. Max ducked behind some bystanders and fired his rifle straight up. The people around him screamed. Through the spaces between the fleeing bodies, Max saw the security team looking around for the perpetrator. He slid the rifle along the floor and blended in with the panicked public. The security team rushed onto the concourse and intercepted Londa's squad, who brazenly carried their rifles out in the open.

Max smiled as he slipped away from his pursuers. Escape was practically in his grasp when laser weapons started going off behind him. He spun around to see the Avalians tussling with the security team. Max picked up his pace, but it didn't save him from being assaulted on his left.

Merthane lurched out of the crowd and grabbed him roughly. "Going somewhere, Maxim? Not leaving without me, I hope."

Max tried to shake off Merthane's iron grip. "How the hell is your gimpy ass finding me all over the place, but Glintock can't?"

"Because, I'm in this for the money."

"I thought you were above all that."

"You're Galactic Enemy Number One, Maxim. You must be guilty of *something*."

"You know I'm innocent."

"All I know is, you've severely vecked up my knee, so I'm inclined to take you in for that alone."

He glanced down at Merthane's leg. A clumsy brace didn't appear to be much help. He wanted to strike, but the pistol digging into his back made him reluctant. "Where are we going? The *Claw?*"

"After we make a quick stop." Merthane hustled Max onto a lift with no one else aboard. "If you recall, I made you a promise last year and I intend to keep it—especially after Dayna."

"You brought her into that mess."

"And you let Memta out of the box. The blame firmly lays at your feet."

"Agree to disagree, I guess."

"Well, I'm holding the pistol, so I must be right."

"You'd fit right in in America."

Merthane emitted a nasty laugh. "Your father used to say the same. Violence made him squeamish too."

Max didn't remember his father that way. After all, the man had taught Max how to fight. Perhaps knowing how to fight didn't necessarily mean one enjoyed fighting.

"Your father also had a tenuous relationship to honor and honesty."

Max's brow furrowed. "What the fuck are you talking about? Dad was honest to a fault."

"No, you knew him as his son. I was a war buddy— completely different relationship. You knew a sanitized version of Jimmy. I knew his real self."

Max's blood boiled. He wasn't sure if it was because Merthane made sense. "He wasn't very sanitized as *galacin* ate him from the inside out."

A shadow passed over Merthane's face. "I'm sorry about that. I hated Jimmy in the end, but I wouldn't wish that fate on anyone."

"You've still never told me why you hated him so much. You were like brothers." He was loathe to admit it, but it was the truth.

"Much like yourself, your father took something from me— something very dear—and he became my enemy." Merthane gritted his teeth. "You might absolve yourself in Dayna's death, but you were vecking well responsible for Gage's."

Max winced. Gage was a sore spot. Even if he hadn't been directly responsible for his death, he'd forever blame himself. "Gage was an adult and made his own choices. He knew the risks."

Merthane's grip on his arm tightened. "You're not very good at taking responsibility for your actions, Maxim."

"Sure I am, when it's warranted. But, your twisted mental gymnastics to make me responsible for every bad thing that's happened to you? No fucking way. The way I see it, I'm pretty much the only reason you've got to keep going."

Merthane chuckled. "Oh, my boy, I'm so disappointed. You don't know me at all."

The lift *dinged* at Level Fifty-One. As the doors opened, Merthane ground the gun muzzle into Max's ribs and pushed him into the corridor. Once they cleared the lift, Max spun to his left. Merthane's grip was tight, but he couldn't brace himself on his bad leg. His shot went astray and Max kicked at his knee brace.

With an agonized scream, Merthane crumpled to the ground. Max swiped the bounty hunter's pistol and blasted Merthane with a stun bolt for good measure. He didn't need him shooting him in the back.

With Merthane down for the count, Max ran for the *Heartbreaker*. If the port followed standard procedure, docking services would have been suspended as soon as the riot started outside *Murrall's*. He hoped the Avalians had been mopped up. He couldn't take any more surprises.

As he approached the docking bay, his heart jumped. The docking bay door was open, which meant Alesha and the others had made it. After his ordeal, he just wanted to see his friends safe and sound, especially Gina. She couldn't have known what she was getting into.

"All right, let's get the fu—" He stopped dead in his tracks.

Litning, Gina, and a couple of Alesha's crewmembers laid motionless on the floor. The rest of the crew, sans Jethan, stood ready, but wary, because in the middle of the area stood the assassin from Earth, holding a sword to Alesha's throat.

CHAPTER 28

Max's heart sat in his throat. Alesha, bloodied and subdued, had the assassin's sword at her neck. The assassin appeared undamaged. His eyes flicked to the others on the floor. Alesha's crewmembers did not move. He was relieved when Gina and Litning stirred.

"*Just the man I've been waiting for,*" the assassin's digitized voice taunted.

He covered his fear with bravado. "That's right. Here I am, baby. I think it would be better if we were alone, though, don't you? Why not let Alesha and all these others go first?"

"*This...refuse thought they could challenge me, so they have earned their reward.*"

"Not gonna lie, that's pretty bleak. You really should talk to someone." Max tried to catch Alesha's panicked eye.

"*Toss the pistol, or your girlfriend is a head shorter,*" the assassin said, pressing her sword against Alesha's neck.

"All right! All right! But...technically, she's not my girlfriend...presently." He wasted no time in tossing Merthane's pistol toward the assassin.

Her head turned toward the weapon. "*Wh-where did you get that?*"

"From a constant thorn in my side. I managed to yank him out."

The assassin was disconcertingly quiet. Her sword tapped against Alesha's neck as it wavered in her hand. "*Did...did you...?*"

Max squinted at the assassin. "Are you losing it?"

The assassin's grip tightened on Alesha, and she cried out. Max's eyes widened. "*Have you taken someone else from me?!*"

Before the assassin could slit Alesha's throat, she pushed her hostage away as she ducked to avoid a crate sailing toward her head. The crate had come courtesy of Jethan, who appeared out of nowhere. The assassin tossed a quartet of small knives in his direction. One nicked his leg. Max rushed to get Alesha out of harm's way.

"Who *is* this horvorka?" she asked.

"I think she's working with Merthane. The woman she keeps talking about must be Dayna."

"Veck, Merthane's here too?"

"Of course. He's off the board for now. We need to get the fuck out of here."

Alesha's eyes went to her fallen comrades. Her face contorted in grief. Having lost crewmembers in the past, Max's heart broke for her. "I...I'll need a new pilot."

"I've got that covered. Just get on the ship. We'll handle Little Miss Stabby."

The assassin landed in front of them, blocking their path to the ship. "*Tell me how you'll handle me, Ultra.*"

Max glanced behind them. "Did...did you flip over here?"

She brandished both her swords. Max recalled seeing the second discarded on the floor when he came in. The assassin's agility was frightening.

"So, I think I've figured out why you're so hot to kill me," Max said. "It's Dayna, isn't it? You think that I killed her?"

"You're also wanted for murdering thousands on Aval," the assassin said, dodging the question.

"Look, I know this is going to sound self-serving, but I didn't do that one either. Sierra Numani killed Dayna. She was—"

"Possessed by Memta. Yes, I know. Your crew let Memta loose on the galaxy. The fault is yours."

Was anyone *ever* going to let him live down the job he'd pulled with Sierra and Kalen? "Well, technically, Sierra was on that job too. I don't know what the hell Merthane has told you, but he's slightly biased. He hates my guts."

"With good reason!" Their impromptu conversation ended as she lashed out with her blades.

Max and Alesha retreated from the slashing attack. As he fumbled in his jacket for his collapsible pistol, he spared a glance behind him to see Litning getting to his feet. He whipped his pistol out and turned it on the assassin.

"Stun won't get through her armor," Alesha said as they kept their distance.

"Oh, I know. Trust me." He switched the pistol to lethal and fired. The assassin energized her blades and managed to block Max's bolts.

"Get out of the way!" came a bellowing cry from behind the assassin.

Max grabbed Alesha around the waist and lunged to the left as Jethan opened fire from the boarding ramp with Alesha's laser cannon she'd used on Earth. The laser bolts sailed in hot and fast, forcing the assassin to direct all her attention to the new threat. Her swords weren't fast enough and she activated an energy shield that took the cannon's punishment.

Her shield encased her in a greenish globe, so her flank was protected from Max, who *really* wanted to shoot her in the side. Instead, he pushed Alesha toward the *Heartbreaker* and rushed over to Gina, who was getting to her feet. Litning picked up Alesha's fallen and carried them to the ship.

Gina threw her arms around Max. "Oh my god, Max! Are you all right?"

"I should be asking the same." She didn't look hurt.

"I'm fine. She just hit me the wrong way and I knocked my head against that wall."

"She *hit* you?"

"Well, yeah. I mean, I was beating her ass with her own sword."

Max's mouth hung open. He couldn't picture it. Despite their long history, there was so much he didn't know about her. "That's…uh, wow. Get on board the *Heartbreaker*. We've gotta take out the trash."

She kissed him. He held her as long as he could. Jethan marched methodically down the boarding ramp, keeping his fire trained on the shielded assassin. Gina ran behind him and into the ship. Max waved to Litning and gestured to the assassin. Litning nodded with a tight smile.

Max looked to Jethan and slashed his hand across his throat. Jethan stopped firing. In the moment the assassin took to reset herself, Litning charged. Her shield remained in place and Litning hit it at full speed. The impact bounced the assassin down the exit corridor. As she crossed the threshold, Max activated the door controls, slamming the entrance closed behind her.

He ran to the ship and slapped the grinning Litning on the shoulder. "Thanks for the save," he said to Jethan.

"It was not for you," the alien grunted. Max was surprised he didn't take the opportunity to lord his timely arrival over them.

As the trio passed into the *Heartbreaker*'s cargo hold, Max spotted the covered bodies of Alesha's fallen comrades. He hadn't known the two well at all, but he'd seen the anguish on Alesha's face. She'd wanted her own crew so badly and to lose two of them.... It was a pain Max never wanted to experience again and it saddened him that Alesha had to live through it. A fright shot through him when he realized how close he'd come to mourning Alesha herself.

An alarm sounded outside the ship.

"*Max! Get up here!*" Alesha's voice sounded from the ship-wide intercom.

He shoved his thoughts away and raced up to the cockpit. The captain's chair was empty; Alesha sat in the co-pilot seat. A wary Gina sat in one of the jump seats. He squeezed Gina's shoulder as he slid into the pilot's seat. Alesha had already powered up the engines.

"They're trying to break into the docking bay," Alesha said.

"Fabulous." He checked his console and saw sparks erupting from the docking bay door.

She clicked the communicator. "Station Dispatch, this is the *Heartbreaker* requesting departure."

A male voice answered. "*Negative*, Heartbreaker. *Station security wants a word. We cannot approve departure request.*"

Alesha's panicked face turned to Max. "We're vecked."

Max's heart hammered in his chest. The security forces were almost through the door.

A loud electronic squelching sound cut through their communication with the station dispatcher. A familiar female voice sounded over the *Heartbreaker*'s communicator. "*Allow me, Maxim.*"

"Murrall!" Max blurted over their benefactor's jolly laughter.

The light on Alesha's console went to solid green and the docking bay's hatch opened above them. Alesha let out a whoop.

"Thanks, Murrall," Max said. "We owe you."

"*And don't think I won't come around to collect, Maxim. Safe travels!*"

The *Heartbreaker* took off, rising out of the docking pod and heading for the open sky. No one pursued them. The skies over Marina were clear thanks to the security lockdown. Max and Alesha shared a sad look; the possibility existed that they might not see their home again.

Gina leaned forward. "Where are we going?"

"It would be impossible to visit every Zeth business in a hope to intercept Sierra," Max said.

The *Heartbreaker* passed the barrier into space to find a logjam of ships attempting to dock in Marina. Max scanned the area, but nothing screamed, "GAC." He steered the *Heartbreaker* into the glut of ships.

"What are you doing?" Gina asked.

"Hoping to get lost in the crowd," he replied. "Then we have to figure ou—"

Grathell's voice came over the intercom. "*Boss, you need to get on the net and see this.*"

"What channel?"

"All *the channels.*"

Alesha pressed a few buttons on her console. Part of the viewport transitioned to a video screen. All three in the cockpit reared back in horror. Cloaked in shadow, an exact duplicate of Max stared into the camera.

"*The attack on Aval was only the start. Soon, the yoke of the GAC will be removed from this galaxy. I call on all other like-minded individuals to rise up and take back their worlds from the control of the GAC. There are no civilians in this war. All those who support the GAC are combatants. This includes the residents of* The Gallant. *Aval is a corrupt cesspool. This is a government that locked me away with no trial for a crime I did not commit. Aval's association with the GAC has only made it more corrupt. The wealthy residents of* The Gallant *benefitted the most from this corruption. They had to die, if only to awaken the slumbering power that can topple this corruption. If you are with us, join our cause. If not...beware.*"

The screen went black and a pink-skinned newscaster with green eyes appeared. "*A disturbing manifesto from the terrorist GAC officials have identified as Maxim Ultra.*"

The rest of the newscaster's words became muffled as if Max's ears had filled with water. His heart pounded in his chest. A cold sweat broke out all over, but he felt like á furnace inside. His hands shook.

"That...that was *me*," he managed to say. Alesha and Gina could only offer wide-eyed, but empathetic stares. "Jesus *fuck!*"

CHAPTER 29

Matthias followed Dilton through the disaster area outside *Murrall's*. Station Security and Marina-stationed GAC agents worked together to mop up the rioters. Unconscious bodies in pools of blood and vomit pocked the area. Matthias felt badly for those who had to clean it up.

Dilton hadn't said anything since they'd seen "Max's" manifesto. Matthias knew that it wasn't Max in the video, but with the manifesto being shown on every news outlet in the galaxy, he was concerned about his partner. The GAC had confirmed that the video was not some kind of AI program—whoever had delivered the message, it was a real live person.

Two large bouncers stood outside the doors of *Murrall's*. Their suits were rumpled and torn. One had a cut on his face, while the other's jaw swelled. Dilton marched up to them. "GAC. We want to see Murrall."

"Murrall's indisposed right now," the bouncer pushed through his puffy lips.

"Right. Beattie?"

The bot stepped up to the bouncer and with one swift motion, delivered a throat punch. As tender jaw doubled over in pain, his partner moved to engage. Dilton stopped him with a pointed finger.

"She's got another one for you. Let us in."

With a defeated look, the bouncer trudged to the doors and admitted them.

"Now, that wasn't so hard, was it?" Dilton said. As the entrance doors closed behind them, another set of doors opened instantly. A smartly dressed, dark-skinned woman with bright blonde hair emerged.

"I'm sorry, we're closed for business right now," the woman said.

"Good. We're not here to conduct business," Dilton said as she whipped out her credentials. "Dilton—GAC. These are my associates, Glintock and Beattie. We'd like to see the lady of the house, please."

"Murrall is not seeing callers presently. Is there perhaps something *I* can he—"

"I'm sorry, perhaps you missed the part where I said *GAC*," Dilton said. "Take us to her, *now*."

The woman's smile was strained. "Very well." She flipped open a small box on the wall and pressed a glowing blue button. A panel opened to reveal steel lift doors. The doors opened. Once the four were inside, the lift shifted sharply, moving horizontally.

Dilton's eyebrows rose. Matthias remained neutral. Murrall was not an enemy they wanted to make, not even as GAC agents. She had vast resources at her disposal and was a limitless font of information. Why sour a potential working relationship?

The lift jerked to a stop, forcing them to brace themselves against the walls. Murrall's associate looked at them apologetically. "Sorry, we don't use this much."

"Why use it now?" Beattie asked in an aggressive tone. "Sending us into a trap?"

"No. I had us take the lift to avoid our main pleasure room. It's full of bounty hunters nursing their wounds after the brawl that broke out in there. It'll take me weeks to get all the blood mopped up."

Matthias decided to step in. "Thank you, Miss...."

"Jhantra. My name is Jhantra. Thank you for finally asking." She punctuated it with a glare at Dilton.

"Jhantra, thank you. You've been most helpful," he said.

"You're at least respectful, Agent Glintock, but I won't fall for cheap niceties." The lift doors opened. "Right this way."

Jhantra led them into a cavernous room decorated in polished obsidian. The walls featured blank alcoves bordered by thin, bright strings of light. They glittered off the shiny floor like a sea of stars.

On the left wall, a bank of video screens showed the interior of the club. A few showed private sex rooms—rooms that Matthias was sure the patrons had no idea were monitored. The largest screen was the main pleasure room. Matthias recognized several of the bounty hunters in there.

Murrall sat in a white armchair, with a roaring fireplace behind her. She wore a white fur coat and a half-full wineglass twirled in her hand.

"Murrall," Jhantra said. "These are GAC agen—"

Dilton pushed past Jhantra. "Murrall, Agent Dilton, GA—"

"Agent Matthias Glintock of the GAC," Murrall said, ignoring Dilton. "Maxim has told me so much about you."

Matthias raised his eyebrows. Dilton's look could have melted steel. "Ah…is that so?"

"Of course! Knowledge is my business."

"I thought prostitutes were your business," Beattie said. The bot cut to the chase.

Murrall's jovial demeanor melted away. "My employees are companions, *robot*. I didn't know androids were so uncouth these days. I don't dispute how I make my living, agents. What I take issue with is the tone. I'm nothing if not a professional."

"Understood. If all these bounty hunters were on premises, how did Maxim Ultra walk out of here unscathed?" Matthias asked.

Murrall gestured to the video wall. "As you can see, Agent Glintock, several of those hunters are otherwise occupied. The others are nursing their wounds."

"I think what Agent Glintock is driving at is, why were all these bounty hunters here in the first place?" Dilton asked.

Murrall sipped her wine. "Perhaps this den of iniquity appeals to those who choose bounty hunting as a profession."

Beattie kept her arms crossed. "All those bounty hunters? Was that part of the plan? Lure Ultra here and feed him to the dogs? Then, he slipped away when the dogs turned on each other? Do I have that right?"

Murrall kept her own unwavering gaze on the bot. "Once again, I do not like your tone, *android*." She turned to Matthias with a softened expression. "I hate to disappoint you, my love, but you're only *half* right. Yes, I lured the hunters here with Maxim as bait, but I sprung the trap knowing they would fight amongst themselves."

"And with all those bounty hunters here in Marina, Ultra would be free to roam," Dilton said. Matthias couldn't hide his smile, but quickly concealed it when Dilton turned to him. "You're happy about this?"

He measured his words. "It was a clever ploy."

"We should bring her up on obstruction charges—harboring a fugitive at the very least."

"I wouldn't say I was harboring Maxim; he was only here for a brief time," Murrall said.

Dilton gave her a phony smile. "You're enjoying this, aren't you?"

"It's not the worst way to spend an evening, no." Murrall's own smile was tight, but a bit more genuine.

"Well, what if I have my agents come in here and pick this place apart piece by piece? Would that be an enjoyable time for you?"

"Agent Dilton, I am sorry if Maxim keeps giving you the slip, but there simply isn't any reason to threaten me. By clearing so many of the hunters off the board, I've made your job that much easier."

"Not all of them," Matthias said.

"Oh yes, my sources informed me that Maxim had run afoul of his old adversary, Talon Merthane. Honestly, I'd thought the man had retired after the defeat he suffered last year."

"Why not keep Ultra and collect the reward?" Beattie asked.

Murrall nodded. "Yes, the reward is a not insignificant sum. However, I believe Maxim when he says he didn't do the Aval thing. In fact, I know he couldn't have done it."

"How's that?" Dilton almost spat the words.

"He and his crew were doing a job for me just prior to his return…ah, home."

"It's all right, Murrall," Matthias said. "We know he returned to Earth."

"He still might have had time to destroy *The Gallant*," Dilton said.

"Impossible, my dear. A job like that takes time and planning—time Maxim did not have," Murrall replied.

"Because he was working for you," Dilton said. It wasn't a question.

"Yes, I believe I mentioned that."

"What was he doing for you?" Matthias asked. He tired of the games. Murrall protected their mutual friend and clearly had no idea where he was headed. He just needed her to say the words to Dilton, so they could move on.

"He was contracted to find a friend of mine."

Dilton stared at Murrall, her expression neutral. "Are you purposely feeding us information one line at a time in the hope that each minute will let Ultra get that much farther away?"

"Ah, not as inept as I'd hoped, Agent." Murrall's wolfish grin belied her sweet old lady appearance.

"Look, Murrall, we know Maxim is investigating Sierra Numani's potential involvement in some robberies at Baron Zeth's companies," Matthias said. "Did you have any insight on that? Do you know where he was headed next?"

"I only know what is officially known. A woman, very much fitting Sierra's description, was involved. Whoever planned these jobs isn't doing it through normal channels. There is a shocking lack of information."

"If the information is that contained, it supports the theory that Numani *is* working with some kind of well-funded rogue actor," Matthias said.

Dilton was incredulous. "What does *any* of that have to do with Ultra? He just released a vecking manifesto to the entire galaxy! Did he record that little love note here in a back room somewhere? Did Jhantra do the camera work?"

Murrall laughed. "If you think that was Maxim Ultra, then you're more in the dark than I'd realized! Maxim isn't interested in revolution."

"And you would know this, how?" Dilton asked.

"Young woman, I have known Maxim Ultra since he was a boy. Whoever is behind this video does not know him. They have a very convincing image, but that was not him."

"So, you have no idea where Ultra was headed next?" Beattie asked, all business.

Murrall shrugged. "It's a mystery to me. I know he was ambushed by Merthane, but managed to escape. Merthane's associate tried to step in, but they eluded her as well."

A light went on in Matthias' head. "*Her?*"

"Yes, Merthane has a sidekick now. Maybe the old man is slowing down and needs the help."

Before Matthias could get in another question, Dilton cut him off. "Well, thanks for nothing, Murrall. I hope the minutes you've bought Ultra serve him well."

"You'd be wise to not underestimate him. He's quite intelligent for an Earthling."

Jhantra escorted them back outside. Matthias looked at Dilton, who clearly wasn't happy. "She gave us some interesting information. We shouldn't have cut off the interview. Max mentioned a female bounty hunter on Earth. Could it be...?"

"Who cares? Our only goal here is to bring Maxim Ultra in—preferably alive. We're responsible for figuring out what the veck happened at *The Gallant. That's it*," Dilton snapped.

Matthias took a deep breath. "But, all of this could be connected."

"It may well be, Glintock, but I'm not here right now to solve a puzzle. Thanks to Talon Merthane and this waste of time, we're nowhere closer to finding our man."

"We should check with the port security and see when Cabal left," Beattie said. "That may give us a clue to where they went."

Matthias stifled his frustration. He felt it was all connected in some way, but Dilton and Beattie clearly weren't interested in pursuing leads that might exonerate Max. His communicator chirped insistently. Producing the device from his jacket, he blanched at the message.

"What is it?" Dilton asked.

"We have to go. It's the *Sequel.*"

CHAPTER 30

The *Sequel* dropped into normal space. The gleaming blue jewel that was the planet Iswat loomed in the viewport. Dozens of ships were scattered throughout Iswat's orbit. There were no warships of any kind. The GAC appeared to be letting this drama play itself out.

"Mercenaries," Robert said with barely disguised contempt.

"It looks like every merc in the galaxy's here," she replied.

"A non-GAC world in a scramble for control of the planet? I wouldn't be surprised if every private army sent a representative here to get in on that flood of cash."

Egar Kowas' recent assassination had thrown the planet into the fires of civil war—their second in almost as many years. This time, there was no clear entity to take power. Kowas' subordinates had tried to take control, but the people wanted free elections. The remnants of the military junta that had controlled the planet for decades were ready to retake power. The former revolutionaries had also split into multiple factions. It was, simply put, a dicey situation.

"Where did our man put down?" Robert asked.

"*We have been unable to determine that,*" Roeger's voice answered over the intercom. Shanta had him stationed at the ship's main computer. "*Iswat's planetary defense grid is down. It will take a few moments to find another source of information.*"

"Do what you can, Roeger," Shanta answered. "I doubt our guy came here, but I just wanted to throw the GAC off our trail for a bit." Her eyes surveyed the various ships. "Keep clear of any media ships. The last thing we need is someone broadcasting our arrival."

"Literally," Robert muttered as he piloted the *Sequel* away from a cruiser emblazoned with the *Zeth Media Systems* logo. "What's the latest?"

"Only what I caught on the news. It's a full-blown, planet-wide civil war. Once Kowas was assassinated, it all went to nakra."

"And the GAC *still* hasn't stepped in?" Robert asked.

Shanta shrugged. "It's not their fight. Iswat isn't a member planet, so they just kind of…throw up their hands."

"That's pretty shitty. These people need help."

"It could also be possible that they're spread too thin. A galactic union sounds great, until you realize just how big the galaxy is." The intercom beeped. "Roeger—you find anything?"

"*I have, yes.*" The control console beeped and its holographic projectors displayed a copy of a video file. The images were grainy, but the visual of a ship zipping by the camera was unmistakable.

"Where is this from?" Shanta asked.

"*A weather satellite,*" Roeger responded.

"Can you figure out where he landed?"

"*I am extrapolating the data now,*" Roeger said.

"Great find, Roeger." Her body buzzed. Was this their guy? She noticed Robert staring at her. "What?"

"What if this doesn't work?"

"Then we check one of the other planets."

"No, I mean, what if we can't clear Max?"

His question hung in the air. She hadn't honestly considered they'd fail. Confronted with it, she had no answer. That scared her more than the question. "We'll figure that out when we get there."

"'Figure it out?' We have to have a contingency plan. Max is my man, don't get me wrong, but no one wants to go on the run *forever*. Aval could throw bounty hunters at us for the rest of our lives." He was spiraling.

An answer solidified in her mind. "If we have to, we go to Murrall or somebody else, get new identities, and stay under the radar."

"I don't know if I can do that," Robert said wistfully. "And please, don't believe I'd *ever* turn Max in or anything like that. Never. I just know that if the deck is stacked against us and there's no way out, he'll turn *himself* in."

"I know. We have to make sure it doesn't come down to that. We're a family, Robbie."

"*That goes for all of us, Robert,*" Roeger's voice came over the intercom. "*I have a path of approach for our quarry.*"

"Throw it up on the display," Shanta said.

Again, the holographic display lit up. Shanta gazed at the model.

"Where did he land?" she asked.

"*In the country of Divtrat. There is not much there,*" Roeger said.

"What is this guy up to?" she whispered to herself.

Robert cut the engines and hit the starboard thrusters, navigating the *Sequel* toward Divtrat. The ship floated away from the traffic jam they'd jumped into and no one appeared to notice their departure.

Shanta smiled ear-to-ear. She patted Robert on the shoulder. "Good work, Robbie."

"Thanks. I'll cut the engines back on once the planet blocks us from prying eyes," he said.

"Sounds good. Christi, let's scan that area as soon as we can."

Christi's console-friendly hologram appeared. *"Of course, Shanta."*

The *Sequel* sailed around the planet, Robbie engaging the thrusters every so often to stay out of Iswat's gravity well. As they approached Divtrat, Christi reappeared. *"I am getting readings from Divtrat. Curious."*

"Did you find our guy?" Shanta asked.

"I cannot find a single individual from up here, but I am reading some unusual heat patterns."

"Unusual how?" Robert asked.

"Unusual in that they should not be there. This particular portion of Divtrat is very sparsely populated."

"What do the readings say?" Shanta asked.

"There is enough heat for a small town."

"Veck *me*," Shanta whispered. She looked at Christi in disbelief. "What is it?"

"There appears to be a single structure at the base of Grijba—one of Iswat's largest mountains."

"Whatever it is, it seems to be a larger concern than random mercenary groups," Roeger added.

"Refugees, maybe?" Robert asked.

"*Unlikely,*" Christi replied. "*The bulk of the fighting is on the main continent around the capital. This location is rather remote for refugees.*"

"But, our guy could be down there?" Shanta asked.

"*Anything is possible,*" Roeger replied.

"I'm really curious about what this is," Shanta said.

"I'm not," Robert replied. "It's none of our business. A big building pops up in the middle of nowhere? None of this is adding up to anything good. This is a GAC problem."

"*But, the GAC does not operate on Iswat,*" Christi said.

"So, it's up to us to investigate? Who's paying us for that? Because, I thought this ship was a business venture," Robert responded.

Shanta paused. Robert had a valid point. Why *was* it up to them? In the end, though, there was only one answer. "We go down there. We owe it to Max to see if our guy is down there." She held her tongue another moment. "And as far as the other thing, it's the right thing to do."

Robert groaned. "People who do the right thing usually end up dead."

"*Thank you for the confidence, Robert,*" Roeger said.

Within an hour, the *Sequel* roared into Iswat's atmosphere. Robert entered a fair distance away from the structure in question.

"What have we got, Christi?" Shanta asked as the *Sequel* passed through the clouds.

"*It's definitely a single structure. There are a* lot *of people outside. I'm reading industrial equipment,*" Christi said.

"Put me on the record as saying that this is a bad fucking idea," Robert said.

Shanta smiled grimly as her stomach lurched with the *Sequel*'s descent. She gripped her armrests.

The ship was low enough that she could see everything that Christi had described. The structure was a wide building roughly two hundred meters across. Industrial equipment littered the area, but more telling was the presence of fabrication bots, which were able to build a structure in a matter of days. Her eyes widened when she saw something Christi *hadn't* mentioned—a large laser turret atop the structure.

"*Nakra!* Bank, Robbie! Bank!" she yelled.

Robert jerked the controls and the *Sequel* peeled away. As the ship passed by the metal fortress, the double-barreled cannon fired successive laser blasts at the *Sequel*. The bolts missed, thanks to Robert's skillful piloting. As the ship tilted to port, Shanta saw that the people on the ground were black-uniformed military types. Her mind raced to what Max had told her about the Memta case and the men who had stormed the *Galactic Dream*.

"Christi! Send a distress beacon out to Glintock! Now!" she screamed.

"*Sending now, Shanta,*" Christi replied with cool efficiency.

"I've got this!" Robert yelled.

"I know, but look what's down there!"

Robert chanced a look at the ground and his eyes bulged. "Fuck."

"We need to regroup. Get us out of here!"

Before Robert could hit the throttle, a bright blue flash of energy rocked the ship. Alarms screamed in the cockpit and the gentle glow of the control console switched to a harsh red light.

"*That was Memta energy.*" Christi's statement sliced through the cacophony.

Shanta clicked the intercom. "Gerry! How bad is it?"

"*It is not a difficult fix, but it cannot be done while we are in the air,*" Gerry responded from the engine room.

Robert glanced at Shanta. "She knew exactly where to hit us."

She swallowed hard. "Get us as far away as you can."

"I'll do my best." Robert managed to land the *Sequel* a few kilometers away from the fortress.

"*Sensors detect a large force headed this way,*" Christi said.

The four crewmembers gathered in the common area. They were armed and ready for a fight.

"Christi, is the repair something you can handle on your own?" Shanta asked.

Christi's voice filled the room. "*I am afraid not, Shanta. I will need at least one pair of hands to aid me.*"

"I can make the most difference here," Gerry said. "I will remain to repair the ship."

"Thank you, Gerry." His selfless act put a lump in Shanta's throat. "We'll do our best to lead them away from here. Now, let's do this. For Max."

Robert sighed. "Yeah, for Max, but let's just hope we don't get killed in the process."

Shanta, Robert, and Roeger exited the ship. The area was desolate but for the mountain behind them. The unmistakable *whine* of approaching vehicles was heard on the wind.

"Not many places to hide," Roeger stated.

"That's an understatement," Robert said. "Up the mountain?"

Shanta looked around. "It's our only chance." The three of them scrambled up the nearest path. Shanta looked to the horizon. A dust cloud moved closer. "If we get to a good vantage point, we can keep them off the ship."

Roeger followed her gaze. His eyes whirred. "There are quite a lot of them."

"We can't just surrender," Shanta said. "Not to her."

"Would we be better positioned on the *Sequel?*" Roeger asked.

"Let's spare any unnecessary damage to the ship. We have to distract them—give Gerry and Christi the time they need so we can get the *veck* out of here," Shanta replied. It wasn't a great plan, but they were dead in the water until repairs were made.

The trio climbed to an outcropping that gave them an excellent view. Crawling to the edge on their bellies, they observed ten hover vehicles pull into the area. At the back of the group of black uniforms, an unmasked woman stood atop the rear of the vehicle.

Roeger turned his head to Shanta. "It is Sierra."

"I figured, but thanks for the confirmation." She glanced at Roeger's sniper rifle. The bot would be able to incapacitate their opponents, but his strict moral code would ensure that none would be killed. For the *Sequel* to make an escape, their foes would have to perish—especially Sierra. "Switch guns with me."

"I am far more accurate than you, Shanta."

"Yeah, but that horvorka's got to die, Roeger. Switch with me, please." Roeger held onto his weapon another moment before reluctantly passing it to Shanta. "Thank you." She lined Sierra up in her scope. Though she'd never met Sierra, Shanta saw that the woman appeared haggard. The blue glow that the others had described was very dim.

"*You can come out,*" Sierra said, her voice artificially amplified. "*Your ship's disabled and there are far too many of us to shoot through.*"

"I only have to hit you, witch," Shanta whispered as she took a shot at Sierra's head.

The laser bolt sailed through the air, as if in slow motion. The hazy blue glow around Sierra flared, absorbing the bolt before it could make contact with her. Sierra pointed at the outcropping with a gleeful smile. *"Take them."*

Shanta tensed for a fight, but six soldiers in jetpacks launched out of the hover vehicles. They shot nets out of the wide-barreled rifles they carried. Shanta raised her rifle, but was caught in a net made of a sticky substance. Robert and Roeger found themselves in the same trap.

Sierra had gotten closer and wore a smug smile. "Bag 'em up. Let's find out what they know."

CHAPTER 31

Max paced in the guest quarters of the *Heartbreaker*. His heart raced. Someone, some*thing* that looked and sounded *exactly like him* had taken responsibility for Aval and threatened the *entire galaxy*. He felt hot. Was that a heart attack symptom?

There was a knock at the door. Before Max could answer, Gina entered and closed the door behind her. She immediately embraced him and Max held her tight. She felt like a life preserver.

"Are you okay?" she asked.

"No, I'm not. Somebody's out there impersonating me and it's so authentic, even *I* believe it." He resumed pacing. "What the fuck am I going to do?"

Gina placed her hands on either side of his head, keeping his focus on her. "Max, it wasn't you. The truth is on our side. We can beat this!"

He knew she was only trying to calm him down, but he couldn't buy into her point of view. "Gina, I love you, but how many times has the 'side of truth' worked out for the FBI?"

Her expression said his remark had put her out. "Fair."

"I'm sorry. I know you're trying to help, but truth is not a prominent power out here."

"But, it's at least a starting point. I believe Shanta and the others will find this guy. I know it."

"And if they don't? Merthane's assassin proved that I can't go back to Earth. I mean, this guy is a terrorist declaring war on the *galaxy*. And, he's *me*."

"We'll figure it out, Max. It's a deadly serious situation—I get that—but, we'll make a plan and work it out together."

"No! You need to get far away from me!" He wouldn't be able to live if harm befell Gina.

"What…what are you saying? You want me to leave?"

"No, all of you! Dump me on a planet and put as much distance between us as possible!"

Despite his instructions, she embraced him again. "I'm not going anywhere. Neither is Alesha, nor is Litning. You're stuck with us."

Her sentiment touched him, but fear consumed him. He couldn't lose his friends again—his family. But, if he pushed them away, wasn't he just losing them another way? Indecision wracked his mind.

Another knock sounded at that door. After a moment, Alesha stepped inside. "Hope you're not fucking in here." Her eyes went to Gina. "Has he stopped freaking out yet?"

Gina glanced at Max. "We're getting there."

"I can't believe how flip you're both being about this! If we don't find this guy, I'll literally be on the run for the rest of my life. Everyone I love will be at risk in attempts to draw me out." He felt a bout of hyperventilation coming on.

"Max, how is that any different from how we usually live?" Alesha asked. "I mean, sure, we have the house on Modan, but how often are we there? I don't know if you've noticed this or not, but our work has won us a lot of enemies. So, there's *always* the threat of someone coming along to ruin our day. As for us being in danger because of you, I can only speak for myself, but that comes along with the territory. We're family. We're going to protect you to the last man, woman, Glutob, robot, and Revash."

While Gina's attempts to reassure him were appreciated, Alesha's words cut through his panic to touch his heart. When was he ever living the quiet life in space? *Never.*

"Are we good?" Alesha asked with that crooked smile he loved.

He nodded. "Thanks. Both of you. Sometimes I forget what I have and only focus on what I can lose. It means a lot to know I have so much love in my corner."

The intercom whined. "*Apologies for interrupting,*" Litning said. "*Alesha, there is a call for you. It is Agent Glintock.*"

Alesha was surprised. "*That's* ominous. We're supposed to be on radio silence. Patch it through to here, Litning." The intercom clicked over. "Why, Agent Glintock, this is unexpected," she said in a coy singsong voice.

"*We don't have time for that nakra. You people need to get to Iswat now.*"

"Why? What's wrong?" Max asked.

"*It's the* Sequel. *They're in trouble.*"

CHAPTER 32

The *Claw*. Deep space.

Talon and Alexis sat in the cockpit, monitoring the *Heartbreaker*'s position. He was bandaged up after his encounter with Maxim in Marina, as was Alexis. She'd succeeded in planting the tracker on Alesha's ship, but Talon remained irritated that they hadn't been able to corral Maxim. The tracker was the backup plan. Now, it was the only plan.

If every bounty hunter in the galaxy hadn't been on Maxim's tail before his "manifesto," they certainly were after the fact. Talon didn't put much weight in the damning video. It wasn't him. Whoever it was certainly *looked* like Maxim, but it wasn't him. Maxim wasn't a political creature. Talon believed he knew him well enough to say that. The goal remained the same. They would simply have more unwanted competition than before.

They stayed out of the *Heartbreaker*'s sensor range. Talon had the *Claw* outfitted with the highest end sensor package. The scanner trilled and some text scrolled onto Talon's console. He sat up and squinted at the screen. "That's strange...."

"What is?" Alexis asked.

Talon double checked the text again. "Their vector and that Cardon Lane will take them to Iswat." He couldn't help but give her a brief glare. Alexis' assassination job on Iswat was still a sore point for him. Yes, he'd taken assassination jobs in his time, but Alexis destabilized a planet and still had no idea who'd hired her. It was unprofessional.

"Why would they go there?" she asked.

He had no idea. All that was on Iswat was civil war. Did they think they could hide Maxim there amidst the chaos? From what he understood, the planet had become a hotbed of mercenary activity, but not bounty hunters so much.

"Talon?"

He snapped out of his thoughts and his hands moved over his console. The *Claw* responded to his commands. "We're going to find out."

CHAPTER 33

Shanta's eyes opened slowly. She was in a room with glaring lights and no furnishings whatsoever. It was essentially a bare metal box. Two black-outfitted guards with laser rifles stood at the lone door. Her crewmates were assembled around her. Like her, they were chained to the floor at their wrists and ankles. Her heart sank when she saw that Sierra's people had captured Gerry as well.

It appeared that Gerry had bulked up for his fight with Sierra's troops, as he was still quite large. A thrill went through Shanta. She didn't know how much Sierra knew about Gerry's capabilities, but the *Sequel* crew had a potential upper hand.

The door to the room snapped open and Sierra stalked inside, surveying the crew like a predator assessing its prey. "Where's your fearless leader?"

"Clearly not here," Shanta replied.

"Not so fearless after all, I guess. So, if Max isn't with you, why are you here?"

"I don't know where he is. We're here on other business. Running into you is a total coincidence," Shanta said.

"I'm sure it is. I'd love to believe you, but I've been hearing rumblings that Max and Alesha are looking for me. So, that tells me you're not being totally honest and really, we can't get anywhere in this galaxy without total honesty."

"Excuse me, glowing, crazy lady," Robert said. "Last year, you were running from these guys," he said with a nod to the troops guarding the door. "Now they're working for you?"

Sierra chuckled. She had that mischievous smile Shanta had seen in the holos Max had. She was quite beautiful—for a psychopath. "How about you, Glutob? Do you want to talk?"

"He doesn't speak common," Shanta blurted.

"How the veck do you communicate with him?"

"That's usually handled by Christi, but she's back on the ship," Shanta said.

"I *know* who Christi is, thank you." Sierra looked agitated. She turned to Roeger, who appeared shut down. "And Roeger? Are you still holding a grudge about what Gelf and I did to you last time? I can make it worse. I promise." Her hand lit up with turquoise energy.

Roeger didn't stir.

"Not talking, hm? There's a fix for that too," Sierra said as her hand stretched toward Roeger's chest plate.

"I see you've still got some of that Memta shine," Shanta said quickly. The last thing she wanted was Sierra torturing her robot friend.

Sierra's attention flicked back to her. "What do you know about Memta?"

Inside, Shanta heaved a relieved sigh. "I know enough. I know that Max drained that witch out of you. I guess he didn't finish the job."

Sierra flew at her, stopping centimeters from her face. "Would you like to become more intimately familiar with the 'witch?'" Her eyes gleamed with blue light. There was something else behind her eyes, though. After dealing with a lot of less than stellar con men in her life, Shanta knew the look. It was fear—the fear that came when the person selling the story didn't completely believe in it.

"I don't think that's necessary," Shanta said calmly.

Sierra's fingertips crackled with blue energy. "Why are you here?"

"I told you, we were here on other business."

Sierra's smile took on a sinister edge. "Well then, I guess we're at an impasse."

Shanta's eyes narrowed. "We are?" She couldn't believe that Sierra would quit that easily.

"Yes. You see, you refuse to answer my questions, but I and my associates need them answered. I don't have to tell you that it's not exactly common knowledge that we're here."

Shanta shrugged. "That doesn't have to change. We can go about our business and forg—"

"*NO*. No, you would never 'forget I was here.' You'd find the nearest GAC outpost or run back to Max, and we'd have a veritable mess on our hands. So, I as I said, I need answers. You're failing to provide them. So, I think you need a little *motivation*."

Sierra's threatening posture sent a shiver through Shanta, but she kept a brave face. "You can torture me, but I won't tell you anything."

"Oh, I don't doubt that. But, I have a feeling that if I start hurting your friends, you'll open up." Sierra stood between Roeger and Gerry. "There's no point in using Roeger, since you can clearly repair him." She looked at Gerry with a strange curiosity. "I...don't even know if I could hurt you and I'm afraid I don't have the time to find out." Her eyes shifted back to Shanta. "So, that, only, leaves..." she took a step back with each word.

"Wait!" Shanta cried.

Sierra's hand latched onto Robert's shoulder and blue energy coursed down her arm. Robert *screamed*. Shanta closed her eyes and gritted her teeth. He sounded like he was being burned alive.

Sierra stopped for a moment. Robert's heaving, gasping breaths forced Shanta's eyes open. They were wet with tears. Roeger had stopped pretending to be shut down. His wide, yellow eyes bored into Shanta. His fear was palpable. The guards at the door looked visibly shaken, even with their faces obscured by masks.

"So, any answers for me? Or shall we have another go?"

Robert took a shuddering breath. "Don't...tell this...bitch *shit!*"

Sierra's eyebrows rose. "Well, I guess I have my answer."

Roeger looked from Shanta to Sierra and back again. "Shanta?"

Before she could open her mouth to answer, Robert cut her off. "Keep it shut, Roeger!"

"Oh, are you sure, Roeger?" Sierra taunted. "You can help him."

She was going to kill Robbie. They couldn't hold out for Glintock. If they told Sierra they suspected she was hiding the bomber—maybe, somehow, she *was* the bomber—she'd kill all of them. Shanta's mind whirled with potential "reveals" that might stay Sierra's hand.

"Max! We're here looking for Max!" she cried.

Sierra paused and turned to her with a dubious expression. "Why would you be looking for Max?"

"Have you seen what the reward is up to? I could retire to some beach and never have to think about people like you ever again."

Sierra laughed. "I can maybe see *you* turning on Max. He's known you for, what, a year? But Robbie? *Roeger?* I don't believe it."

Robbie was the first to fall into line. "I had a good thing going on the *Galactic Dream*, until Max showed up and fucked it all up for me."

"No, that just proves you're angry with me and my friends here," Sierra said. "You're not making your case."

"Max made things worse for me there. People saw us together and then saw him shooting up the place. Believe me, if he hadn't been there, I could have talked my way out of losing my job." Robbie was so convincing, *Shanta* almost believed him.

Sierra's eyes narrowed. "All right, you might sell him out, but not sweet, sweet Roe—"

"Maxim does not let me do anything," Roeger was so quick, Shanta believed he and Max might need to clear the air.

"What does that mean?" Sierra asked.

"I am an emote. I have dreams and goals, but Maxim keeps me on the ship like a mascot. I want my own life."

Shanta's heart broke for Roeger. He *couldn't* lie.

The bot's words gave Sierra pause. She was about to open her mouth when she touched her ear. "Wait. Ship approaching Iswat. It's the *Heartbreaker*."

Shanta hid the joy that surged through her. Glintock had gotten their message after all.

"Scramble the fighters. Activate defensive measures," Sierra said to her unseen minions. She smirked at Shanta. "Looks like you might collect that bounty after all."

CHAPTER 34

The *Heartbreaker* emerged from the Cardon Lane; Iswat was dead ahead.

"What are all those ships over there?" Alesha asked from the captain's chair.

Max sat in the pilot's seat, looking at the readout from the sensors. "A lot of mercenary outfits and media. Half are here to join in the civil war, while the other half is here to cover it."

"The *Sequel*'s distress call came from the other side of the planet," Litning said from the co-pilot's seat.

"Well then, let's get over there," Alesha said. "And maybe steer clear of those media ships. The last thing we need is someone seeing the galaxy's most wanted fugitive."

Soft steps sounded on the stairs. Gina wrapped her arms around Max's neck. "Hey, Sweetie," he said, turning back to his console.

"Wow," she said, gazing out the viewport. "It's beautiful."

"Yes, it is."

Iswat *was* a gorgeous planet. A prismatic dust, the result of multiple asteroid collisions—strays from a nearby belt—created a heavenly glow around the Earth-like planet. The picturesque scene was marred by a dark cloud emerging from the planet portside.

Max redirected the sensors to get a read on the cloud. A sting of panic shot through him. "We've got a squadron of fighters— just came into view."

"They are vectoring toward us," Litning said. "We cannot hope to fight them all."

"Gina, you may want to strap in, honey," Alesha said. "Ideas?"

"I've got a few," Max replied as Gina buckled herself into a free seat.

"Great. Let's do it," Alesha said. After a moment, she added, "Don't veck up my ship."

"I'll do my best." Max looked over the controls. He didn't know the little nuances and intricacies of the *Heartbreaker*. Double-checking the system, he made sure to pull up his personal preferences.

"Seriously, don't fucking wreck it."

"I *have* done this before." Max tapped the controls and the *Heartbreaker* shuddered to a stop. The fighters were close enough that he could individually pick them out. "All right, what the fuck did I do?"

Alesha frantically punched a code into the pad on her armrest. "She's just a little temperamental. Give me a second."

"Those ships are getting closer," Gina said.

"I *said* give me a second!" Alesha snapped. More tapping. Finally, the engines surged back to life. "See? All yours, Max."

Alarms blared as the fighters came within firing range. They were small, one-man vessels, agile and very deadly. Max prodded at the controls calmly, while Gina looked on warily.

"Are we going to go?" she asked.

Max glanced at the fighters. "Just a second…."

"They're practically on top of us!"

"Just a second…."

"They're powering up their weapons." Litning said with urgency.

"Annnnd…*now!*" Max threw the *Heartbreaker* into a dive, pinning everyone in their seats. The mobile fighters flew by, but regrouped to give chase.

"Maybe a little warning next time, Max," Alesha forced through gritted teeth.

"I have to use every trick I can. Sorry."

"Well, they are back on us," Litning said. "And gaining."

"Thanks for stating the obvious. You know, you really are a fantastic co-pilot," Max replied. "Just keep your eyes on the shields. This is going to get sticky."

With a flick of his wrist, the *Heartbreaker* cut to starboard. A glance at the sensor display showed that the fighters remained in tight pursuit. The ship shuddered as they opened fire.

"Are we going to *do* something about that?" Alesha asked, an edge in her voice.

"Do you have any charges on board?" Max asked.

She didn't answer. Instead, she punched some keys on her armrest. An alarm sounded as a star charge—a barrel-sized defensive weapon—launched out of the rear of the ship. As it exploded, it created a dazzling shower of sparks and light that resembled a cloud of stars. The fighters scattered in its wake.

"That should hold them for a sec," Max muttered as he set the ship on an ascension course.

Alesha sat bolt upright in her chair. "What are you doing?"

"Flying the ship."

"Straight into that flotilla! The goal here isn't to smash my ship!"

"I'm *not* going to smash the ship! Have a little faith!" A massive media vessel loomed ahead of them.

The fighters had regrouped. Max guided the *Heartbreaker* under the media ship, but then cut to starboard, streaking between the big vessel and a smaller merc ship. Out of the corner of his eye, Litning winced as Max pushed the throttle higher.

The *Heartbreaker* weaved over and around the orbiting ships. The fighters split up, the spacing too narrow for them to pursue in formation, but a few stayed with the *Heartbreaker*.

"The other ships are interfering with our sensors," Litning warned. "I cannot see the other fighters."

"It's okay. That should mean they can't see us either."

"Oh my god, watch out!" Gina screamed.

Another mercenary ship drifted into the *Heartbreaker*'s path. Max barely cleared the obstacle. One of the fighters behind them wasn't so lucky, smashing against the merc's shields. The other two fighters dove under the merc ship.

"You're going to get us killed, Max!" Alesha yelled, her hands clutching her armrests.

He knew his tactics were dangerous, but it was the only way to even the odds. Survival was his only goal. His crew, both on the *Heartbreaker* and down on the planet, was counting on him. "Anything on scanners?"

"Nothing," Litning replied.

"Shit."

"Wait. One of the mercenary ships is powering up its weapons," Litning reported.

"They're going to shoot at us?" Gina blurted.

"No," Max replied with a grin. "No, they're not." Within moments, a fighter streaked into view and the merc ship blasted it into oblivion.

"Why aren't they shooting at us?" Gina asked.

"Because, we look like fellow mercs and the fighters are the aggressors," Alesha answered.

The glut of ships began to break up and fire on the fighters, who forgot about the *Heartbreaker* as they flew for their lives. The only ships that didn't participate in the shooting were the media vessels. They elected to withdraw from the scrum.

The biggest ship, a *Zeth Media Systems* transport, pulled away as fast as the lumbering vessel could go. Max directed the *Heartbreaker* toward that ship.

"Where are you going?" Alesha asked. "Let's get to the distress call."

"In a minute. Notice who's *not* here right now?" Max replied.

Alesha scanned her instruments. "I don't see any GAC signals."

"Exactly. These fighters aren't Iswat pilots. I have a feeling we're going to need some GAC muscle to resolve this."

"But, the GAC has no authority here," Litning said.

"They will if the mass murderer of Aval is here," Max said as he piloted the ship close to a large viewport on the media vessel. He hit a switch, turning on the cockpit lights, making them very visible to anyone out in the darkness of space.

"Gods, Max. What are you doing?" Alesha asked.

"Duck down if you want," Max said. He waved big and grinned. Litning and Alesha hid.

"You all look ridiculous," Gina muttered as she covered her face with her hand.

"Just making it as obvious as possible," Max said. He clicked the communicator. "Greetings and salutations, *Zeth Media Systems*. Maxim Ultra here. Welcome to Iswat."

"Hey, boss! We're on the holo news!" Grathell called from down below.

"Max, I hope you know what you're doing," Alesha said from her crouched position on the deck.

"Whatever's going on down on the planet, I have a hunch we're going to need as much confusion as possible up here to get our people out," Max said as he guided the ship over the media vessel and streaked toward the planet. *Hang on, guys. We're on our way.*

CHAPTER 35

"So, he's ignoring you?" Dilton asked as she and Matthias stalked the streets of Apex on Modan. They headed for GAC Headquarters—a towering, obsidian spike in the pristine landscape of High City. The building extended all the way to Low City and beyond.

"It seems so," Matthias replied, jaw clenching. "Max and his people need help, but we'll leave that part out when we confront this piece of nakra."

Dilton stayed quiet. Matthias made note of it.

They marched through the main entrance. The interior of the tower wasn't as intimidating as the exterior. Armed officers ran security, but they exuded an affable manner. Matthias and Dilton passed through the security checkpoint and made their way to the lift bank. Within moments, a lift arrived, and they boarded.

Once alone, Dilton turned to him. "What's your plan when we get up there?"

"Well, if I was certain you wouldn't report me, I would say, beat him so there are no marks. But, since I can't be sure of that, I'll try to convince him to help us."

"You really don't trust me, do you?" she asked.

"Should I? I'm sure you don't answer to Brontin, but beyond that, I have no idea. You have a GAC-issued android duplicate walking around with you with no real explanation why. Why *should* I trust you, Dilton?"

She stared at him with hurt in her eyes—or was it conflict?

The lift stopped and the doors opened. Matthias strode onto the executive floor, heading to Brontin's office with purpose. Those GAC employees that he encountered scurried out of his way. Dilton followed behind him at a measured pace. He'd grown fond of her, but her secretive nature prevented him from fully embracing her. Who was she really? Would she have his back when needed? He was about to find out.

Matthias burst into the anteroom that led to Brontin's office. The assistant at the desk outside the door leaped to her feet and tried to impede his progress, but he stepped around her.

"Agent Glintock! Agent Glintock, you cannot go in there!" the assistant cried. She held out her arms to block him.

Standing a full head taller than the assistant, he glowered at her. She balked, but held her ground. Dilton put her hand on Matthias' shoulder, getting between him and the assistant. "Stop scaring her, Glintock." Her touch made him dizzy. She turned to the assistant. "Step aside, dear. Agent Glintock is far too much of a gentleman to rough you up, but I'm not. And I'd hate to ruin that lovely tunic you have on."

The assistant shrank back into her chair. Once she was out of the way, Matthias hit the door release to Brontin's office. It opened into a spacious room decorated in reds. Brontin sat behind a large black desk, incredulity etched on his face. "What the veck are you doing, Glintock?" His one arm rested at his side, hidden by the desk, potentially reaching for a weapon.

"You've been ignoring my communications, *Captain*, so I thought we'd pay you a personal visit," Matthias said. The rage inside him made it almost impossible to get the words out.

"I've been ignoring your communications, because they're absolute nonsense! Now, get the veck out of my office!" Despite the venom, Brontin remained seated.

"There's a situation on Iswat and we have to respond!" Glintock said.

"Iswat is not part of the GAC. It's not our problem, Glintock."

"What about Maxim Ultra?" Dilton asked.

"What about him? He's clearly eluded you two. *Vecking* useless," Brontin muttered the last part under his breath.

Out of the corner of Matthias' eye, Dilton's body stiffened. "Then apparently, you aren't aware of the reports coming out of Iswat," he said.

Brontin looked perplexed. His hand resting on the desk moved toward a small console built into the desktop. He clicked a button and a wall panel opened to reveal a hologenerator. His other hand remained behind the desk.

The hologenerator switched on. A multi-colored beam of light shot out and depicted a female newsreader with a tall, blonde hairdo. "*…a remarkable turn of events over Iswat today as a civil war continues to rage on the planet's surface. A ship arrived in the area, pursued by star fighters of an unknown origin. The star fighters were destroyed or otherwise chased off, but the real story is that the fugitive Maxim Ultra appeared to be aboard the ship that started all the commotion.*"

Brontin's brow furrowed. He looked at Matthias. "What are you playing at?"

"We have to send a strike team to Iswat," Matthias answered.

"To capture one man? You *are* slipping, Glintock," Brontin said with a harsh laugh.

"No. To deal with whoever is controlling those fighters."

"I told you, Iswat is none of our business."

"We have reason to believe that the individuals behind those fighters are the same that attacked the *Galactic Dream* last year," Matthias said.

"Well, unless you've been completely disregarding the case I assigned you, there's no way you could have any evidence of that," Brontin said. His face darkened. "Or, maybe your information came from Maxim Ultra and you're not disregarding the case, but undermining it." He clicked another switch on his desk console. A loud buzz sounded and two GAC officers in tactical gear burst into the room, their laser pistols trained on Matthias and Dilton.

"Brontin, what the veck is this?!" Dilton cried.

"I would think it's obvious, Dilton. You're clearly conspiring with wanted fugitives and that makes you a security risk. Officers, take them."

Matthias tensed as the officers stepped toward them. He hadn't imagined it would go this way, but was ready to fight if Brontin forced it.

"Stop," Dilton said.

"Hah! I don't think so, Dilton. Take them!" Brontin yelled. He pulled his hand from behind the desk and stopped pretending like he didn't have a pistol.

"No, seriously, stop," Dilton said.

"These men are loyal to me. Period. There won't be any smooth-talking your way out of this. Honestly, I'm surprised at you, Dilton. I can't believe you threw in with Glintock. I thought you were a career woman." He stood up. "I'm just completely in the dark as to why you would join up with an agent that's been a constant thorn in my side."

"So, what are you going to do, Brontin? Throw us in holding cells?" Matthias asked, his mind racing.

"Oh, you misunderstood me, Glintock. I discovered you were collaborating with the most wanted man in the galaxy and I called these officers in to help apprehend you. However, you attacked me and we had to put you down. Sadly, Dilton here was cut down in the crossfire." Bontin's chilling preciseness sent a shiver through Matthias.

"*That's* your plan?" Dilton balked. "*Kill* two GAC agents in your office and attempt a cover up?"

"Well, I did tell you that these men are loyal to me," Brontin replied with a sinister smile.

The three of them took aim. Matthias' body tensed. Before he could strike, the door to Brontin's office exploded and knocked the officer closest to Dilton to the floor. Through the smoke and debris, Beattie entered the office. "I apologize for my tardiness. I was parking the hover car." Matthias had never been so happy to see a bot in his life.

Brontin appeared paralyzed with indecision. Dilton made it easier for him. She produced a small button-operated device from her pocket. "This, Glintock, is why I have Beattie. With a click of this button, I not only called her, but she recorded everything you said, Brontin. You're going to prison."

Brontin started stammering before aiming his pistol at Matthias, who had no time to get out of the way. The laser bolt erupted from Brontin's weapon, but deflected off Beattie's outstretched hand. Her other hand gripped the lone standing officer's neck, immobilizing him. Dilton swiped Brontin's pistol away, smacking him in the face once she wrenched it from him. The captain collapsed, staring into space.

Matthias was lost. "What the veck just happened?"

Beattie finished subduing Brontin's officers and moved over to their boss. Dilton kept him covered with his own weapon. "I'm afraid I haven't been totally honest with you, Matthias," Dilton said.

"Oh, *no?*"

She made a face. "No need to have an attitude about it. The higher ups paired me with you. They didn't fully trust Brontin here—with good reason—and they wanted to see if there was any validity to your reports about the independent army."

He hadn't been expecting *that*. "And what was your conclusion prior to Brontin threatening our lives?"

"That you're on target. Beattie filed my report before we came up. This little drama just sealed Brontin's fate."

Matthias couldn't help but feel slightly betrayed. They'd been working so closely together, but he hadn't an inkling of Dilton's true allegiance. All the bigwigs had to do was call him up. He could have told them Brontin was slime. "So…now what? Oh, and thank you for the save, Beattie." In the wake of Dilton's reveal, he'd forgotten that he'd cheated death.

"Think nothing of it, Agent Glintock," she replied. "You proved yourself worthy of the effort."

Dilton smiled. "Aw, look at the two of you getting along."

"That generally happens when someone saves your life," Matthias said. "You didn't answer my question."

"What's next?" she asked. "Well, I suppose after they take out the trash here, they'll probably give you Brontin's job."

Matthias couldn't suppress the thrill that surged through him. "What about Iswat?"

Dilton shrugged as other GAC officers entered the office to haul Brontin away. The man looked positively catatonic.

"I figure that if the job's about to be yours," Dilton said. "You can make the order yourself."

A smile teased the corners of Matthias' lips.

"Go ahead and smile, Glintock. Things are starting to go your way," Dilton said.

"I'm generally cautious by nature."

She put her hand on his shoulder. He thought he might melt at her touch. "We can talk all about it on the way to Iswat."

CHAPTER 36

"How do we want to do this?" Max asked as the *Heartbreaker* broke into Iswat's atmosphere.

"We have a signal from the *Sequel*, but it looks like it's been moved to this structure here," Alesha said as she pointed at the holo-map.

Litning squinted. "What is all the red on the map?"

"It's people," Gina said.

"Yes. Thermal imaging. Whatever Sierra's got going on down there, there are a lot of people with her," Alesha said.

Max looked at the map. There were dozens of red dots all around the facility. "We can bet that's where the gang is. But, we're never going to get through the front door."

"We'll have to sneak in," Alesha said.

He studied the map. "We'll come in low and wide, park the ship about three klicks away, and come in on foot. That should keep us off their sensors."

"How will we get into the base?" Gina asked.

He shrugged slightly. "Without a schematic, I have no idea. We'll just have to take a look." He gazed at the map a little longer. "There's a small rock formation behind the facility, but close enough that we can camp out there and observe."

"Not very smart placement," Alesha said.

"Well, who said Sierra was a brilliant military tactician?" Max asked.

"*If* she is the one in charge," Litning said.

"That's true," Max conceded. "With a force this big, there's *got* to be someone else behind this. Maybe the people who tried to buy Memta from her? But, we're here for one reason—getting our friends out of there. If Sierra's behind my little problem and we can resolve that too, great. I don't want to be here any longer than we have to. After my little stunt up in orbit, the GAC has *got* to be on its way and there's no guarantee they're going to play nice with us."

"Hopefully, they'll be enough to keep these other people busy—whoever they are," Alesha said.

"All right, let's get down there," Max said as he took the controls again.

Within an hour, Max had the *Heartbreaker* planet side. After gathering weapons and supplies, Max, Alesha, Gina, Litning, and Jethan set out. Alesha's remaining crew stayed with the ship. Max parked in a clear area. It wasn't ideal, but they didn't have much choice. Time wasn't on their side.

As they walked to the facility, the terrain became rockier. A path revealed itself, trending downward. The group followed it. As they descended, the path became a small canyon. Litning and Jethan were so wide, Max wasn't sure they'd be able to fit down the narrow corridor. Litning struggled, turning his body sideways as he hiked behind Max.

Max glanced behind him, but had to do a double-take—Litning was practically on top of him. "You wanna give me a little breathing room here, Fuzzy?"

"I need to talk to you," the Revash said through clenched teeth.

Max barely made out what he'd said. "Okay, talk."

If possible, Litning leaned in even *closer*. "It is a private matter."

"Clearly. You're practically humping my leg. What's up?"

Litning looked behind him, nearly stepping on Max's foot. "Jethan stinks of fear." Max could barely hear him.

"Well, anyone would be afraid out here. Hell, *I'm* afraid."

"No. I observed him on the ship. He is jittery, nervous. It started when it was decided we would be coming to Iswat. Since then, I have not been able to ignore the signs that he is agitated."

Litning hadn't liked Jethan since they'd met, but the fact that he'd take time out of their mission to address it made Max think it was more than simple suspicion. "Keep an eye on him. If he bolts, he may lead us to treasure."

"Or a quick death," Litning deadpanned as he gave Max some more room to walk.

After another quarter hour, the ground leveled out and Max slowed his approach to the canyon's exit. The rear of the facility loomed large—about a football field away—but what drew Max's immediate attention was the pair of black-clad troops patrolling the area.

"I can take the two of them out easily," Litning growled.

"Or, we could just let them pass and keep it quiet," Max muttered back.

"You never let me have any fun," Litning grumbled.

The troops completed a circuit and headed back to the facility. Through his scope, Max saw the facility's rear hangar was open. The *Sequel* was inside.

"Fucking stole my ship…" Max mumbled.

Dozens of troops in black fatigues milled about the hangar entrance, but based on the scans from the *Heartbreaker*, there were far more out front. The land separating them from the facility was marked by several metal wedges that looked wide enough to protect two or three people. They were designed to prevent vehicles from approaching the facility, but their size suggested they were also meant to protect infantry from potential bombardment from the air or space. *The blast-proof panels Sierra stole. How are we gonna get inside?*

Gina swiped the scope away from Max. "Hey! What're you—"

"Of the people on this little excursion, who has successfully breached several drug dens?" She held for an answer. "Oh, just me? Then pipe down and let me work."

Alesha smiled slyly. "Gods, I love this woman more and more."

Max threw Alesha an annoyed look.

Gina continued looking through the scope. "Those guards aren't just loitering around on a smoke break. We'll need a distraction."

Max's eyes locked on the *Sequel*. "I've got just the thing."

"Once we have that, we can move up the field, using those barriers as cover until we're on top of those guards."

He beamed at her. "Good plan."

"What about our distraction?"

"Well, I really don't want to put the *Heartbreaker* in harm's way…."

"Thank you," Alesha chimed in.

"So, I've got something else in mind." Looking down at his wrist unit, he saw they were close enough to make contact. He tapped out his access code, hoping for success.

"*Yes, Maxim?*" Christi's voice came like a tidal wave of relief.

"Christi! It's great to hear your voice."

"*You as well, Maxim. Where are you?*"

Not knowing who might be listening in on their conversation, Max was wary to reveal their position. "Always in your heart, sweetie."

"*What can I do for you?*"

"I need a distraction—Fourth of July."

"*Understood, Maxim.*"

He switched off communications, keeping his eyes glued to the hangar.

"Now what?" Gina asked.

"Now we let Christi work her magic," Max replied with a sly smile.

"Hussy," Alesha muttered.

A few moments passed. Without warning, a loud *BOOM* echoed across the landscape and laser bolts erupted out of the hangar. The troops in black scrambled. Many fired back at the *Sequel* with small arms, but the laser bolts deflected off the shields.

"*Voila*—distraction."

Alesha squinted. "I don't see how this helps us get in…"

"Is she looking at me?" Litning asked.

"Yeah," Gina replied.

"You and Jethan don't really blend in," Max admitted. "We'll have to chance it. Come on."

Max led the way, weapons at the ready. Following Gina's instructions, he stopped behind one of the metal barriers littering the field. It appeared the soldiers had the same idea, hiding behind the barriers to protect themselves from Christi's assault. She hadn't been able to get the *Sequel* airborne, but she'd done just about everything else she could.

As Max and his comrades pushed up the field, he spotted another group of soldiers coming up the left side of the facility. Confidence was high that the crew would make it inside first. The *Sequel*'s cannons continued to fire haphazardly. A trio of panicking troops stopped to intercept Max's team. Litning and Jethan made short work of them.

"Okay, I guess they blend in fine," Alesha said as they paused behind the next row of barriers.

Some of the soldiers had gotten over the initial shock and turned their weapons away from the *Sequel* and focused their fire on the crew. Max and the others maintained their cover, but they were stuck about halfway to the hangar.

"Christi! We could use a little help out here!" Max yelled.

"*I cannot get out of the hangar, Maxim. This is the best I can do from here.*"

The grating sound of metal grinding on metal pierced the din of battle. Max looked up. A giant cannon on the facility's roof rolled to cover the building's backside.

"Jesus fuck."

"What's wrong?" Gina asked.

He pointed to the cannon. "We've got to wrap this up quick."

"That's not good," Gina said.

Alesha swiped Max's scope from him. "Hey! What's with you two today?"

Ignoring him, Alesha directed the scope at the approaching

cannon. "If we get to at least the... second row of barriers from the hangar, we should be safe."

"How do you figure that?" Max asked.

She gave him an incredulous look. "It's called geometry?"

"Yeah, well I flunked geometry," he muttered as he peeked around the barrier. The cannon was almost in position. Movement to the left caught his eye.

Litning and Jethan were having an argument. Jethan attempted to grab Litning's arms. Litning pushed the alien firmly against their barrier. Then, he jumped up, grabbed the top of the barrier, and landed on the other side. Before the soldiers behind the next set of barriers could swarm him, Litning jumped into their camp. The soldiers' screams carried over to Max.

"Come on, let's go!" he hissed.

The crew froze at the sight of Litning positively *thrashing* the soldiers. The soldiers appeared apprehensive to shoot into a mass of their allies, but Litning had no such limitations. He tossed the troops around like a child's playthings, but Max noted that he avoided any killing strikes. After all the progress Litning had made in trying to atone for his past, killing was the last thing he wanted to do. Of course, the troops in black didn't know that.

Max and the ladies fired their weapons at the unsuspecting troops, stunning them and evening the odds for Litning. Jethan was conspicuously absent.

With a sickening thud, the Revash knocked out the last of the troops, but more were on their way. "Great job, Fuzzy, but we've gotta go. More of these goons are coming up the side and, well," Max said as he pointed up at the cannon.

"Thank you, Maxim. It would have been quicker with some help," Litning said with a glare at the cautious Jethan, who slunk out from behind his barrier.

"Yeah, what the veck were you doing while Litning did all the work?" Alesha asked. "What do I vecking pay you for?"

"You pay me to protect you, not charge into a foolish fight. I'm not getting killed for these people," Jethan replied.

"*I'm* one of those people! What's gotten into you?" Alesha asked.

"We don't have time for this!" Max said. "Let's hustle!"

With a loud *CLANG*, the cannon locked into place. Powerful red laser bolts pounded the ground and impacted on the metal barriers surrounding them. After three or four shots, they became jagged slag.

"Split up!" Alesha cried. "Get to the front barriers! It won't be able to hit us there!"

Jethan took off without any encouragement and Litning ran in the same direction. Max put his arm around Gina and turned his back to the cannon.

Gina squirmed in his arms. "Max, it's sweet and adorable that you want to protect me, but doesn't this make us a bigger target?"

"Honey, I wouldn't know what to tell your mom if I got you killed in space." He keyed his wrist unit. "Christi, stop shooting out here. We're coming in."

"*Affirmative, Maxim. I will maintain pressure inside the hangar. Quite a few troops are gathering to welcome you.*"

"Sounds good." The cannon fired again, pummeling another nearby barrier.

"How can we escape that gun?" Gina asked.

"It's on a cycle. It fires five times and recharges. We've got to move while it's recharging."

"Gotcha."

The cannon fired one more powerful bolt. Max pulled Gina with him and scrambled over to the barrier Alesha had been occupying.

"Trying to cut down on the angle?" Gina asked. "Do you want me to keep it from Alesha that you followed her advice?"

"Alesha and I have a strong professional relationship based on trust. But, yes."

The cannon fired again, but this time, it hammered the barrier protecting Gina and Max. He winced at the crippling force and intense heat of the laser. A second bolt impacted against the barrier, which buckled with a sickening groan. Max knew what was next. He threw Gina to their old barrier and leaped after her as the cannon reduced the other barrier to a broken, twisted monument to death. The next shot sent dirt and grass flying as it carved a hole in the ground.

Max grabbed Gina's hand. "Come on!"

"It's not recharging yet!"

"It's locked on! Let's move!"

He pulled her over to the barrier that Litning and Jethan had been using as cover. Once the cycle completed, Max led Gina around the corner and raced for the last row of barriers before the facility.

The cannon fired. Max heard the air sizzle as a bolt blasted the ground behind them. The shockwave propelled them forward, but they kept their balance. Once they reached the row of barriers, Litning caught them.

"What's going on?" Max asked. "Where's Jethan?"

"He ran into the facility," Litning said.

"Thanks for the save, Litning," Gina said.

A grateful expression took hold of Litning's face. "Thank you, Gina. *He* never thanks me."

"*What?* That's a fucking lie! I offered you a job when you saved me!" Max blurted.

"Hey!" Alesha hissed from another barrier. "Can we focus up here?"

Max looked up warily at the cannon. The powerful gun moved side to side slowly, searching for a target. Max turned to Alesha and shrugged.

"Told you so," she muttered just loud enough for him to hear.

Max peeked around his barrier. Christi had the troops inside the hangar pinned down. The hangar was completely wrecked—fires burned everywhere. Christi couldn't keep it up forever, though, and more troops were imminent.

"We'll go in now. Stay close to the *Sequel*. Christi's got them under control, but this could get messy," Max said. "We get in there, find our people, and get the fuck out."

"I am going after Jethan," Litning said.

"Yeah, I'd like to know where he's gone," Alesha added.

Max sighed. "Fine."

"What about Sierra?" Alesha asked.

"What about her?"

"We need to take her down."

"'Lesha, she's the GAC's problem."

"If she still has Memta's powers, she's the galaxy's problem, Max!"

"We're not messing with her. We find our friends. We leave. End of discussion."

"But, what about Jethan?" Gina asked.

"Well…I guess he's still *technically* a friend. Though depending on what he's up to, we may be leaving his ass here. Okay, go now!"

Max led the way into the hangar, pistol at the ready. Some of the troops in black fired at them, but the *Sequel*'s cannons kept them in check. The *Sequel* was parked over to the right. Its shields sopped up the majority of the troops' lasers.

"How do we get out of here?" Gina asked

"I'm workin' on it," Max said. He searched the hangar for a door that would lead them deeper into the facility.

"I have Jethan's scent," Litning said.

"Get after him," Max said. "The three of us should be able to find—"

"*Sierra!*" Alesha yelled.

Max's head snapped up. Flanked by a group of troops, Sierra stalked toward them. Her body flared blue as her eyes locked with Max's. She flashed a sinister smile and ran toward the back of the hangar.

"She's mine!" Alesha cried as she took off after Sierra.

"Alesha! Alive! We need her alive!" Max called after her in frustration.

"I'll watch her back!" Gina called out as she rushed off after Alesha.

"Gina! No! God dammit!"

Max was about to chase her until another cadre of troops arrived from the other side of the facility. They immediately started firing at him. Max ducked behind the *Sequel* and chased after Litning. "Can I have *one* thing go right today?"

CHAPTER 37

Shanta and the *Sequel* crew were still chained to the floor and under guard. Of all the beings in her charge, she was most worried about Gerry, who was still in his bulked-up form, but shaking and sweating. *Just hold on a bit longer, buddy.* She'd lost count of the booming explosions she'd heard in the last half hour. Clearly *a* cavalry had arrived, she just wasn't sure *which* cavalry.

The guards' body language screamed uneasiness. If the GAC were invading, Shanta figured the guards would be running for their lives. The fact that they maintained their posts, told her the explosions that echoed through the facility were the product of some other unknown invader. Either that, or the Sierra was so terrifying, they refused to disobey her orders even in the face of their potential deaths.

Whatever. No one forced them to take this job. Shanta gave Gerry a nod.

Gerry slowly nodded back. She knew he was in pain. He had a malleable form, but holding those forms for too long hurt. She wasn't sure how effective he'd be in their escape, but it was the only option they had.

Gerry's body slowly shrank from his bulky form to a softer, more flexible one. His shackles slipped off, but he caught them before they could clatter to the floor.

One of the guards looked in Gerry's direction. "Hey, what…?"

Gerry slithered across the room in the blink of an eye. As their captors reached for their close-quarters weapons, Gerry turned his appendages into tendrils and wrapped them around the guards' throats.

"Uh oh, he's gotcha now," Robert said as he calmly looked on at the proceedings. They'd seen this part before. He turned to Shanta. "I could really go for a cheeseburger. What have we got on the ship?"

Shanta shrugged. "Dunno. Roeger?"

"The inventory does not contain bovine," Roeger replied.

"Well, I figured that, but what do we have that's close? Cheeseburgers sound good, huh, Gerry?"

Gerry tightened his grip on the guards, who slapped uselessly at his arms. "Cheeseburgers are always good. With our lack of bovine, I would substitute thandras meat."

"Yeah…thandras could be good," Robert said with a wistful expression. "Still, we should try to get some beef."

"I will add beef to the shopping list," Roeger said.

"Let's get out of here first," Shanta said.

The guards' bodies went limp and Gerry dropped them to the floor. He then unlocked the crew's bonds.

"Great work, Gerry," Shanta said. "How're you feeling?"

"A little drained, but cheeseburgers will definitely hit the spot."

"You are a magnanimous hero, Gerry," Roeger said as he patted their friend on the arm.

"Yeah, what he said," Robert added. "Thanks for the save. Now, let's get out of here."

Shanta and Robert picked up the guards' rifles. She searched the two of them until she found a keycard. The door opened. She and Robert stuck their heads out. The hallway was deserted. Another explosion rocked the facility. Without the door muffling the noise, Shanta picked up on a familiar sound.

"Where to?" Robert asked.

Another explosion.

"The hangar," Shanta replied.

"Why there?" Gerry asked.

"Because I'd recognize the *Sequel*'s firing signature anywhere."

CHAPTER 38

Max and Litning pounded down a hallway, Litning's nose leading the way. The *Sequel* kept the facility's defenders busy, so they had free reign of the halls. Jethan had some questions to answer, but he had a good head start.

"You still got him?" Max asked.

"If I did not, we would not be running," Litning responded.

"Well, see if you can catch a whiff of Shanta or Robert. They're the priority."

"You do not want to know the truth about Jethan?"

"Sure, but let's remember why we're here."

"Understood."

As they headed down the hall, Max looked around. Everything was the same, like it had rolled off an assembly line. Something felt off.

Litning stopped and put his arm out to stop Max. "He is near."

"Really? How did we catch him so fast?" Max kept his voice to a whisper.

Litning raised his nose. His ears twitched. "He is…frustrated." He looked down at Max with a slight grin. "I think he is lost."

"I guess no one gave him a map," Max said.

"Shall we help him find his way?"

"Let's."

Litning led the way down a couple of corridors until they arrived at a dead end to find—"Nothing?"

Max arched his eyebrow, searching as he drew his pistol. "You're sure he was here?"

Litning sniffed the air. "I am positive he is *still* here!" He scanned around, sniffing. His outstretched arms almost touched both walls. He took a deep breath and lowered his arms. "He is gone."

"Damn."

Suddenly, Litning's left arm shot out. His clawed fingers wrapped around something Max couldn't see. Whatever he had in his grasp shifted in color. What had appeared as a wall mere seconds ago took a humanoid form. Litning tightened his grip and the figure revealed itself.

"Jethan!" Max's head spun. "H-he's some kind of chameleon. Shit, if I'd known that, I might have changed the entire plan to get in here!"

"Max, he was not helping us," Litning reminded him.

"Right. Why were you trying to sabotage us? Who do you work for?"

Jethan didn't seem interested in answering Max's questions. His craggy green hands clawed at Litning's. "Re…lease me…Re…vash!"

"Answers first," Litning said calmly.

Jethan gave no answers. Instead, he delivered shots to Litning's mid-section. Litning growled, but held him tight.

"You look sleepy, Jethan," Litning said. "Why not answer our questions before you nod off?"

"You...have...never...trusted me...Revash," Jethan choked out.

"And?"

"You...were...*right!*"

Jethan slashed at Litning's torso. The attack made him flinch, which loosened his hold on Jethan's throat enough for the alien to get free. He pushed Litning away and swiped at Max, whose stun bolt merely hit the wall.

Jethan grabbed Max by his jacket. The alien's putrid breath was hot on his face. "You have been *nothing*, but a dagger in my side, human!"

Max had no clue what Jethan was talking about, but before he could ask, Jethan slammed him against the wall, knocking the breath from his body. The alien wound up for a punch, but it never landed.

Litning's massive hand grabbed Jethan's shoulder and threw the green-skinned being across the hallway. "Are you all right?" he asked Max, his eyes never leaving Jethan.

"Yeah..." Max groaned. "Go get him."

"My pleasure." Litning moved toward Jethan with purpose.

Jethan wore a wicked smile, but said nothing. He allowed Litning to advance. Before the Revash could lay hands on him, Jethan's body shimmered and disappeared.

Litning lunged at where Jethan had been, but came up empty. He turned in a slow circle, eyes darting around the corridor. "Ack!" Blood splattered the wall as the disguised Jethan cut Litning. Another attack, slashed Litning's leg. He swung his fist in that area, but to no avail. His reward for the failed strike was a gash in his back. Litning leaned heavily against the wall, looking haggard.

"Where is he?!" Max cried as he moved in a tight circle, pistol at the ready. His eyes widened. Litning came at him with a wild punch. Max ducked to avoid getting pulverized. Clearly, the Revash believed Jethan had been in front of him.

"He has somehow masked his scent," Litning said, his words slurring with exhaustion. Max could see his friend struggled to stay upright. Another cut to Litning's back elicited a howling Revash curse. He swung his arm back in an arc so wide, Max had to duck again.

The wild swing caught Jethan in the head. As Litning connected and Jethan's body slammed against the wall, he became visible for a split second. It was all the opening Litning needed. He grabbed the invisible Jethan and started whaling on him, hammering him with his furry fists. Every punch that landed made Jethan visible for an instant. Litning delivered a final, powerful shot that knocked Jethan to the floor.

"Gods..." Litning whispered.

Max stepped from behind Litning. His eyes bulged. "Are you seeing what I'm seeing? I'm not starting to have rimi hallucinations am I?"

"No, we are definitely seeing the same thing," Litning replied.

Jethan spat up blood on the floor, but he didn't look like Jethan—he looked human. He wasn't a chameleon, he was a shifter. The pieces fell into place for Max. "Jesus fuck.... *You* blew up *The Gallant!*" Max cried in disbelief. "You motherfucker! This is all your fault!"

Jethan laughed. "Only the beginning, human!"

"This scum did not concoct this course of action on his own," Litning said. "Who are your compatriots?"

"There is no need for a pair of dead men to know such things!" Jethan spat before vanishing again. Max fired his pistol at Jethan's last position, but hit nothing. The shifter left a blood trail, though.

"We've gotta get that fucker!" Max yelled as Litning slumped against the wall. Max rushed to his friend's side.

"You…need to…go after him," Litning managed through gritted teeth.

"He'll keep. We need to find our friends and you need medical attention."

"I am…fine."

"You can barely stand up. Come on." Max let Litning lean on him for support. He thought his knees might grind to dust under the weight. They took several steps down the hall. Max's eyes strayed to the blood trail.

"Thank you, my friend," Litning said.

"Please. You've saved my life more times than I can count. This is the least I can do."

"This is true, but I still appreciate your help." They continued down the halls and came to a crossroads. The blood trail stopped. "He must have…found a way to…staunch his wound."

Though Max's primary concern was getting Litning to safety, his heart dropped at losing Jethan's trail. The shifter had framed Max and made his life a living hell. He needed to bring him to justice—not only to clear his own name, but to also bring closure for *The Gallant*'s victims.

As Max and Litning worked their way back to the hangar, they came upon another junction. Rounding the corner, they were practically run over by a group coming in from the right.

"What the veck…Max!" It was Shanta and the others. "It's about time!"

"Hey! We came to save *you!*" Max said as Roeger and Robert took the injured Litning.

"You didn't think we could handle that ourselves? Pfft," Shanta said.

Max's face broke into a relieved smile. "It's great to see you all. Is everyone okay?"

"Gerry's a little worn out," Robert said. "But, he saved the day."

Max smiled at Gerry. "Proud of you, buddy."

"Thank you, Maxim," Gerry said with a weary smile.

"Your ex-girlfriend was ready to fry us," Shanta said. "But apparently, Litning ended up the worse off. What happened?"

"We found out who framed me. It's Alesha's crewmate, Jethan. He's a shifter."

"Then, he must have returned here after the bombing," Roeger said.

"That is how we ended up here," Gerry said.

"He must be working with Sierra," Shanta said. "Vecking horvorka."

"He may have a ship here, still," Roeger said.

"Get back to the *Sequel* and relay a message to Glintock. They need to track any ships leaving the planet. Have Christi do the same," Max said.

"Where are you going?" Shanta asked.

"I'll see if I can track him down and find Alesha and Gina. They ran off after Sierra."

"Great," Shanta sighed. "We're never getting off this planet."

"Get the *Sequel* prepped and patch Litning up. We'll be along shortly." Max went back the way he and Litning had come, hoping to pick up Jethan's trail.

He couldn't believe that Jethan could have stopped his wounds from bleeding while running away. The blood pattern wasn't exactly as he'd remembered it. Some of it still looked fresh.

The hairs on the back of Max's neck stood up. Keeping his attention on the floor, he whipped his pistol out and fired directly in front of him. There was a loud grunt and the sound of something large slumping against the wall.

"Cut the shit, Jethan. Show yourself."

The camouflage fell away to reveal Jethan in his usual hulking green form. "You'll need more than that to stop me, human."

"Believe me, I'll happily plug you again if I have to. Is this really you?"

"I have assumed so many forms, I sometimes forget my original one."

"Can you walk?"

Jethan spat out a laugh. "You think I am coming with you? I will die first."

"I'm not taking the rap for this, you piece of shit."

"I am afraid you will, Ultra. No one will take the word of a mass murderer and his fugitive Revash."

"Get up."

Max kept his distance as Jethan clawed his way back to his feet. The shifter grimaced, holding one of the wounds Litning had gifted him. "After you."

Max laughed. "Yeah, sure, let me walk in front of you. I'm offended you think I'm that stupid." He motioned with his pistol for Jethan to start walking. "Pretty smart, holding your position and letting us walk away."

"I know when I am beaten. Your Revash is a formidable opponent."

"I'll be sure to let him know that. And, he's not *my* Revash. We're equals."

"How ever you define your relationship—I care not."

They continued toward the hangar, but Max's brow furrowed. A door was open on the right side of the hallway. It hadn't been open before. His eyes darted around, anticipating a threat. As he and Jethan passed the doorway, the shifter spun around and pushed him into the room before Max knew what was happening.

The door slammed shut, plunging Max into darkness. He kept his pistol at the ready. The feeling that he wasn't alone hung over him like a shroud.

"Hello, Maxim." The unmistakable voice echoed, revealing the size of the room. It was Merthane.

Max turned around slowly to see Merthane grinning in the dim light. The assassin stood beside him. "Je-sus fuck."

CHAPTER 39

Alesha had Sierra in her sights. The witch randomly tossed bolts of blue energy behind her, but most impacted harmlessly against the walls. For any that didn't, Alesha glanced behind her to make sure Gina was all right.

She was grateful for Gina coming along. It showed that she understood the gravity of the threat Sierra represented. Either that, or she simply didn't want to sit on the sidelines. Whatever the case, that made Gina Alesha's kind of girl.

As Sierra led them deeper into the facility, Alesha stopped running to take aim with her pistol. One shot put a hitch in Sierra's stride, but that was all. Gina lined up a shot with her rifle. She squeezed the trigger once. A fiery red laser bolt hit Sierra square in the back, sending her sprawling to the floor.

"How…?" Alesha asked in astonishment.

"Top of my class at Quantico."

Alesha shook her head in awe. "I think I'm in love with you a little bit."

"Just think how much more you will be once you really get to know me."

"Ugh. Alesha, you're incorrigible," Sierra panted from her prone position down the hall. "Do you two want me to leave so you can just veck here on the floor?"

"Maybe some other time, Sierra," Alesha replied as she approached, pistol at the ready. "For now, why don't you toss that gun away and we'll get to the part where we take you into custody."

"Why, Alesha, you almost sound like a law-bringer. Don't tell me you've bought into that nakra. Who's your girlfriend?"

Alesha held her hand out to Gina, preventing her from giving her name. "Max's old flame."

"Well, she *was*." Sierra whipped her arm out and a glowing blue energy bolt slammed into Gina's chest. The impact threw Gina against the wall—*hard*. She crumpled to the floor.

"*No!*" Alesha cried. She started toward Gina, but stopped mid-step. Whispers built in her mind.

"*Alesha, child...join with me.*" It was the heavenly, but sinister voice of Memta.

Her head snapped back to Sierra. "How? We sealed her away."

"So…you hear her song too? Isn't it magical? She still gives me strength!" Again, Sierra lashed out with more blue energy, but the fresh bolt lacked the power of the first, almost fizzling out in midair. "*Nakra!*"

Alesha took the opportunity to charge Sierra. She led with a hook that Sierra easily blocked, but followed with a leg sweep that took Sierra back to the floor. "Not so hot without your magic, huh?"

"*Alesha….*" Again, the voice stopped her cold.

Sierra sat up and delivered a strike to Alesha's mid-section. A wave of pain radiated through her body. Sierra delivered a shot to her jaw. Alesha went down on one knee as Sierra got back to her feet.

"Can you hear her, Alesha? Embrace her *power!*" Sierra emphasized the last word with a Memta-powered punch.

Ringing filled Alesha's ears as she spat a mouthful of blood. Another blow raced toward her head, but she had the wherewithal to deflect it. She struck out with her other hand and connected with Sierra's knee. Sierra cried out and fell back several steps.

Fog filled Alesha's head, but Memta's voice lingered, like a bright blue light cutting through the haze. "*Alesha...join with me.... Complete your life.... Join with me....*"

She shook her head and threw up her hands to defend herself. Sierra tackled her to the floor, clawing at her with glowing hands. Her nails dug into Alesha's flesh as she wrapped her hands around Alesha's throat.

"We're going to change the galaxy! But, you people keep getting in the way!" Sierra screamed as she tightened her grip. She leaned close as Alesha's vision dimmed around the edges. Her strength ebbed. "And once I kill you, I'm going to make your little girlfriend over there beg for death."

A sizzling laser bolt struck Sierra in the chest, knocking her off Alesha. Alesha rolled and coughed uncontrollably. Gina, her body propped against the wall, lowered her rifle.

"I don't fucking beg, bitch," Gina said.

Alesha chuckled and smiled at her new friend. Gina returned a relieved smile of her own.

"You two are pathetic. Did you really think this fight would change anything? Oh, Alesha, I expected so much more from you." Sierra cackled; she held up a green box and pressed the single button.

"Oh...veck," Alesha said.

"*Self-destruct sequence has been activated. Evacuate in an orderly manner*," a voice echoed through the halls.

"Oh, fuck!" Gina cried.

Alesha staggered toward Sierra, who continued laughing. Memta's voice was louder than ever. "*Join with me, Alesha! You can save them all!*"

Alesha struggled against the desire in her heart. She then kicked Sierra in the head. The voice dissipated. Alesha had passed her trial. Her next challenge was to escape with Gina *and* Sierra.

CHAPTER 40

"*What are we waiting for?*" the assassin asked in her digitized voice. "*Let's kill him and be done with it.*"

"You know we can't do that, Alexis," Merthane said. "The reward is for bringing him in alive."

"Well, you fucked that up," Max said. "You just let the guy responsible for the Aval massacre walk away scot-free."

Merthane sneered. "The man responsible is standing right in front of us."

"You know I didn't do this. That's not justice."

"You're talking about truth. That's not my goal. Bringing in the man society holds responsible—that's my job. The other guy did it? Make the case. Then I'll bring him in."

"Good luck with that. He's a shifter."

"That's certainly rare. And it would be quite a challenge."

Max nodded, his eyes scanning the room for any advantage. "Let me guess, Jethan actually *did* run away from us, ran into you, and cut a deal. Am I warm?"

Merthane's smile widened. "You always were a smart boy, Maxim."

Again, Max nodded. "So, you can't kill me, but I'm sure it's perfectly fine if you beat the shit out of me."

"*It'll have to do*," Alexis said, taking up a fighting stance. Merthane didn't move.

"And what are you going to do? Watch?" Max asked.

"Something like that," Merthane replied.

"I don't get it. She's already tried to kill me. *Twice*. Was she not supposed to do that?"

"Let's just say that Alexis and I have different goals."

"Ah. You want the dough and the orgasmic pleasure of throwing me in prison and she wants to kill me for…reasons."

"*YOU MURDERED DAYNA!*" Alexis cried.

"Now, we talked about this. Hopefully, the perpetrator of that particular crime is being bagged right now. I actually left Dayna unconscious and out of the fight."

"*So, you're saying her death was her own doing?*" Alexis' shoulders moved up and down as if she were breathing heavily.

"Well, I mean, no one *made* her go up on that roof." He winced as soon as he'd said it.

Alexis screamed, drew her sword, and charged at Max. She swung her blade wildly, giving Max ample time to dodge the attack.

What am I doing? I've gotta get out of here. "Look, I'm truly sorry about Dayna. I didn't know her long, but I'm sure she was a lovely person. She'd have to be to stick it out with this asshole." He gestured at Merthane. "But, you've got to believe me when I tell you, I had nothing to do with her death."

"*LIAR!*" Again, she charged at him and again, Max sidestepped her attack.

"What the fuck have you been telling her?" Max asked Merthane.

"The truth," he replied with a sneering grin.

"*Bull*-shit! Alexis, Merthane hates me, okay? He's going to tell you anything he can to make me look like a villain…."

"*But, you* are *a villain, Ultra*," Alexis replied. "*Not only did you let Memta loose on the galaxy, you also killed Talon's son.*"

Max had a retort ready, but held his tongue. Gage's death hadn't been his fault, but he'd blamed himself for it every day since. No matter what he saw as the truth, this young woman would never see him as anything *but* a villain. It was a hard truth to swallow, especially when Merthane was such a piece of shit.

Alexis came in with a more controlled attack. Max tried to side-step, but she pivoted and punched him in the stomach with the back of her hand. He hunched over to get his wind back, while Alexis pivoted again, brandishing her sword. He hit the floor, eluding the blade that would have removed his head.

She's not fucking around. He rolled on the floor, only to be met by the bottom of Merthane's boot. "You fuck! I thought you were just watching!" he cried, rolling away from Merthane.

Merthane chuckled as Alexis struck again. Max kicked out at her ankles. Before he could connect, she flipped into the air, landing deftly by Merthane, who grinned wildly.

There was no way Max could beat them both, but all he really had to do was incapacitate them long enough to make his escape. The problem was, his belt of tricks was either on the *Sequel* or back on Earth.

He got to his feet, studying Merthane. He drew his pistol and snapped off a couple of shots, separating the allies. The weapon was set to lethal, as Max knew stun would have no effect on Alexis. He rushed Merthane, who took up a defensive position. With a push of a button, Merthane's energy shield extended from his wrist, protecting him from the front.

Max feared his knee would shred as he switched targets to Alexis. He fired his pistol repeatedly as he charged toward her. She deflected the laser bolts with her energized sword, as Max predicted she would. He fired at her feet and, when she tried to defend, he tackled her to the ground. The maneuver stunned her. Max was able to wrest her sword from her and roll away. He got to his feet, pistol holstered and sword in hand.

Alexis rose and drew her second sword.

"*Do you actually think you can beat me?*"

"No, but maybe I don't have to."

"*If you expect to leave here alive, you will.*" She immediately launched into an attack, swinging her blade with powerful, precise strikes.

It took everything Max had to keep up with Alexis' offensive and he only blocked half of her swipes. The ones that broke through his defenses nicked up his arms and legs. He moved his body enough to avoid any serious damage, but the cuts still stung like a bitch. She was fast. *Too* fast.

He glanced at Merthane, who watched with barely-restrained glee. "Are you just going to stand there, looking like you want to beat off?"

"You have bigger problems to worry about," Merthane replied. As if to prove his point, Alexis nicked Max's leg. "I want to watch her destroy you. If I can get a few shots in without getting in the way, all the better." Merthane said the last part with a kick in Max's direction, keeping him in Alexis' sights.

Alexis' sword connected again, slashing Max's forearm. He cried out, but managed to keep hold of his sword. Sweat poured down his face. His arm throbbed. Blood dripped from his wound.

Alexis lunged. Max escaped her and flanked Merthane behind his energy shield. Max energized his sword and swiped downward, cutting Merthane's utility belt free. The belt clattered to the floor. Merthane moved and was knocked off balance by Max, who scooped up the belt.

Max swept the sword in an arc, keeping Merthane and Alexis at bay. He opened the first pouch on the belt and threw whatever he'd found at the pair. The two of them dove in opposite directions as the spheres exploded in thick gray smoke.

Max slung the belt over his shoulder as he backed toward the door. The smoke inched toward him. Footsteps sounded to his left. Alexis emerged from the smoke, swinging her sword wildly. Max dodged, but met Merthane's boot. As Max hit the deck, the sword clattered away from him.

Alexis flipped to the discarded sword. She sheathed it and charged at Max. Before he could react, Merthane came at him with a haymaker. Max blocked and Merthane's fist only connected with his arm, which already hurt like hell.

"*Motherfucker!*" Max cried as he attempted to disengage from Merthane. He took a step back and ran smack into Alexis. She thrust her sword forward, but Max spun to the left. The blade only cut his jacket. Merthane punched him in the stomach. Max bent over, leaving himself defenseless to Alexis' next attack. She kicked him in the back of the knee, forcing him to the floor.

As Max hit the deck, he pulled out his pistol and blasted Merthane in his injured knee. Blood and bits of bone exploded from Merthane's leg. The bounty hunter screamed as he went down. Max kicked up at Alexis, separating her from Merthane. Then he fired his pistol at her repeatedly. As her energized sword deflected the bolts, she backed up. Once she was several feet away from him, Max again fished around in Merthane's belt and tossed a few plum-sized capsules at Alexis. Upon impact with the floor, the capsules burst into a gooey pink substance. It stopped Alexis in her tracks, suspending her in a sticky web.

Max lay back on the floor, exhausted. He wasn't sure how much blood he'd lost, but his jacket and pants were uncomfortably wet. The room echoed with Merthane's moans and Alexis' grunts as she struggled. Her sword hung above her, out of reach. As she thrashed about, the goo latched to her helmet and removed it. Her short, spiky blonde hair framed a face that was familiar. She snarled at him as she struggled.

"Sorry, but you need a time out," Max said as he slowly got to his feet.

"You vecking shot me!" Merthane screamed. "I can't walk!"

"That's your fucking problem," Max replied as he scanned around the room. "Where the fuck is the exit?" He swayed on his feet as a wave of lightheadedness swept over him.

"We'll never help you, murderer!" Alexis spat at him.

"Yeah, yeah, yeah, struggle some more, why don't you?" Max said with a chuckle. He was about to move to the supposed exit when a cord wrapped around his ankles. Max tripped and hit the floor. His pistol and Merthane's utility belt were jarred from his hands. Before he knew what was happening, his body was being dragged across the floor toward Merthane.

"You thought you were walking out of here? After what you've done?!" Merthane screamed as his gauntlet winched Max closer.

Max grasped for his pistol. His fingertips brushed the grip as Merthane's other gauntlet produced a large, serrated knife. Max stretched his arm as far as it would go, gritting his teeth. Finally, his hand grasped the pistol. Merthane jerked the cord. Max fired. Merthane's movement knocked Max's aim off. The laser bolt sliced through Merthane's cheek, leaving behind a sizzling wound.

Merthane howled.

"Yeah, hurts, doesn't it?" Max asked as he freed himself from the cord. Movement led Max to turn his pistol on Alexis. Her armor was full of tricks. She'd almost burned herself free from the goo. "Not so fast, sister." He fired several bolts at the floor to keep her in check. Then he aimed the pistol at Merthane. "Call her off! Or I'll give you another hole in your head."

Merthane chuckled. His laughter built in pitch and frequency until it was a wail.

"What's so fucking funny?"

"You…you called her, 'sister.'"

"Yeah, so?"

Merthane laughed again, turning his mangled face into a horrific mask. "That's exactly who she is!"

CHAPTER 41

The planet shifted under Max. *That's impossible*. "You're fucking lying. No way."

Merthane's freshly scarred face twisted into a grin. "Space is lonely, Maxim. And cold. Jimmy just needed someone to cuddle. That happened to be Alexis' mother. While *your* mother sat home. On Earth. All alone."

"Shut the fuck up!" He didn't accept it. His father wouldn't. Couldn't. That's not who he was. However, when he looked at Alexis, the evidence was in her eyes. His father's eyes. Max's eyes.

His mind reeled back—twenty years into the past. He was thirteen. Jim had just recently started taking Max into space with him. Staring at Alexis, one particular trip stood out in his mind....

The *Hunter* had touched down on a lush world with purple skies. The foliage had a unique green color. Max felt like he was looking at a video game. His dad had departed the ship and walked toward the lone home near the landing area. The rest of the crew—Pepper, Benton, Roeger, and Merthane—hung around the landing ramp as Max and Gage goofed around.

"Where are we, Father?" Gage asked Merthane, who wore a sullen look.

"A planet that's very special to us."

"Where's my dad going?" Max asked.

Merthane practically sneered. "To visit an old friend."

Max thought Merthane's behavior was odd. He looked after his father, but the setting sun washed the whole area in a golden glow. "Hey, Roeger. Let me see the scope."

"Why?"

"I wanna see what Dad's doing."

"Maxim, if your father wanted you to know what he was doing, he would have taken you with him."

"Oh, Roeger, don't be such an asshole. Just give me the scope."

"I do not approve of your language, young man," Roeger chastised him.

Before Max could retort, Gage nudged his arm. "Use mine."

"Thanks," Max said. He trained the device on his father, who stood at the front door of the house with a very pretty blonde woman. His dad handed the woman a small box. In the front yard, a little girl with long blonde hair played. And still, Merthane wore a sour look....

"I...I remember." Max looked to Alexis. Her eyes were wild—face a mask of confusion. "You were the little girl. You couldn't have been more than three."

She shook her head, squeezing her eyes shut. "No," she whispered. "No, no, no, no!" Her eyes locked on Merthane. "How? How could you keep this from me?!"

Merthane's expression showed he hadn't expected his reveal to go this way. "He was no father to you! *I'm* your father!"

Alexis grunted as she worked to free herself from the pink goo. Once freed, she stalked over to the incapacitated Merthane and punched him in the face. He screamed. "You had no right to keep this from me. You knew who my real father was and said *nothing?* You kept the information to use it as a weapon against my…my *brother?*"

"Don't forget, he tried to trick you into murdering me," Max offered.

"I never said you don't deserve that, Ultra," she said, keeping her eyes on Merthane. "You betrayed me, all to get back at a man you blame for Gage's death. That's not how you treat a daughter. That's how you treat a pawn." She hit Merthane again, which knocked him unconscious. Then, she spun and kicked Max in the chest, sending him to the floor.

A klaxon sounded. "*Self-destruct sequence has been activated. Evacuate in an orderly manner.*"

Despite the pain radiating through his chest, Max sat up instantly. Alexis had vanished. All she left in her wake was her unconscious father figure. The alarm continued to blare. No matter how much he hated him, Max preferred Merthane rot in prison rather than let him find potential forgiveness in death. Unfortunately, nothing in life was free. If he wanted Merthane in a cell, he'd have to drag him out.

CHAPTER 42

The emergency klaxon continued to blare as Max lugged Merthane toward the hangar. His own injuries hampered him. It was all he could do to drag the older man down the hall by his leg. Max glanced at Merthane, wondering how the man was so heavy after he'd stripped him of all his equipment. Max needed answers and Merthane was the only one who could provide them.

Where's Litning when I need him? It was a reflex. He hoped his friend had gotten the medical attention he needed on the *Sequel.*

"*Self-destruct in five minutes. Please evacuate in an orderly manner.*"

"Jesus fuck," he muttered as he redoubled his efforts to drag Merthane's ass down the hall. As he struggled, his wrist unit lit up.

"*Ma—im? Re—u—ere?*" It was Christi. Something in the facility's construction prevented the signal from getting through.

"Christi! I need help! Send Gerry or Roeger!"

His only response was static. It was a shame the terrorists were blowing the place up. He was curious about the composition. He huffed and puffed as he winced through his injuries and continued pulling Merthane down the hall.

Another alarm blared. "*Self-destruct in three minutes. Please evacuate in an orderly manner.*"

"God dammit!" Sweat poured down his face. He knew he should drop Merthane and run for it, but he couldn't. The man had opened a door into his father's life that Max had never known existed.

Footsteps sounded down the hall, metal on metal. Max drew his pistol to greet, "Roeger!"

"Maxim! What are you doing? You are injured."

"Help me get him to the ship, buddy!"

"Merthane? Why?"

"No time to explain!"

Roeger nodded. In one fell swoop, he threw Max over his shoulder and picked Merthane up by his belt. "If his belt snaps, I am leaving him."

"Go! Go! Go!"

With a strength belied by his wiry frame, Roeger hefted the two men and took off at a run. With all the bouncing around, Max was sure he'd vomit.

"*Self-destruct in one minute. Please evacuate in an orderly manner.*"

"We'll never make it to the ship and get out!"

"The ship is safely outside," Roeger said. "*We* are the only ones in danger."

"Well, that doesn't make me feel any better…."

They crossed into the hangar. Destroyed and burning vehicles littered the room. Christi had done her job *too* well.

"*Self-destruct in thirty seconds. Please evacuate in an orderly manner.*"

Max looked over his shoulder. They were a little more than a hundred yards from the exit. They weren't going to make it, not with Roeger carrying both of them.

"Roeger, I'm sorry, buddy."

"We are not beaten yet, Maxim!" With his last word, Roeger took two leaping steps and heaved Merthane toward the exit. He pulled Max into his arms like a groom carrying a bride over the threshold. Merthane landed on his face just outside the hangar, while Roeger poured on the speed.

"*Self-destruct in ten seconds. Please evacuate in an orderly manner.*"

Another ship exploded to the right. Roeger turned his body to shield Max from any debris. A piece of shrapnel lodged in his shoulder.

"*Nine.*"

Some fleeing black-clad soldiers took shots at the pair as they made their escape.

"*Eight.*"

Max fired back, steadying himself as best he could as Roeger ran. He caught one in the chest, but the others scattered for the exit.

"*Seven.*"

With a horrible groan, a beam snapped free from the hangar ceiling.

"*Six.*"

It crashed in front of Max and Roeger, forcing the robot to change direction.

"*Five.*"

Roeger's feet pounded on the hangar deck. They were still about fifty yards away.

"*Four*"

His metal arms tightened around Max.

"*Three.*"

Roeger ran.

"*Two.*"

And ran.

"*One.*"

He leaped into the air, sailing out of the hangar and onto the grass as the first explosions rocked the facility. Roeger picked Merthane up by his belt again and carried the two rivals to a safe distance near the parked *Sequel*.

Max embraced Roeger. "Thank you, buddy. Really. You saved my life."

"I would not let you die."

Max smiled at his friend. "Chain this piece of shit up and get that shoulder looked at."

"With pleasure, Maxim."

The field was littered with black-uniformed soldiers. Unfortunately for them, it was also filled with GAC transport ships and shock troops. Glintock had gotten their message. He stood beneath the *Sequel* with Alesha and Gina, who had a bound and unconscious Sierra at their feet. Max limped over to them with a wide grin.

"Isn't this a beautiful sight?" he asked as he embraced Gina and then Alesha. "Thank God you two are still in one piece."

"Your girl handled herself admirably against this vecking horvorka," Alesha said with a soft kick at Sierra. "After this, she and I are going out for drinks. Where's Jethan?"

"Escaped. He's a shifter, so guess who he's been impersonating across the galaxy? How's Litning?"

"They're patching him up on the ship," Gina said, rubbing his back. "You're hurt. What happened?"

"Too long a story to tell right now." He turned to Glintock. "Am I under arrest?"

"Not today." He shook Max's hand. "I'm glad to see you all made it out alive."

"Thanks. *I'm* glad you brought the cavalry."

"You'd have to thank Agent Dilton. After she put Brontin in his place, she made all this happen." Glintock smiled, he actually smiled, as Dilton and her android duplicate joined the group.

"Ultra," Dilton said with a nod.

"Dilton." Her expression said she wasn't completely sold on letting Max walk away. "We found the guy who blew up *The Gallant*—a shifter—but he got away thanks to that asshole," he said, gesturing to the bound Merthane. "You can put him away for aiding and abetting, if that's a crime out here."

"It most certainly is," Dilton said with a slight smile.

"Do we know of any ships that left the planet? We may be able to track him," Max said.

Dilton's doppelganger didn't smile. "Two ships left. One was Merthane's ship, the *Claw*."

"That'll be Merthane's protégé, an assassin named Alexis." *My sister….* "She'll keep for now."

"The other was a ship designated, the *Pike*."

"Can you cross-reference that with ships that left Aval in the wake of *The Gallant* bombing?" Glintock asked.

The android paused for a moment. "Yes, the same ship left Aval after the destruction of *The Gallant*."

"I think we have our man," Glintock said with a tight smile. "Where is he headed?"

Beattie looked at Max. She almost had sympathy in her eyes. "He is going to Earth."

CHAPTER 43

The *Sequel* emerged from the Cardon Tunnel nearest to Earth. Max, behind the controls, pushed the throttle as far as it would go. Robert, sitting in the co-pilot's chair, balked.

"Max, you gotta watch your speed. They could pick us up on their radar," Robert warned.

"I don't fucking care about that. We're the only people who worry about the GAC rules concerning Earth. So, this time, fuck that," Max responded.

He caught Robert's wary gaze out of the corner of his eye. "I hope you know what you're doing," Robert mumbled.

"Relax, Robbie. I've been doing this a long time."

"So have I, Max. And a pilot that's emotionally distracted is no good to anybody."

Robert knew what he was talking about. Ever since they'd left Iswat, Max hadn't been thinking clearly. His mother's life was at stake. They'd tried to communicate with Sam, but had no luck.

The *Sequel* approached Earth at maximum velocity.

"Max, you're going to take out a few dozen satellites if you don't slow down!" Robert yelled. He grabbed Max's arm. "Let me take the helm. I'll get us there as fast as possible. I promise."

Max let Robert's words break through his temporary madness. It made no sense to race headlong into the planet, wreaking all kinds of havoc on the way in. He wouldn't be able to help his mother that way. He keyed control over to Robert and got up from his seat with a grimace. "Just get us to her house. I'll take the elevator down. And I don't care if we're seen."

"Will do," Robert replied as he settled back into the co-pilot's chair.

"And Robbie—thanks."

"Anytime, Max. Anytime."

Max eased down the stairs into the common area. Alesha had stitched him up after his fight with Alexis and Merthane, but he still felt like an exposed nerve. Roeger stood at the main computer, running numbers. He had a patch on his shoulder where the shrapnel had damaged him. "Well, Roeger? Is Jethan down there?"

"It is difficult to say, Maxim," Roeger replied. "Christi and I have been running possibilities, but the *Pike* hit so many Cardon Lanes on the way, it has been tricky to determine where he finally ended his journey."

"Also, the lack of any Earth-based space defense makes it impossible to discover unwanted visitors," Christi added.

"Well, we'll just have to go to the house and hope for the best. Where's Shanta?"

"With Alesha and Gina, tending to Litning and Gerry. Of the two, you will be surprised to learn that Gerry is the more difficult patient," Roeger said.

"Will they be okay?"

"*They will be fine, Maxim,*" Christi said. "*They just need time.*"

"*Max, we're just about to the house,*" Robert's voice sounded over the intercom.

"All right. I'm heading for the elevator." As Max headed for the lift, he checked his newly-restored utility belt and the charge on his pistol. He had everything he'd need. One way or another, Jethan was going down.

Gina entered the common area. "Max, wait."

"Yeah, what's up?"

That seemed to take her aback. "You were going down there without a goodbye?"

"No, I just need to get down there *right now.*"

"Take me with you."

"Gina, no. I'm sorry. I have no idea what I'll find down there and I want you as far away from this as possible."

"I can help, Max."

"I know you can, but…I need you safe. I can't go down there and do what I need to do while worrying that Jethan might rip you in half."

She nodded in understanding. "Be careful." She kissed him on the cheek.

"Always."

Stepping into the lift, he locked the waist-high cage behind him. He took a deep, calming breath. His anxiety wasn't due to the coming conflict, but to what he might find at the house. He gave Gina a half-smile to reassure her. It didn't seem to do the trick.

The *Sequel* lurched as it came to a stop. Max didn't even wait for Robbie's confirmation before hitting the lift's release. The underside hatch opened and the lift dropped at an accelerated rate.

Max gripped the railing tightly as he sped to the ground. As his mother's backyard lawn rushed up to greet him, the lift slowed to a soft landing.

He exited the lift and looked up at the ship. Despite what he told Robert, the fact that the *Sequel* loomed over his mother's house, for anyone to see, bothered him. It was late, but still, it wasn't a good look.

"Robbie, take the ship to one of our rendezvous points. I'll call you when I'm done," he said into his wrist unit.

"*But, what if you need help?*"

"To be completely frank, the two best guys to help me are laid up in the infirmary. I've got this. Thanks."

"*Your call, boss.*"

The *Sequel* peeled off, leaving Max alone. After taking a moment to get his bearings, he realized that the whole street was dark and deserted.

That's…not good.

It was possible that the street had lost power, but the timing was suspicious. He drew his pistol and moved toward the house. There was no sign of another ship. Jethan had a big head start, so he could have stowed it somewhere. As a shifter, he could have been anywhere.

Max looked up at the rear of the house warily. He headed for the deck steps. Squinting at them in the moonlight, he tried to recall which ones creaked the worst. He moved as lightly as he could up the stairs. That didn't stop the second and fifth from issuing a loud *CREAK*.

As he landed on the deck, he peered through the glass patio doors. Pitch black, just like the street. No candles shone from inside. He reached for the sliding door handle. Locked.

He couldn't see anything amiss in the moonlight. No cracks in the siding. No broken or open windows. Was Jethan even there? His stomach dropped into his boots. Could he have gone to Sam's? He took a deep breath, trying to reassure himself that Jethan *couldn't* know where Sam lived.

Patting down his pockets, he found his keys and unlocked the patio door as quietly as possible. If the alien was inside, Max still hoped to get the drop on him. Slowly, he slid the patio door open and eased into the darkened house. He closed the door behind him and re-locked it with what sounded like a deafening *CLICK*.

After a moment of unsuccessfully peering into the darkness, he pushed a button on his pistol. A small cylindrical extension popped out, providing a powerful light. He swept the kitchen. Nothing. *Like it fucking matters when the guy can turn invisible*.

His light scanned the family room. Again, nothing. *Where are you, you son of a bitch?* He moved tentatively, his anxiety a whirling top in his chest. He crept through the kitchen. The laundry room door was ajar on his left. Keeping his aim as steady as his trembling hands allowed, he nudged the door open. His light illuminated nothing out of the ordinary.

The door to the garage inside the laundry room was shut; he didn't think Jethan would have gone in there. Then, all he could picture was a triumphant Jethan looming over the dead bodies of Sam, Cindy, Billy, and Kate. He *had* to investigate the garage, even though the rational side of his brain told him they were all safe at Sam's.

What's stopping this asshole from impersonating me and killing them?

With little thought to staying quiet, he marched into the laundry room and swung open the door to the garage, pistol ready. Nothing. The large concrete and brick room smelled faintly of gasoline, but was empty.

Max wiped his brow with the back of his hand and exhaled a shuddering breath. The fear he felt for his mother was the exact reason why he lived in space. His home planet was no longer off-limits. Jethan and Alexis had broken all sorts of GAC laws by coming to Earth.

Alexis. How was he going to explain *her* to his mother? *Oh, hey, Mom! Did you know I was almost murdered by my secret half-sister? I'm sure she'll be in town to kill you soon!*

Max spun around at a sound from the foyer. He left the laundry room and spied a body on the foyer floor. His pistol light revealed his mother, unconscious on her back.

"Mom!" Max holstered his pistol and rushed over to her. She was breathing, but her eyes were closed. He shook her gently. "Mom! Are you okay?"

His mother's eyes snapped open. Her hand shot out and latched around Max's throat. As he clawed at her tightening grip, he felt her hand growing and changing. *Jethan!*

The shifter kept Kate's face and rose from the floor. Max continued to try and free himself from the alien's grasp. His mother's visage didn't jibe with his predicament. Jethan walked Max over to the basement, opened the door, and threw him down the stairs.

Stupid! Stupid! Stupid! Max thought as he hit every stair on the way down. He crashed on the landing toward the bottom of the staircase, but continued his momentum down the last few stairs to the floor. Dim lights burned in the basement. Max couldn't make out much of anything.

Jethan, still in Kate disguise, jumped down from the top of the stairs to the landing in a single leap. Max scrambled to his feet. He drew his pistol, but Jethan lunged at him and knocked the weapon from his hand.

"Moronic human," Jethan sneered. "I knew you would follow me here."

"Well, she *is* my mother."

Jethan took a swipe at Max, who jumped back to escape harm.

"Imagine my disappointment when I found she was not here. No matter. Now that you are here, I can kill her at my leisure."

Jethan's threat against Max's mother struck him to the core. "Why?"

"For the fun of it, of course." Again, Jethan lunged at him, but Max avoided his grabbing hands. "Once you are dead, I will have fulfilled my contract and can move on to more personal interests."

"Like murdering senior citizens? Nice hobby." Max threw a flash capsule from his belt, but Jethan batted it away. The capsule exploded in light behind Jethan as Max made a lunge for his pistol. Jethan kicked him in the torso like a goalie defending the net. He fell back a few steps. "Why kill me now? Why not on Iswat?"

Jethan shrugged. "I just follow orders."

"That's what the Nazis said."

Jethan's brow crinkled. "Who the veck are the Nazis?" He swung again at Max, who kept his distance. "Perhaps they think you will work better as a martyr of some kind."

Max was surprised. "Who are *they?*"

"You will not be alive long enough to care."

Jethan managed to grab hold of Max and threw him into a wall. Max was shocked he hadn't crashed through it. He fell onto the couch, but was unable to get up before Jethan was on him again. He tried to move his arms, but Jethan's legs had him pinned. Before his eyes, Jethan morphed from his mother back to his normal form.

"When I kill you, I want to do it with my own hands."

"Unlike on Aval, right?"

Jethan's mouth parted in a toothy smile. "Yes. I have to say, Ultra, it was enjoyable playing you—watching the hunters chase you around the galaxy. I often laughed about it in my quarters on the *Heartbreaker*." He reached behind him and dug his claws into Max's leg.

Max grunted in pain, but needed to keep the alien talking. "It started to gnaw at you, didn't it? Especially when they ordered you to make the video."

Jethan sneered. "Yes. While I was happy to stick you with the blame for *The Gallant*, I found myself desiring the notoriety." Jethan put his hands around Max's throat and squeezed. "That video just firmly made you responsible. My employers provided the text. I do not know what they are playing at. It was all nonsense to me."

Max struggled. Jethan's smile seared into his mind as panic built in his chest. The inability to fight off his executioner made it worse. He never thought that this would be the way he'd go out. A guy admits to framing him for a horrific crime, but gets to kill him at the same time? How the fuck was that fair? He thought of Gina. Then he thought of Alesha.

"Goodbye, Ultra. Be happy! You will live forever in infamy," Jethan said.

Three laser bolts slammed into the alien's back. His hands went limp and his body slid off Max and onto the floor.

Max gasped for breath. He looked up to see his mother holding his pistol, a determined look on her face. Max coughed and sat up slowly. Kate rushed over and embraced him.

"Thank God you're all right!" she said as he wearily hugged her back.

"What are you doing here?" he asked, his voice raspy. "You're supposed to be at Sam's."

"I told you, I wasn't going to hide at Sam's house. Did you think I was married to your father for all those years and I never had any way to defend myself from something following him home?"

"Where were you?"

"The panic room behind the wall back there. Come on out, Billy. It's all over."

Billy crept out from behind the corner. "H-hey, Max."

Max gave him a weak wave. "Thanks for the save, Mom, but I sure hope you didn't kill him." He spoke into his wrist unit. "Did you get all that?"

"*Yes, Maxim,*" Christi's voice came back. "*Every word.*"

Max sat back on the couch. It was over. Relief flooded his veins. One look at Jethan confirmed that the asshole was still breathing. "Have a seat, Billy. We're okay now."

Billy pointed at Jethan. "What is that thing?"

"A shapeshifter named Jethan. I'm actually not sure what species he is."

"Oh, I see." Billy looked completely out of his depth.

Max hugged his mother again. "I'm just relieved you're okay."

"Honey, you need to trust that I can take care of myself."

"She's very independent," Billy chimed in.

"Yeah, I'm beginning to see that." Max looked down at Jethan again, making sure the stun blasts still held. He didn't smoke, but suddenly felt like he needed a cigarette. "So, did my mom tell you everything, Billy, or do you still think I work overseas?"

"Uh…she's told me some of it."

"Well, let's tie this asshole up and sit down for a talk."

CHAPTER 44

A few days had passed since Jethan's home invasion. Glintock's small ship sat beside the *Sequel* in an empty field. The crew, Sam, and Max's mother milled around the ships.

"So, this is it?" Sam asked.

"'Fraid so. We've gotta get Jethan back to Aval, so I can go back to a normal life," Max replied.

"I can't believe you had to deal with all that, Max," his mother said.

He winced, not because he didn't appreciate his mother's concern, but because he'd been putting off the Alexis talk and he wasn't thrilled that the time had come for it. The crew had been evenly split on whether he should tell his mother about his sister.

Sam pulled him into an embrace. "Well, I'm gonna miss you, buddy. Don't stay away so long next time."

"Sure, I'll try to stay out of prison." He clapped his friend on the back and Sam moved to say his goodbyes to Alesha and the others. Max then turned to his mother. "Billy didn't want to come out for this?"

"No, unfortunately. He's still a bit in shock over what happened at my house."

"Understandable." He thought of Alexis and grew somber again. "Mom, I...I have to tell you something."

Her brow furrowed. "What is it, sweetie?"

He grimaced. "The woman, the one who, uh, tried to kill me? Merthane told me...she's my sister."

His mother's face was blank. "Oh."

"*Oh?* That's all you have to say?" Max was shocked.

She bit her lip and turned away, arms crossed as if holding herself together. "I've known about Alexis for some time now."

He recoiled. "*What?* And you never told me?"

"*We* never told you, Max, because it wasn't any of your concern."

"It wasn't my concern that I might have a sister out there somewhere?"

"To be frank, no." She took a deep breath. "Things up there aren't like things down here."

"I know, I know," he said, looking over at Alesha. "She's always telling me that."

"She's a smart woman. Talon told me that Alexis' mother, Ejora, wanted privacy. I honored that."

"Merthane is in touch with you?" he asked, incredulous.

"No, no! He snuck down here and approached me. He let me know that Ejora had passed and he'd raise Alexis."

"When did that happen?"

"Not long after your father died." She set her jaw. "Your father loved me, Max. With all of his heart, he loved me. It was one moment in time that resulted in a minor miracle."

"Mom, she almost killed me!"

"I assume she didn't know the truth about you and your father?"

He closed his eyes. He didn't want to make excuses for Alexis, but he couldn't lie to his mother. "No, of course not. Merthane hates my guts. He used that information as a weapon."

"Then, shame on him for keeping that girl in the dark for so long."

"Why didn't you tell me any of this?"

She paused. "You idolized your father, Max. I thought that seeing him as so...human would have crushed you. I'm sorry."

He didn't know what to think. She was right. His father was his hero. The fact that his mother appeared at peace with it helped him keep it all in perspective. It was hard to see his father with all his flaws, but it actually made Max feel closer to him.

His mother hugged him. "I know it's difficult, honey."

He held her tightly. "Thank you for telling me."

She released him. "Find her, Max. Find her and tell her the truth." She squeezed his hand and wandered over to Alesha.

Glintock sidled up beside him. "You tell her about Alexis?"

"She already knew. I was completely in the dark."

"They were protecting you. It's what parents do." Glintock looked up at the *Sequel*. "Speaking of protection, what's the plan for Jethan?"

Max brightened at the question. "Litning and I are going to deliver him to Aval. He's locked up on the ship."

"Are you sure that's a good idea? You're not exactly a popular character there."

"Now that Christi's recording of his confession exonerates me, I kind of want to flaunt my freedom a bit."

"Well, be careful. It's their justice system, so they can hold him until they bring him to trial—unless he meets with an *accident* while in prison. You won't have any problems from the GAC, though. As far as we're concerned, you're completely absolved."

"Do I have you to thank for that or your lady friend?" Max asked with a wink.

Glintock's posture appeared to get even straighter. "Dilton is a colleague and I'm pretty sure she's my boss now."

"Yeah, but I saw the way you looked at her. You should pursue that."

"It wouldn't be appropriate. I will say, though, it was nice to have a partner to rely on."

"I'm hurt you didn't feel that way after we worked together last year," Max said.

"Dilton didn't run off at every moment's notice to chase around an old girlfriend. Is your current flame going to be that flighty when I hire her?"

"Gina? No, she's solid. I know you know this, because I'm sure you found some way to get at her files at the FBI."

Glintock's lips pursed. "She's a stellar applicant. It will be nice to have her under my wing for a time until we station her here on Earth."

"Is the GAC thinking of making overtures to Earth?"

"Gods, no. This planet is nowhere near ready to join the GAC. However, with all the action that took place down here recently, I convinced them that we at least need a presence here. Gina will be my eyes and ears."

"And who did you present that to? Your *girlfriend?*" Max asked playfully.

Glintock grunted.

"So, Sierra was stealing from Zeth to build that facility? Just to blow it up?"

"It looks that way. Those burglaries were handled locally, so no one made the connection."

"We did," Max pointed out.

"Well, you were more interested in finding Sierra; she *was* the common thread."

"It's strange, though. When we were looking at what was stolen from these places, it seemed like a lot more than what ended up in that facility on Iswat."

Glintock scowled. "*How* much more?"

Max felt sick in the pit of his stomach. "Enough to build at least…two—oh, shit."

Glintock closed his eyes. "We got played."

"What the fuck were these people up to?"

"I don't know, but it's not good. We have to stay vigilant."

"That sounds ominous."

"It's meant to be. These people are a threat to the galaxy." Glintock cleared his throat. "I want you to know, Max, I *do* see you as a partner."

"Anything you need, Matthias. You know that. Just give me a call."

"That call may be coming sooner than you think."

Gina approached them. Her eyes were red. "Well, that wasn't hard." She wiped her eyes as discreetly as possible.

"Your folks?" Max asked.

"Yes. Mom called for one last goodbye." Gina and Max had taken a quick trip down to Florida so that she could properly say goodbye to her parents. They seemed to take it well enough, but Max knew it was hard.

"They should be proud," Glintock said. "You're going to be doing important work."

"I have that already, Captain, but thank you."

"You sure about this?" Max asked. "It's not too late."

She looked up. "You guys live out there. Space is old hat for you. But, when you see it for the first time, in all its grandeur…it's like a drug. I can't go back to the FBI knowing what I know now."

"I could wipe your memory, if you'd like," Glintock said.

"Well, I know one person who wouldn't let that happen," she replied, glancing at Max.

"Oh, I'm pretty sure the might of the GAC can handle him," Glintock said as he turned to Max. "Good luck on Aval. Call me if you need anything." He shook Max's hand. "I'm glad this worked out the way it did."

"Me too. I wasn't keen on dying just yet." He gave Glintock a firm handshake and the GAC agent walked toward his ship. Max turned back to Gina. He sensed she was pulling away. "So, are you ready to go?" he asked, gesturing to the *Sequel*.

"I'm going with Glintock. I know you want to get after Alexis."

"Are you sure that's all?"

She smiled at him sadly and took a deep breath. "This is hard."

"Then I'll make it easier for you, don't do it."

"Max…."

"No, I'm serious. What's stopping us from being together?"

"Well, once my training's complete, I'll probably be here most of the time and you…you'll be up there. We both know you don't do long distance relationships."

"That doesn't mean I'm not willing to try. I think we have a good thing going here."

"We do, but…our lives are just on different paths." It was a gut punch.

"Then come with me. Forget about Glintock and just travel the stars with me."

She touched his face, her eyes welling with tears. "That would be lovely, but I can't make that my whole life."

He drew a shuddering breath. "That's fair."

"I love you, Max, and I'm so grateful that we had this time."

"But…."

"But, I just don't see our lives lining up to make it work long-term."

Heartsickness spread through his body. "But, I'm the only person you know up there!"

"I'm sure I'll make more friends. Besides, I think there's already someone a little closer to home who's perfect for you." Her eyes flicked over to Alesha, who tried to appear like she wasn't snooping. "I mean, you already share a house with her."

"How much did she tell you?"

"Enough to tell me that I'm perfectly welcome to crash there whenever I make it to Marina."

"You'd be all right with that?"

"Are you kidding me? I think she's my new best friend."

He gave her a tight smile, despite his stomach being an empty pit. It was hard enough walking away from Gina in high school. He was losing her all over again. "I didn't want it to go this way."

"I know you didn't. Neither did I. But, I think we both knew this was the logical end, whether I went to work for Glintock or not. I mean, were you prepared to chuck everything to come back to Earth?"

He frowned, knowing she was right. "I was kind of hoping you'd choose to come with me."

"And I can't do that. Please, you need to see how it might look from my perspective."

He thought back six months to when Alesha left to captain the *Heartbreaker*. All he'd wanted was for her to stay, but he didn't stand in her way. That was all Gina was asking of him— not to stand in her way. "I get it." He pulled her into an embrace and kissed her cheek. "I really enjoyed our second chance."

"Me too." She gently pulled away from him and started toward Glintock's ship, but turned back to face him. "Thank you for opening up my world, Max."

"You're gonna be great. Trust me."

She flashed him a smile. After she boarded, the ship lifted into the sky and streaked away for the stars. As Max watched the departure, Alesha leaned into him.

"You okay?" she asked.

He sighed. "Yeah, I think so."

"I'm glad I met her. She's a special lady."

"That she is, but I've got an equally special lady standing right here."

"A special lady that almost got you killed by harboring a murderer on her ship."

"You didn't know what Jethan really was, 'Lesha. I know that."

"Still, it doesn't make me feel any better about it. I'm sorry."

"Next time you're hiring, maybe do a better job vetting your applicants." He couldn't keep a straight face.

"Oh, fuck you! You're making fun of me!"

"Hey," Max tried to be serious. "I know it couldn't have been easy fighting Sierra and Memta again."

She got uncomfortably quiet. "I got through it, but while we were drying you out from the rimi, everything hit me. I had constant nightmares about Memta. I craved her power. Am I really that person, Max? Am I that...evil?"

"No, of course not. You're very…passionate. I think that's why Memta is drawn to you. Remember, she was much happier inside a willing host like Sierra. You're stronger than you think."

She smiled at him warmly. "Thanks."

"I wish you'd told me all this before."

She waved him off. "You had a lot you were dealing with. Kicking a rimi addiction—twice—is no small feat. How did your mom take the news?"

He pursed his lips. "Turns out she knew about Alexis the whole time."

Her mouth dropped open. "*What?* Way to go, Kate. I didn't know she could be so sneaky."

He made a face.

"What? Clearly, your mom didn't want to revisit the whole thing and your dad wasn't proud of what he'd done."

"It's just…now my dad is…now he's…."

"Human. He's human, Max."

Her reassuring smile helped. He couldn't wallow in angst. The rest of the crew headed up the loading ramp onto the *Sequel*. "So, where are we dropping you?" he asked.

"Nowhere. I'm coming with you."

"Why?"

"I'm your Space Girl and you're my Earth Boy. You're not shaking me that easily."

They walked toward the ship, arm-in-arm. "Oh, I never thanked you for sending Shanta my way through Pepper. She's worked out great."

"Shanta? I…have…no idea..." She really was a terrible liar.

"I saw you two cutting it up over here while the adults were talking; you've known her for a long time."

She was crestfallen. "Dammit, I promised I wouldn't interfere when I left."

"It's okay. She's great. We both know you did it because you're hopelessly in love with me."

"Gods, you're going to get a big head from this. Where are we headed first?"

"Well, before we go looking for my…sister, we need to make a quick stop on Aval to drop off your traitorous crewmember."

She gave him a dubious look. "Are you sure that's a good idea?"

"I have to set things straight there." He shrugged. "What could happen?"

CHAPTER 45

Majis.

Alexis had barely escaped Iswat with her life. After Talon's revelation, she'd fled to a safe distance. From there, she had observed the GAC taking Talon and Sierra into custody as the freshly-built facility exploded and burned to the ground.

She was reeling. Talon had lied to her, then encouraged her to kill the last source of any information about her father. *Her father*. A week previously, she'd been convinced that Talon Merthane might be her real father. Discovering he'd been grooming her to murder her half-brother made her sick to her stomach. She didn't attempt to free him from the GAC. She let them have him. He needed humbling.

Instead, she made her way to the *Claw* and left the planet. Just prior to hitting the Cardon Lane, she received an alert on her personal network. Upon opening the alert, coordinates were fed into the *Claw*'s navigation system to a planet called Majis. She'd heard the name before—it was one of Baron Zeth's pleasure planets. Along with the coordinates, all the alert said was, "Join us!"

A few days later, she sat in an opulent office at one of the resorts on Majis. The décor was covered in dark blue and gold. A wall-sized window looked out onto a sun-drenched beach with a conspicuous lack of guests. A cold sweat dotted the back of her neck. Her weapons had been confiscated upon entry, but her body tensed for action—any action.

The office door slid open and a smartly dressed older woman strolled into the room. Her shiny, steel-gray hair was worn up in a tight bun. Her clothes and sparse jewelry made Alexis feel like a pauper. She was, possibly, the most glamorous woman Alexis had ever encountered. The woman offered her hand.

"Sestra Zeth," the woman said. Alexis took her hand. "Very good to finally meet you, Alexis…Merthane?"

Alexis was speechless for a moment. "N-no. I use my mother's surname, Turnal."

Zeth took a seat beside Alexis on the couch. "Her death must have been awful. I am truly sorry. However, Talon Merthane has trained you quite well."

"You know my fath—you know Talon?"

Zeth smiled tightly. "Our paths have crossed, yes. I have to be honest. He is not my favorite person to deal with. Do you have any plans to extricate him from his current predicament?"

Hot anger flashed through Alexis' body. "He can rot."

Zeth's eyebrows rose. "Well, not exactly the answer one would expect from a surrogate daughter. You two must have had a grievous falling out."

"You could say that."

"Very interesting…. I pride myself on knowing all the goings on in the galaxy, but this has greatly surprised me."

"Is there a reason I'm here, Madam?"

"Oh, please my dear, don't be so formal. You may call me Sestra or Lady Zeth if you prefer. I have a proposition for you."

"How do you know so much about me?"

"It's unnerving, isn't it? I must say, you have performed admirably these last few weeks." Alexis wore a perplexed look. "My dear, I am your client. I sent you to Iswat to start all that trouble."

Alexis' brow furrowed. She knew who Baron Zeth was, but Sestra Zeth was a mystery. "Why…would a businesswoman want to assassinate a world leader?"

Zeth clucked her tongue. "Merthane shortchanged your education. *All* business leaders want to assassinate world leaders, my dear." She chuckled, but stopped when she saw Alexis wasn't in on the joke. "Perhaps I should have been clearer when I introduced myself. You probably know my buffoonish brother. He is the public face of our empire, while I toil behind the scenes. Nothing happens at Zeth Enterprises without my knowledge. I needed Egar Kowas eliminated to prepare for the future. But, I'm getting ahead of myself." Lady Zeth gazed at her. "You still seem somewhat confused. May I take you on a little ride? I think if you see my current project, you'll understand."

Alexis shrugged. "It's your money, Lady Zeth."

She smiled. "Yes, it is, isn't it?"

Zeth led Alexis over to an opening wall panel that revealed a lift. The two of them descended several levels before the door reopened. They stepped into a cavernous space that appeared to be hollowed out from the mountain that Zeth's building sat atop. An exit as wide as the cavern was on the far end of the artificial cave. A luxury hover vehicle, complete with robotic chauffer, awaited them.

"Good afternoon, Lady Zeth," the robot said. Its voice was male and the body design was made to look like it was wearing a suit.

"Thank you, Roderick. Please take us to the site," Zeth replied.

The bot ushered them into the vehicle. The interior sported cream-colored leather, contrasting with the black exterior. The vehicle rose into the air smoothly and sped toward the exit. Once they started moving, Zeth touched the space between the cockpit and the passenger section. A lavender glow and hum met her touch, revealing the force field between them and the driver.

"We can speak freely now. Roderick wouldn't tell anyone anyway, but why chance it?" Zeth said as the vehicle escaped the cavern and sailed into the warm, sunny sky of Majis. "I understand you have been spending your time making Maxim Ultra miserable." A playful smile teased the corners of Zeth's lips.

A spike of fear shot through Alexis at the mention of Ultra's name. Did Zeth know the secret that Talon had revealed on Iswat?

"He's a meddlesome young man. He and that GAC toady he works with, Glintock. Were you after him for personal reasons or to collect the bounty?"

"Both, I guess. But apparently, he was innocent."

"Oh, I know." Zeth let out a lilting laugh. She leaned in like she was telling Alexis a secret. "I had to keep the GAC busy while I proceeded with my plans."

"But, all those people inside *The Gallant*. You murdered them." The sickness in her stomach threatened to manifest all over Lady's Zeth's glamorous clothing.

"A regrettable necessity, my dear. I needed a crime that would consume all of the GAC's attention, while I and my allies worked toward a stronger galaxy."

"How does murdering thousands of civilians make the galaxy stronger?" Alexis began thinking of escape.

"Alexis, I will not lie to you, the galaxy faces dangers that the GAC cannot protect us from. My allies and I believe we can."

"What dangers?"

"Dangers from the uncharted sectors of space."

"And the GAC is completely unaware? Ridiculous." Alexis wasn't buying Zeth's conspiracy theories.

"They may well be aware of it, but they are woefully under-prepared. The GAC is too strangled by bureaucracy. Corruption reigns. My organization will be a shield to protect the galaxy from the coming storm. You saw my manifesto on the information net, no?"

"The one that Ultra—well, the *fake* Ultra—delivered?"

"The same. All of that was true. The only falsity was that Maxim Ultra was one of us. The people that lived in *The Gallant* were rich and corrupt. Not all, of course, but no one will miss them. You must trust me and my plan."

"Death doesn't bother me. Involving civilians does."

Zeth chuckled. "You mean civilians like Alesha Cabal and Ultra's other female companion you bloodied on Modan? What about Cabal's crewmates? Did *they* deserve death?"

"They...were in my way. They attacked me."

"Because you were trying to kill their friend, who wasn't even in the area! He was busy fighting with your father or...whatever he is to you."

Alexis looked out the window of the vehicle at the shimmering water below them. *Where is she taking me?*

"Alexis, I need someone like you—someone who isn't afraid to get their hands dirty. I recently lost my best operative and I need to fill that hole. We are trying to supplant the GAC, an organization that has ruled the galaxy for centuries. Spectacular demonstrations need to be made to discredit them. They are incapable of keeping us safe."

The hover vehicle climbed into the sky as it crested over a ring of mountains. Inside the ring was a flat valley and a familiar facility under construction. It was almost an exact match for the one on Iswat where she had fought Maxim Ultra. As opposed to the black-clad troops on Iswat, this new facility had white-uniformed soldiers.

Alexis' eyes widened as she turned to Zeth. "You...you were working with Sierra Numani?" The name cloyed to her tongue like rancid honey.

"Indeed. Sierra is a valuable asset, but her exposure to the Memta artifact made her quite unstable. I had hoped that with the power stripped from her person, she might revert back, but alas."

Alexis wanted Numani's head on a pike for Dayna's death. "Numani was working for you, but robbing you at the same time?"

Zeth shrugged. "Again, it's all about subterfuge. Until we are ready to go fully public with our intentions and operations, secrecy is the rule of the day. How best to ensure that everyone believes Zeth Enterprises has nothing to do with this? Make ourselves the victims."

Zeth's scheming mind impressed Alexis. "With the GAC busy dealing with the fallout of *The Gallant*, they wouldn't notice some high-profile heists at various Zeth facilities."

"Exactly. Join us, Alexis. You are a skilled warrior, but you've proven yourself to be cunning as well. I need someone like you—someone who won't fall into madness at a moment's notice. You will never need to take another independent contract in your life. Join me and reshape the galaxy."

Alexis knew she couldn't completely trust Zeth, but the offer was tempting. She'd lived in Talon's shadow her whole life. With him in prison, she had no idea what to do next. Zeth might get her access to Sierra Numani. That was worth all the money in the galaxy. "Lady Zeth, you have a deal."

"Excellent."

CHAPTER 46

The sun set on the Dorgan Province of Aval. Maxim and Litning zipped across the landscape in a rented hover car. They drove with the top down, a bound and gagged Jethan in the backseat. The wind blew through their hair—a massive undertaking for Litning—and they both wore sunglasses to protect from the sun's glare. All-in-all, they looked pret-ty cool.

"How much longer?" Litning asked.

"About twenty minutes," Max replied. The three of them were headed to Aval's prison towers—the same place where Max had spent almost three years of his life. He wasn't thrilled about going back, but it was a symbolic gesture. He had to be the one to deliver Jethan to his final, cramped apartment.

The sky was a beautiful, fiery orange and red as the sun's final rays kissed their side of the planet. The rocky terrain was less beautiful. The towers were in a remote area of Aval and housed some of the vilest criminals in the galaxy. Max only hoped they had a way to subdue Jethan's powers and contain him, so that he couldn't harm anyone again.

The towers rose from the desolate landscape like a supervillain's lair. Max tried to count the numerous towers as they approached, but kept losing count as he kept his eyes on piloting the car. Eventually, he spotted the main administrative building and directed the vehicle that way. He was surprised at the lack of fences or walls of any kind, but menacing gun turrets lined the towers vertically. They could handle any incoming problem from multiple angles—well, except Kalen Vandier, apparently.

Max brought the hover car to a stop near the admin building. Five individuals approached them—four beefy-looking guards, and one in the middle, who wore a suit. "Get him out of the car. I'll do the talking," Max said to Litning as they disembarked.

"Consider me completely at ease." The Revash's sense of humor was definitely improving.

"Hello!" Max called out to the five as he walked toward them.

"The infamous Maxim Ultra," the man in the suit said with contempt.

"I'm afraid you've got me at a disadvantage," Max said. "Where's the warden?"

"I *am* the warden," the man replied. "Wentin Empton. A pleasure to meet you." Empton's tone told Max that it was anything *but* a pleasure to meet him. Litning dragged Jethan to where Max stood.

"Well, here he is, fellas. *The Gallant* bomber. Do I collect the reward from you or…?"

Empton chuckled. "There is no reward, Mr. Ultra."

"That's interesting, considering people have been chasing me all over the galaxy, clamoring for some big payday. I figured since I'm bringing in the real culprit, the reward would come to me, or at the very least, Mr. Litning here."

"How do we know this is the real culprit?" Empton asked. "How do we know it's not you?"

"Because we have a recording of his unprompted confession. Agent Matthias Glintock of the GAC should be delivering that to your Minister of Justice as we speak."

"Do we collect the reward from her?" Litning asked.

Empton motioned to his men and two of them stepped up to take custody of Jethan. They each took hold of one of Jethan's arms and dragged him toward the admin building.

"Do you have a facility to hold him?" Max asked. "He's a shifter."

Empton gave him a tight, condescending smile. "We have it covered."

"Okay…well, if there's no reward, we'll be on our way," Max said as he and Litning turned back to their vehicle.

"Guards, take Mr. Ultra and the Revash into custody."

Max froze. The remaining two guards approached them. "I'm sorry? I thought I heard you tell them to take us into custody."

"I did."

"Yes, but I just handed *The Gallant* bomber over to you. Why would you arrest us?"

"Because, Mr. Ultra, you're still a fugitive of justice on Aval."

"The GAC cleared all that up."

"Yes, the initial charge, but do you not remember blasting your way out of this prison just a year ago? Many injuries and damage to account for."

"And why would you arrest me?" Litning asked, his body tensing for action.

"For aiding and abetting this fugitive, of course."

Max laughed. "Yeah, fuck this. We're leaving. Come on, Litning." He turned to leave and got a shock stick in his back. Crumpling to the ground, he could only watch helplessly as both guards subdued Litning.

"I hope you'll enjoy your stay, Mr. Ultra. We have much to discuss," Empton said with a sinister smile.

What the fuck is happening? Max looked off to the side and balked. As plain as day, his father stood there, watching the events unfold.

"*You fucked up this time, pal*," his father said in a voice that reverberated in his mind.

Max's head swam. *Bad time for those rimi hallucinations to kick in*. His heart thudded in his chest. Despite the price on his head, Merthane, Alexis, Sierra, and all of it, his greatest fear was coming true—he was going back to prison.

END